BEACON AND ICE

THE CHRONICLES OF TERRASOHNEN
BOOK 3

N. K. CARLSON

ALSO BY N. K. CARLSON

Novels

Shadow and Sword

Water and Blood

The Smelly Gospel

The Things that Charm Us

Anthologies

Phantoms

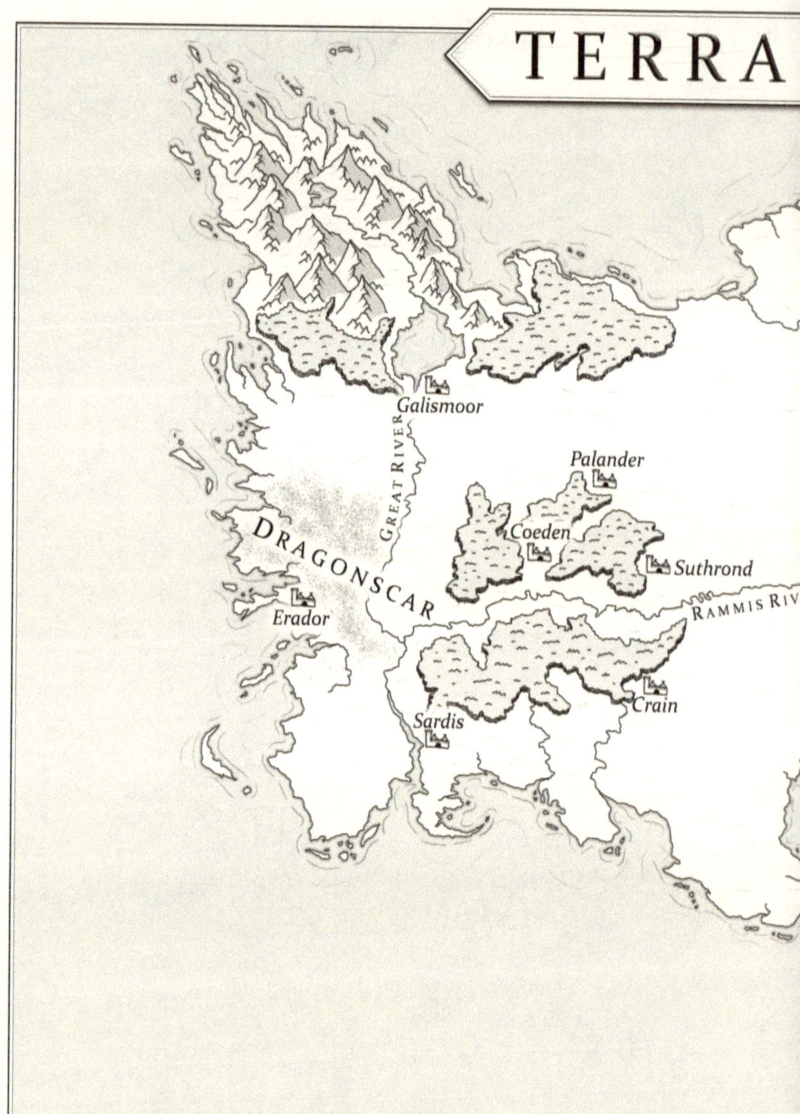

TERRA
Galismoor
Palander
Coeden
Suthrond
GREAT RIVER
DRAGONSCAR
Erador
RAMMIS RIV
Crain
Sardis

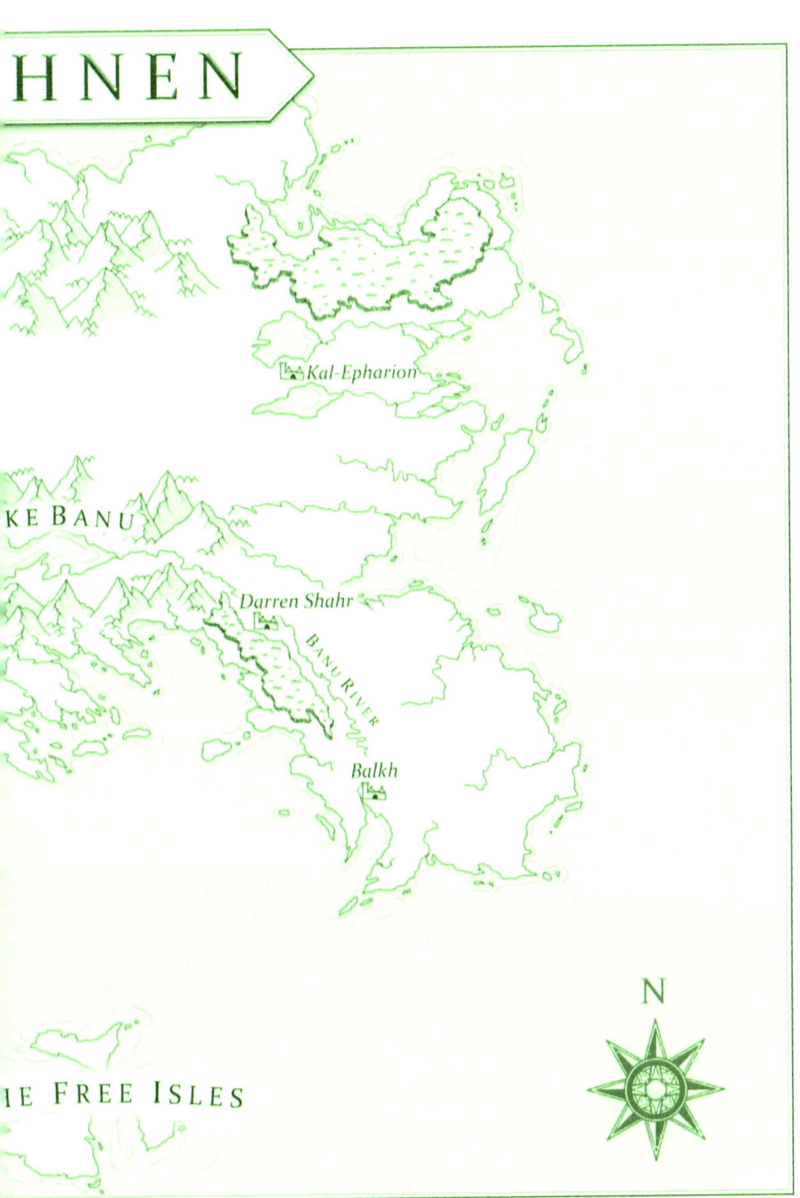

HNEN
Kal-Epharion
KE BANU
Darren Shahr
BANU RIVER
Balkh
N
IE FREE ISLES

Published in the United States by Creative James Media.

www.creativejamesmedia.com

978-1-956183-78-8 (trade paperback)

First U.S. Edition 2024

For Elijah,
"The night is nearly over; the day is almost here. So let us put
aside the deeds of darkness and put on the armor of light."

PART ONE
REITH

ONE

As he approached the Elven city of Crain, Reith couldn't help but think of the last time he had been there. He had been fleeing his homeland, the land of the humans, with the survivors of the Gray Man's devastation of Suthrond. At that point in his journey, he thought he may have been the lone survivor of the Gray Man's attack on his own town, Coeden.

But he wasn't the only survivor. Vereinen, his master, the chronicler, had escaped right before the attack. He had left a note for Reith to meet him in Erador, the ancient, ruined city on the west coast of Terrasohnen. Reith had traveled there, all by himself, only to find the Gray Man there too. And there was no trace of Vereinen.

There, he heard the Gray Man plotting to attack the survivors of Suthrond, so he stole a horse and raced the Gray Man to Suthrond, where he warned their survivors. They all crossed the river and traveled onto Crain to seek refuge.

Though they were temporarily safe from the Gray Man, they did not find the refuge they sought. Though initially received warmly, Pryderus had led a coup and took over the city. He enslaved the humans and killed his predecessor, Gwandoeth.

This time, though, Reith's arrival at Crain would be different. For one, he had an official reason to be there. He was ambassador to the elves, appointed by King Calmon himself. If Pryderus wanted to cause trouble, he had to contend with the whole might of the human army.

But the main reason for Reith's confidence was everything he had been through and how that had shaped him. No longer was he a scared boy fleeing from more powerful people. He was a warrior in his own right. He had held his own in battle and defeated many in combat. He was a slayer of beasts and monsters. He was becoming a man.

But other things had changed, too. Vereinen was dead, killed by a sword blow meant for the Gray Man. The loss of Vereinen felt like a hole in his chest. Even thinking about it made his chest tighten up and he felt like he was on the verge of tears. It had been a few short days since Vereinen had passed, and Reith didn't think he would ever be over it.

And the Gray Man, Solzar, somehow he was no longer a deadly enemy. Reith couldn't explain it, but somehow, this former foe was now a tentative ally. When the blow meant for Solzar fell instead on the willing sacrifice Vereinen, something about Solzar had changed. He ceased to be gray and the Shadow, the Dark Power using him, left him. He was made new.

It was for this reason that he was most excited to be going back to Crain. Ellyn, the lore master, lived there. For a brief, happy period, Reith had apprenticed under her at the temple in Crain. He had read books and had many conversations with her about the God of Light, as well as the Guardians and Dark Powers. If anyone could explain what happened to Solzar, it would be Ellyn.

Beside Reith, on his right, rode Pallin, commander of the legion of Crain. On Pallin's other side rode Laneras, a close friend of Ellamora. These two elves had facilitated his escape from Crain with Ellamora, Dema, and Kydar, when they fled to Sardis.

At the thought of Ellamora, Dema, and Kydar, Reith's chest tightened with emotion. It took his breath away for a minute. Ellamora was now one of Reith's closest friends. They had traveled the width and breadth of Terrasohnen together, and they had the casual familiarity and playfulness of longtime friends. Now she was an elf living in the land of the humans, and he was a human going to live with the elves. He would miss her.

Dema, well, Dema was a torch in the night. She blazed with passion and intensity and Reith had found himself pleasantly surprised to be falling in love with her, and she with him. Dema would be leaving soon to go back to Darren Shahr to be an ambassador to the dwarves. The distance between them would be unbearable for however many months they were apart. He hoped to see her again soon, but there were no plans for it in his immediate future.

And Kydar, he missed Kydar in a different way. Kydar fell in battle as they escaped Sardis and the wrath of Solzar. Reith's sadness over Kydar was different, deeper. It was like a scar that had healed, but still remained as a visible mark of pain.

The company rode in silence. The river was miles behind them, and Reith knew they would probably reach Crain slightly before nightfall, if he remembered the terrain rightly.

"Now, Reith," Pallin began, turning slightly in his saddle to look at him. "When we arrive at Crain, it would be best for you to remain outside the city, in light of the, uh, unpleasantries that accompanied your last visit to our city."

"We don't want anyone's head to end up in a bag," Laneras chimed in.

"Yes, quite right," Pallin replied. "We will enter the city and bring Pryderus to the rampart above the city gate, and when you see him, you should hold up your commission and declare you are an ambassador seeking safe conduct and lodging in the city. He will have no choice but to accept you in."

"And what if he doesn't?"

"We'll just knock him off the wall," Laneras said with a shrug.

"If it should come to that," Pallin replied, ignoring Laneras completely, "then we shall *gently* persuade Pryderus."

"Can I stay with Ellyn again?" Reith asked, eager to make his way back to the temple and see his old mentor.

"I don't see why not," Pallin answered. "At the very least you can stay there for a night or two while official lodgings are prepared which are worthy of your status as ambassador."

They rode on, and the only sounds were the horses' hooves and the jingling of saddles. Reith lost himself in the ride, the gentle breeze in his face, the feel of the horse beneath him, and the light dancing across the sky. In what seemed to be no time at all, Reith saw the ramparts of Crain looming over the world, and to his surprise, he encountered a peach grove.

"Your gift kept on giving in your absence," Pallin noted upon seeing Reith's surprise. "You planted miracle fruit."

Reith still didn't understand the miracle behind the fruit. He had plucked various types of fruit from a grove of fruit trees in Dragonscar, outside of Erador, the only green things in that charred, ruined land. And everywhere he went, anywhere a seed from the fruit fell, new trees sprouted almost instantaneously, creating orchards and groves where there had been none before. The fruit from these trees retained some of that magic too, and fresh fruit and new growth were spread across Reith on his travels from Erador to Suthrond and down to Crain.

"I can't explain it," Reith said.

"Nor can any mortal," Laneras replied. "But the God of Light's hand is upon it, there is no doubt."

"Yes, yes," Reith said. He dismounted and went to one of the nearby trees and plucked a peach bigger than his two fists combined. After rubbing it on his shirt, he took a bite and juice exploded from the fruit, refreshing him after a long day in the saddle.

"We're going into the city now," Pallin said. "Be ready to announce yourself when Pryderus comes to rampart."

The two elves went away, and their company followed suit, leaving Reith alone among the peach trees. He settled himself at the base of a tree and faced the city gate. He allowed his horse to graze contentedly nearby. He continued eating the peach, and when he was through, he took the pit and placed it in his bag. *I'll bring it to Sardis and start a new grove there.*

It seemed fitting to him that he continued the work he had started all the way back in Erador, those long months ago. Perhaps it was his duty to spread the seeds of those trees far and wide across Terrasohnen. He resolved to take some to Galismoor and Darren Shahr if he could.

Reith spied movement on top of the walls and stood to his feet. After brushing off the dirt and grass clinging to his pants, he straightened up and walked toward the gate. High above him, he recognized Pallin and Laneras, who gave him encouraging smiles. Between them, Pryderus glared at him with fire in his eyes.

"Greetings, Lord of Crain," Reith called up to him. "It is I, Reith, ambassador of King Calmon of the humans. Here is my charge," and he held up the king's commission in his left hand. "I request safe conduct and suitable lodgings within your city until such a time as my official duties press me to move on."

Pryderus surveyed him for several long seconds before he seemed to shrink within himself. He said nothing, but simply lazily waved his hand to summon Reith in the city. Reith grabbed the reins of his horse and entered.

Pryderus, Laneras, and Pallin were descending stairs from the wall to the square below when Reith entered. Pryderus ignored him and stomped off.

"Pay him no mind," Pallin said as Pryderus walked out of sight. "You shall stay with Ellyn. We'll accompany you to ensure your continued safety. You should be able to have an official audience with Pryderus in the morning."

"That sounds fun," Reith said, rolling his eyes. "I suppose I have to play nice."

"That's really up to you," Pallin replied. "And of course, what you think your king wants. You represent him, of course."

"True, true," said Reith, begrudgingly. "I suppose I have to build bridges."

"A bridge can only be built from both ends," Laneras replied.

They wound their way through the city, and Reith recognized most of the way. *Good, I won't have to worry about getting too lost.*

Reith walked between Pallin and Laneras, and elves greeted those two warmly. When they saw Reith, most were struck temporarily dumb. He recognized a few from the temple when he had worked there on his previous stay in Crain, but he did not remember any names.

They came at last to the small temple. It looked just as Reith remembered it before. It was made of white marble, carved expertly as if from a single block of marble. It was small, no taller than the surrounding two-story buildings. Stained glass windows blazed in the light of sunset.

At the door stood Ellyn, lore master of Crain and keeper of the temple. She was tall and wore a simple green robe. She beamed at him and the two reached for each other simultaneously and pulled the other close in tight embrace.

"It is good to see you," she whispered into his ear.

"And you, too," he whispered back. They broke apart again.

"There is someone else who wishes to see you," she said. They bid farewell to Laneras and Pallin, and Ellyn led Reith around to the back of the temple, where a small hut stood, which Ellyn used as a stable. A splendid white horse stood there.

"Aspen!" Reith exclaimed and rushed forward to stroke the horse. Aspen whinnied with delight.

"I spoke to her every day," Ellyn explained. "I told her you would return."

"Of course I returned," Reith said. "Shall we ride tomorrow?" he asked the horse. Aspen gave a soft neigh, which Reith took as an affirmative.

"Come, Reith," Ellyn said. "The night has come. Let us retire inside. I will make us warm drinks and you can recount all your journeys for me."

Ellyn let him in through a back door and they walked the familiar hall toward the library which Ellyn used as a study. The smell of books and leather was intoxicating, and Reith soon nestled down in a comfortable chair while Ellyn busied herself in the kitchen. She returned carrying large, steaming mugs of tea. She handed one to Reith, and he sniffed it, letting the steam and aroma wash over him. She seemed to have added peach juice to it. *I wonder if that's from my peach grove.*

"I have heard some of your tale from Ellamora," Ellyn said

after taking a sip of her tea. "But I see the sorrow in your eyes. Tell me what has happened to you since we last met."

"Well," Reith began, thinking back on his travels, "We went to Sardis, as you know, fleeing from Pryderus and his treachery. When we arrived, Ellamora gained us entrance into the city, and we went to see the king. But the Shadow, the Gray Man, Solzar is his real name, he beat us there. He was already spinning a web and trapping King Koinas in it."

"You say his real name is 'Solzar'?" Ellyn asked. "How did you find out this information?"

Reith launched into the story of their arrest and imprisonment and of finding Vereinen in prison. With sorrow, he conveyed Vereinen's regret of pointing Solzar toward becoming a Shadow.

"Ah, it all makes sense," Ellyn said, nodding when he had finished that part of the tale. "How did you escape prison?"

Reith explained to her how Romulus had gone against his father and rescued them. Over the next hour, he recounted Kydar's death, their travels to Amisos, their voyage to the Free Isles, their flight to Balkh and the battle that was fought there, of the siege of Darren Shahr, the victory won there, the travels to the plains of Palander and the battle where Vereinen fell, and the Gray Man shed his Shadow and became Solzar again.

"You have experienced much and known great sorrow, Reith," Ellyn said when he finished his tale. "I am so proud of you."

Tears welled up in Reith's eyes at those words. They, combined with the emotions of speaking about several deaths of those close to him, pushed him over the edge into sobs. Ellyn scooted her chair closer to his while he cried and gently laid a hand on his shoulder. She said nothing, but she didn't need to. Her presence was enough.

After several minutes, Reith's tears dried up.

"Sorry," he mumbled, wiping his eyes with the back of his hand. "I haven't lost control like that in a long time."

"You didn't lose control," Ellyn replied softly. "You were simply reacting to everything that has happened to you. You can't bury your grief forever."

———

Reith slept soundly that night in his old room. Despite only staying there a short time so many months ago, it felt more like home than anywhere else he had stayed since leaving Coeden after Solzar had destroyed it.

He rose with the sun and joined Ellyn in the duties of the temple. There was a simple rhythm to the tasks that he found enjoyable. *Maybe I should become a priest.*

Around midmorning, Pallin and Laneras entered the temple.

"It is time to meet Pryderus," Pallin said with a sigh.

"What's his mood like today?" Reith asked.

"Hard to say," Laneras replied. "But he can't do anything to you, so you needn't worry."

After saying goodbye to Ellyn, Reith stepped out onto the street with the two elves. They led him back toward the center of town to the familiar stone tower from which Pryderus ruled. There were several armed guards blocking the door and several more with crossbows on top of the tower. Reith noticed that Pryderus had increased the number of guards from Gwandoeth's time.

The guards were obviously expecting Reith, Laneras, and Pallin, for they stepped aside for Reith to pass.

"We won't go in with you," Pallin explained. "We are not allowed."

"But we will wait out here," Laneras clarified, giving the guards a sharp look.

Reith stepped past the guards and pulled open the wooden door set in the wall. He stepped into a dark room lit by candlelight, which flickered in the draft of the open door. In the center of the room, where Pryderus' desk had been when he was Gwandoeth's assistant, stood even more armed guards. Reith gripped the hilt of his sword tightly.

"Up the stairs," one of the guards said, pointing toward the staircase along the side of the room. Reith took a deep breath and then slowly climbed up to the office of the Lord of Crain.

Two

"Enter," came the familiar voice of Pryderus when Reith knocked, though muffled by the wooden door.

Reith gently opened the door and stepped into Pryderus' office. It was different than it had been with its previous occupant. Gwandoeth's office more closely resembled a library with the wisdom of ages on his shelves. Pryderus had removed nearly all the books and the shelves as well. Now charts and graphs filled the empty spaces on the wall and stacks of papers resided on a table behind his desk. On Pryderus' desk were a variety of official looking forms and contracts, organized into neat piles. Clearly, Pryderus' main business was business.

Behind the desk, Pryderus was bent over a page with a quill in hand, busily scratching out something written there. He did not even look up as Reith approached.

Reith stood before the desk for a long minute, peering down at the elf who had given him so much trouble all those months before. He fingered his sword hilt, determined not to make the first move.

Pryderus lingered over the page as long as he could, before

setting down his quill and placing the paper onto one of the neat piles of paper in front of him. Only when it was safe in its place did he bring his pads together and raise his eyes to meet Reith's.

For several long seconds, they stared into each other's eyes, daring the other to blink or turn away. Pryderus blinked first.

"Well," he said in a bored voice.

Reith let several seconds of awkward silence pass before replying.

"Well, what?"

"Don't be smart with me, boy," Pryderus snarled at him. "You and your kind befouled my city once, and here you stand again. What do you want?"

"I am an ambassador of King Calmon, here on a diplomatic mission. I aim to stay in your city for a few days before traveling on to Sardis to meet with the new king there."

"And what does your king wish for you to do in Crain on your diplomatic mission? Spy on us? Study our defenses so you can attack?"

"Nothing of the sort," Reith said calmly. He sensed Pryderus was nearing some sort of violent outburst. "I am simply here to improve the relationship between our two races."

"Bah, what should elves have to do with humans?" Pryderus spat. "We were all better off when you stayed in your land, and we stayed in ours. We have a new king, and I am sure you had something to do with it, filthy human."

The words hung over the room like smoke. Reith closed his eyes to gather himself, then looked upward and sighed.

"The world is changing, Pryderus," he said gently. "I know you think that is for the worst. But I have seen the elves and the dwarves, I have seen kings fall and seen kings and queens rise from the ashes."

"Is that a threat?" Pryderus said loudly, hastily standing to his feet. As he rose, he knocked a pile of papers to the floor. He swore and stooped to gather them. Reith made no move to help.

"It is no threat," Reith said. "But a statement of fact. You think mighty highly of yourself if you would place yourself in the same category of kings and queens. You are a small man, cowardly and vile."

Pryderus made to straighten up but slammed his head into the corner of his desk and fell, sprawled out over his precious papers.

"I pity you," Reith added, standing over the prone form of Pryderus, who groaned in pain. "This interview is over. If you should wish to speak to me in an official capacity again, please summon me from the temple. I shall stay with Ellyn until I depart."

Reith turned and swept from the room.

———

"How did your meeting with Pryderus go?" Ellyn said when he was back at the temple.

"It went exactly how I expected," Reith said with a sigh. "He is a horrible man. Sometimes I think he might be a Shadow."

"Not every villain becomes a shadow. Some are simply evil and mean."

"Speaking of Shadows," Reith said, "I have questions about what happened to Solzar."

"Ask away, though I don't pretend to be an expert on such things," Ellyn stated.

"How did Solzar cease to be a Shadow?" Reith asked.

"Ah, the first thing you ask, I can only speculate," Ellyn replied.

"Have a guess then."

"On this subject, we are in uncharted territory," Ellyn said. "Why, what happened with Vereinen and Solzar perhaps is the only time such a thing has happened in the history of Terrasohnen. So, let's start at the beginning. Do you remember what a Shadow is?"

"Yes, a Shadow is someone who is wholly taken over by a Dark Power."

"You are correct in broad strokes, but I would make a slight change to that definition. A Shadow is wholly *given* over to a Dark Power. Do you see the difference?"

"Yes, I suppose. Dark Powers don't go around overwhelming people and turning them into Shadows. The person seeks them out to become a Shadow."

"Precisely," Ellyn said, giving Reith a smile. "It is a matter of will. The will of the person who would be a Shadow is what matters. Dark Powers can only enter where the recipient is willing. Though they would like to be the main characters of history, the Dark Powers can only act in the background and through willing people. In short, it means we don't have to go about our days worrying that a Dark Power might suddenly come upon us and make us Shadows."

"So what does this have to do with Solzar and Vereinen?" Reith asked, bringing the conversation back to the initial subject.

"It has everything to do with them. Solzar gave himself over to the Dark Powers and so became the Gray Man, a Shadow. His will brought about that change. But another will came into the situation."

"Vereinen?" Reith asked.

"Yes, Vereinen," Ellyn replied. "When Vereinen stepped in front of the sword meant for Solzar, he placed not only his life, but his will in front of the death blow. Why do you think he did such a thing?"

"I don't know," Reith said honestly. He had been

wondering why ever since Vereinen had died. "Instinct I suppose."

"Now we are getting to the heart of the matter," Ellyn said. "By stepping in front of Solzar and taking the blow meant for him, Vereinen undid the Shadow."

"So if there are other Shadows, we just need to throw someone in front of them and kill them?"

"No!" Ellyn protested. "You need to remember it is the life and the will together that made all the difference with Solzar and Vereinen. Anyone can die before a Shadow, but to unmake a Shadow, the will must be there, too."

"So because Vereinen willingly stepped in front of Solzar, that made all the difference?"

"Yes, but it goes deeper than that," Elly explained. "Tell me, would you step in front of a blow meant for Pryderus?"

"No, I suppose I would more likely be the one delivering the blow," Reith said, wondering why this had any bearing on the conversation about Shadows.

"Quite right," Ellyn agreed. "Pryderus is a despicable man. But Shadows are even worse. You would perhaps be willing to step in the way of a blow meant for a close friend, Dema or Ellamora, perhaps, am I right?"

"Yes, I suppose so," Reith said, still confused.

"One would die for a family member or a close friend," Ellyn said. "It is the nature of such relationships. But to die for an enemy, no one would dare."

"I don't understand," Reith said.

"When Vereinen stepped in front of Solzar, he was stepping in front of a bitter foe as well as a cherished friend. Solzar represented both to Vereinen. But he stepped in front of him and died in his place. Why?"

"I suppose he thought he was dying for a friend," Reith responded.

"That he did," Ellyn replied. "So in short, it was love that caused Vereinen to jump in front of Solzar and die for him. Even though Solzar was now an enemy, Vereinen loved him unto death. Vereinen loved Solzar enough to put his blood on the line for him. And if there is one thing the Dark Powers despise, it is love. They do not love, nor do they comprehend love. Love is repulsive to them. The Dark Powers care only for themselves. The idea that someone would sacrifice themselves for another is beyond their comprehension. And now we reach my speculation. I believe it was Vereinen's love, proven by the ultimate sacrifice, that freed Solzar from being a Shadow. His love brought about a victory over the Dark Powers."

"Love can do all that?" Reith asked, incredulously.

"Yes," Ellyn replied. "Love is more powerful than the Dark Powers and also the Guardians."

"How can that be?"

"Because of the God of Light. The purest light in the world is love. It is by love that the God of Light made Terrasohnen. It is the God of Light who gives power to the Guardians and the Dark Powers, though the Dark Powers have rebelled and twisted that power for evil purposes. The God of Light is greater than the Guardians and the Dark Powers, and therefore love is more powerful than either."

"So if more Shadows rise," Reith began.

"And they will," Ellyn interjected.

"How do we get rid of them?"

"You see the dilemma. Not just anyone can step in front of a Shadow and die for them. It has to be the right person, with the right life, with the right will, with their blood on the line. It has to be someone given over completely to the God of Light in love."

———

The next few days were the most restful that Reith had had since Solzar had destroyed Coeden and sent Reith on the run. He did not go to see Pryderus, nor did Pryderus send for him, and Reith was just fine with that. He spent his time in quiet conversation with Ellyn around the Temple, reading books in her library, and with Laneras and Pallin in the evenings.

One evening, he found himself playing a card game he had little understanding of with Laneras and Pallin.

"So, Reith," Laneras said, as he placed two cards down on the table. Evidently, they were good cards, because he looked satisfied. "When will you depart for Sardis?"

"Perhaps in a week," Reith replied, looking at his own cards in his hand. He either could win the game right then and there, or he had dismal cards. Trouble was, he couldn't tell the difference. "I am enjoying my time in Crain."

"Well, Pryderus is not enjoying your time in Crain," Pallin said. "Never before in all my time commanding the Legion has the Lord of the city demanded so much personal protection from my soldiers." Pallin placed his cards on the table with disgust, and Laneras smiled.

"Does he think I pose a threat to him?" Reith asked, still looking at his cards. He didn't know what to make of them, so he simply placed them on the table. Laneras groaned.

"How does he always do it?" Laneras said to Pallin with exasperation in his voice. He shoved a small pile of coins toward Reith, who began sorting them into stacks in front of himself.

"Your very presence in the city itself is a threat to Pryderus," Pallin said, ignoring Laneras. "He drove you out before. And now you're back, and you do not fear him. That is threatening to one such as he."

"He needs to get over it," Reith muttered.

"He may not have the chance," Pallin said. "I have heard

from scouts that an army from Sardis is marching this way with the king's brother at the lead."

"Remus?" Reith said with interest.

"The very same," Pallin replied. "I do not think Pryderus will last much longer as lord."

"Then I shall stay here until Remus departs for Sardis again," Reith declared. "Oh, I would like to see Pryderus put in his place, especially after what he did to Gwandoeth."

"Pryderus may be a cowardly and vile ruler, but he has supporters in this city. Removing him will not be easy."

"Come to think of it," Reith wondered, "How are you still in charge of the Legion? Doesn't Pryderus know you oppose him?"

"Of course he knows," Laneras interjected. "But Pallin is strong too. He also has supporters. And his supporters are well armed."

———

It was three days before Remus' forces arrived at Crain. Reith was kept up to date with the latest scouting reports from Pallin and Laneras and was well prepared when Remus made his appearance. He stood by Laneras and Pallin by the city gate as Remus and his soldiers approached. When Remus drew near, he and Reith greeted each other like old friends, despite knowing each other for a short time.

"Reith, how good to see you," Remus said, embracing him. "Or should I say, 'Your Ambassadorship?'"

"Reith is quite alright by me," Reith said with a chuckle. "Tell me of Romulus and Sardis."

"All is right in the world, friend," Remus said with a smile. "We marched into the city and my father had no choice but to surrender without a fight. He is imprisoned, and Romulus is on the throne. He will welcome you most warmly to Sardis when you choose to take your mission as ambassador farther south."

"I hope to ride with you when you depart," Reith said.

"Then we will welcome you most gladly," Remus replied. "But as to the timing of that departure, I do not know. I think we shall have trouble here. My brother has filled me in on all the struggles and difficulties you had in Crain. He is most disgusted with the current Lord. Shall we pay him a visit?"

"By all means," Reith said.

Remus entered the city to crowds of elves who did not quite know what to make of him. Several clapped and cheered, but when the rest failed to join in, those who initially were exuberant succumbed to silence rather quickly, looking sheepish. Others looked at him with bemused curiosity. And still others looked on Remus with hostility.

"Tough crowd," Remus remarked to Reith in a voice just loud enough for Reith to hear as they marched through the streets. Soon enough, they arrived at Pryderus' tower. It was just as Reith had encountered the week before. Many guards stood sentry outside, though this time they were at attention.

"Halt!"

The lead guard had stepped forward from the rest and was holding out a hand to stop the prince from advancing any further.

"Who are you and what business do you have with the Lord of Crain?"

Remus glanced at Reith with annoyance at the guard's zealousness for his duty.

"I am Prince Remus, brother to King Romulus, here on the king's business. I demand an audience with the Lord of Crain."

"King Romulus?" the guard protested. "We recognize no king by that name. Our king is Koinas, long live the king!"

The other guards echoed with their own 'long live the king!'

"King Koinas has been removed from the throne because madness has overtaken him," Remus explained calmly. "He has no more authority than you do. I am here on the orders of my brother, King Romulus. With his troops at my back, I demand to speak to the lord of this city."

"Very well, my lord," the guard replied with a sigh. "I shall check with his excellency to see if he is available for a meeting. He is terribly busy, you know."

"Make sure his answer is favorable," Remus said, with a note of threat finally entering his voice.

The guard turned and walked through the midst of his soldiers and disappeared into the tower.

For several long minutes, they waited for the guard to return. The crowds grew bored with the proceedings and one by one left to go about their business. Remus began to pace in frustration.

"Is this what it's always like in Crain?" he asked.

"No," Reith said truthfully. "This is actually way better. So far, no one's head has been put in a bag."

After several more minutes, the guard finally returned.

"I'm sorry, my lord," the guard replied. "Lord Pryderus is too busy for any callers today. If you would like, I can introduce you to his secretary who would be glad to make you an appointment for his next available opening."

Remus swore and spat on the ground at the feet of the guard.

"So, this is how he wants to play the game," he said in a low voice where only Reith and the guard could hear. "Very well," he said more loudly. "I shall inspect the administrative function of the city and determine what, if any fines, should be levied against Pryderus' personal purse for negligence of duty. Unless of course, he could squeeze me in for a quick meeting."

Remus looked expectantly at the guard, who swallowed before stammering, "Right this way, my lord."

"Thank you," Remus said to the guard. "Reith, I shall send for you if and when I need you. For now, I must go in alone."

Remus followed the guard into the tower and the door shut with a bang behind them.

"I am anxious to get this nasty business over with," Pallin said, looking at the tower with concern.

"Do we need to go in with him?" Laneras asked.

"No," Pallin replied. "Prince Remus can handle himself."

They waited in silence for another minute before the door to the tower burst open and Remus strode out into the street.

"By order of the king," he declared in a loud voice to those gathered, "This tower is hereby deemed to be the king's prison. Pryderus, formerly lord of this city, is charged with the murder of Lord Gwandoeth and shall remain locked in this tower until such a time as he can be brought to Sardis to sit his trial before King Romulus, long may he reign!"

There was silence at the end of the pronouncement, then the sound of muttering rose like the sound of insects in the street.

"That was quick," Reith quipped to Remus.

"The villain was quick to admit to his deed. Now he must suffer the consequences. And we must suffer his company on our way back to Sardis."

"Who shall be Lord of Crain, my lord?" Pallin asked.

"Laneras," Remus replied, turning to the younger elf. "How would you like to be Lord of Crain?"

THREE

The new Lord of Crain's first order of business upon taking office was to declare Crain to be a free city for members of all races, where humans and dwarves would be welcome to live alongside elves to build a community together.

"As the only human here, and on behalf of King Calmon," Reith said, "I enthusiastically support this order. If my people should ever need to flee their land again, they shall find a find a friend in the Lord of Crain!"

"So it should have been, and so it was, when Gwandoeth held this office," Laneras replied. "But Pryderus poisoned the imaginations of the people. We must bring healing, and this is the first thing to do."

The next two days were a flurry of activity in Crain. Preparations were made for an official ceremony for Laneras and a feast to follow. The people of Crain, after their initial shock at the change, enthusiastically threw themselves into the preparations, except for Pryderus, who could be heard bellowing insults from the tower at all hours of the day. His cronies all abandoned the former lord when he could no longer grant them special favors and tax exemptions. They each in turn presented themselves to Laneras and asked for his special favor, which he denied.

"It is not right for the Lord of Crain to prefer the rich and powerful over the poor."

And so Laneras' rule began with justice and righteousness.

In addition to preparing for the ceremony, at which Reith would be a guest of honor as ambassador and give a short speech, he had to prepare to leave, as Remus said they would be traveling back to Sardis the morning after the ceremony.

He sat in Ellyn's library that night and wrote down some of his thoughts for his speech. His preparations were interrupted by Ellyn's arrival.

"I hear you will be leaving shortly," she said.

"Yes," Reith replied sadly. He enjoyed his time with Ellyn in the temple. "My official duties will take me to Sardis. I will miss you terribly!"

"I don't think you will miss me," Ellyn answered.

"Of course I will," Reith protested.

"It's hard to miss someone who you will still see every day," she said simply.

It took Reith a few moments to process what she said.

"You're coming to Sardis?" he asked, hope rising in his heart.

"I am, indeed," she said with a smile. "I just asked Remus if I could accompany you."

"Why are you going to Sardis?" Reith asked. "What about the temple?"

"Oh, there are others who can look after the temple while I am gone," she said. "But as for my traveling to Sardis, it is my desire to visit the great temple in Sardis and to study there before returning to Crain. I think there is much to learn and experience there."

"Well, I will be glad of another friendly face on the road and in Sardis," Reith said with delight.

The next days passed quickly. Reith packed his few possessions and readied Aspen for the journey to Sardis.

"It will be good to ride with you," he said to her as he stroked her mane. She whinnied as if responding.

The ceremony took place a few hours before sundown in the city square. A small stage had been erected with prominent chairs for Laneras, Remus, Pallin, Reith, and several other elves. Reith took his place alongside the others and listened as Remus spoke about Laneras' character and qualifications for the post. After Remus spoke, it was Reith's turn.

"People of Crain," he began, a bit nervous to be in front of a crowd. Their eyes were fixed on him, and he felt his hands shaking a little from the pressure. He swallowed and continued.

"On behalf of King Calmon and the entire human race, it is my pleasure to congratulate Lord Laneras. This is a momentous occasion. His first decree ushers in a new era, and new age, where the races of Terrasohnen can live and work together for the good of all, not just a few. He has been my friend and now our friendship can transcend our borders as we work together for the peace and prosperity of all Terrasohnen."

He sat back down after his short speech and many in the crowd applauded, though there were some boos and jeers mixed in.

"Great job, Reith," Remus said, leaning over and whispering in Reith's ear. "The quest for unity continues."

Pallin and a couple of the other elves gave speeches, and finally Laneras stood to give his speech.

In his speech he cast a grand vision for Crain as a center of commerce and culture, a city where the whole of Terrasohnen could come together and build things together. Several times throughout, he had to stop for a tumult of applause and cheering. The crowd seemed to hang on his every word.

When Laneras finally finished, the crowd rose to their feet as one, cheering and clapping.

"That's how you win the hearts of the people!" Remus exclaimed, clapping Laneras on the back.

The celebration lasted long into the night. The fires remained lit roasting meat and beverages flowed freely. Reith was happy to see peaches were plentiful in the party, from his peach grove outside of the city.

When his head finally hit the pillow that night, his last night in Crain, he was exhausted and fell immediately into a dreamless and restless sleep.

———

At dawn, Remus, Ellyn, and Reith gathered outside the tower. Remus instructed his soldiers to enter the tower and remove Pryderus. When they came out, Pryderus' wrists were chained together. He looked small, out from behind the desk he ruled behind. A caged wagon was waiting for him, and he was placed inside to be dragged to Sardis. Surprisingly, he had nothing to say as they placed him in there.

"Now that he is dealt with, it is time to depart."

The company departed Crain as the city began to stir in the early hours. Laneras, Pallin, and the legion of Crain saluted them as they left. Reith said goodbye to the two elves, and then they were out on the road. Remus, Reith, and Ellyn were at the front of the procession, with Remus' soldiers behind them, and then wagons laden with supplies, and finally the wagon bearing Pryderus brought up the rear. Reith was happy to be in the saddle again, and patted Aspen's neck as they rode.

"Tell me about what happened when you and Romulus left Darren Shahr," Reith prompted Remus.

"There's not much to tell, to be honest," Remus said. "You would think two princes deposing their insane father would make for a more thrilling tale, but it actually was nothing of the sort."

"So what happened?" Reith asked.

"Well," Remus began. "We traveled back from Darren Shahr. Once we reached elven territory, it seemed that at each town and village, news of our coming had preceded us. We rode into each and there was much celebrating."

"What were the celebrating?" Reith asked.

"The lost prince's return," Remus said simply. "News of my death seems traveled far and wide."

"Oh, yeah, I forgot about that part of the story."

"It is a part I often wish I could forget," Remus said mournfully.

"So, each town you entered welcomed you heartily," Reith said, bringing the conversation back. "What happened when you arrived at Sardis?"

"More of the same, though much grander. Sardis welcomed us back with a parade all the way to the palace. We were glad of it, because we did not want our father to silently oppose us. With the people's support, there was nothing he could do."

"What happened when you reached the palace?" Reith asked.

"Our father welcomed us in and spoke privately to us. He was furious. Furious with me for failing in my initial mission, and furious at Romulus for stopping the attack on Darren Shahr."

"Is he a Shadow?" Reith asked.

"I don't think so," Remus replied. "Romulus does not think he is, and he met the Gray Man, Solzar, when he came to court. But something is not quite right with him. He may not be a Shadow right now, but I think he is susceptible. I saw it in his eyes."

"What did you and Romulus do then?"

"We soothed him with calm words and escorted him to his chambers. Once safely inside, we locked him in and posted a guard outside the door."

"I bet he did not like that."

"No, he did not," Remus agreed. "But Romulus and I had discussed on the road that something must be done with him. He fraternized with a Shadow and put our whole kingdom at risk with a foolish war against the humans and the dwarves. Many elves, humans, and dwarves have perished. So, the next morning, we summoned him to the throne room. Romulus at this point had not ascended to the throne. We sat beneath the throne, the three of us, and talked."

"Were your minds already made up?"

"Mine was," Remus answered. "I thought Romulus should be king. But Romulus was not so sure."

"Why not?"

"Well," Remus began slowly, choosing his words carefully, "I think Romulus was worried about the precedent. Who's to say that if he took the throne in this way at this time, that the same could not be done to him in the future, by his own son or by someone else. When king's take the throne in Sardis, they are anointed by a priest. It symbolizes the king's divine right to rule granted by the God of Light. It's not something to rebel against lightly."

"But he did make the decision, right?" Reith asked. "He's the king now."

"Yes, he did. But not until after this conversation."

"What happened?"

"Romulus shared his concerns about our father's recent decision making, specifically naming three things: sending me on the assassination mission, welcoming a Shadow to court, and sending troops out to attack the Free Isles, the dwarves, and the elves. After detailing his complaint, Romulus sat and let my father speak. And what terrible words he spoke. He weaved a sinister tale of how the elves are the God of Light's special creation, and how we deserve to rule over the humans and dwarves. He spoke of long ago wars between the races and the harm done to elves by the other races. He justified his actions with such rhetoric. And when he finished, he told Romulus that if he was going to be a good king, he must put the elves first and try and take throne of emperor of all Terrasohnen."

"That's monstrous," Reith said.

"Quite," Remus said, nodding. "Well, when he said those things, that stirred Romulus to action. He stood again and spoke. He said, 'Father, you are shrouded in darkness and vile in your thinking. You are no longer fit to be king.' So I took my father by the arm, and Romulus sat down on the throne."

"What did your father do then?"

"He screamed profanities and insults at Romulus and myself, disowning us and vowing revenge. He was quite deranged. We called in guards, who saw the madness of my father, and we took him back to his chambers, and locked him in. He has been well cared for ever since, though he bellows vile words at any who approach his door. And thus began the reign of Romulus, King of the Elves."

———

The days passed swiftly as they drew closer and closer to Sardis. Reith, who was accustomed to sleeping under the stars, was pleasantly surprised to find they slept in the finest inn in each town they passed through. Each night was spent in merriment with fine food and drink in the inns with Remus, Ellyn, and the others, and in the morning, a hot breakfast sent them back out. On the road, he spent his hours conversing with Ellyn about the finer points of theology as well as elf culture. If he was to be an ambassador to these people, he pledged to do it right and get to know everything there was to know about the elves.

On their last day of travel, they rounded a bend in the road and Sardis, that splendid city, came into sight. Reith remembered the last time he had been there, how he had spent days in a dungeon cell and fled for his life after escaping. He thought of those who perished in that desperate flight. Several elves had fallen helping them. Cassius, Ellamora's uncle, had died in the escape. But the one that hurt most of all was Kydar. Kydar had become a close friend in the short time Reith had known him. And now he was gone.

The thought of his friend unexpectedly brought tears to Reith's eyes.

"Are you alright, Reith?" Ellyn asked Kindly.

"I'm sorry," Reith said, wiping tears from his eyes. "I was just thinking about what happened the last time I was in Sardis."

"Never apologize for your grief, Reith. Your tears prove the light resides in you."

Prince Remus led the way into the city. At the city gate, a company of elven soldiers stood at attention as their prince passed by. A herald was brought forth and announced the return of Prince Remus to the crowds as they walked the streets of Sardis to the palace. Everywhere they went, the people stopped and inclined their heads down in respect.

Upon arriving at the palace, Reith and Ellyn were permitted to accompany Remus to the throne room. They entered the great hall and saw Romulus seated on the throne at the other end of the hall. His head was adorned with a thin circlet of gold. Beside the throne, on a lesser chair, sat Myon.

At the entry, Romulus and Myon stood and greeted them warmly.

"Brother! Reith! Welcome back to court," Romulus exclaimed.

Reith embraced Romulus, and for a moment realized just how much he had missed the elf. Reith turned and embraced the older elf as well. Myon smiled at him, and Reith returned it.

"Good to see you, Reith," Myon said warmly.

"And who might this be?" Romulus asked, turning to Ellyn.

"My name is Ellyn, my Lord," Ellyn replied, bowing to her king. "I am lore master of Crain. I have chosen to travel to Sardis with my friend Reith to study here for some days before returning to my own city."

"You are very welcome in Sardis," Romulus replied. "However I can be of assistance, you may ask anything of me, my brother, Myon, or our friend Reith, and we will take care of it."

"My Lord is too kind," Ellyn replied.

"Now, let's get some food and drink, and you can tell me all that has befallen you since we parted at Darren Shahr, Reith. I trust my brother has told the tale of our return to Sardis and my ascension."

The next two hours passed quickly, as wine, bread, grapes, and cheese were to be had in abundance. It was a merry time, except of course for the ill tidings Reith brought of Vereinen's death.

"And Solzar is blind, you said?" Myon asked.

"Yes, he is."

"Peculiar," Myon muttered to himself. "What does it all mean?"

"It is another puzzle to mull over," Romulus agreed. "Darkness, ironically, clouds the subject."

After their meal and discussion, Reith and Ellyn were shown to their rooms. Reith's room was large, with huge windows overlooking the city. Heavy curtains hung to the sides of the windows, ready to be drawn in the evening. A fireplace stood opposite the magnificent bed. In the corner was a large stone basin, filled with hot water, from which steam gently rose. Reith stripped and plunged himself in the bath, and stayed in until the water was a bit too cold for him.

In anticipation of his arrival, Romulus had asked for fine clothes to be hung in the wardrobe along the side of the room, and Reith was pleased to find they fit quite well. The fabric was soft and smooth, lighter than his usual clothes, and adorned in greens and blues.

His room was splendid, and the hospitality was tremendous, a far cry from his last experience in this palace, many floors below in the dungeon.

Dinner was served in the great hall, and Reith was seated, in the position of honor at the king's table, at Romulus' left hand. He was served the finest food and drink Sardis had to offer. Joining Romulus and Remus at dinner were Myon and Ellyn, as well as several leading elf lords from the city. They all eyed him suspiciously, evidently unhappy that a human would be honored over all of them at this meal. They generally ignored Reith, and Reith spent most of the evening listening to their conversation.

Most of the lords wanted Romulus to grant them tax breaks or royal permission to use land belonging to the king for farming or hunting. But one lord wanted something else.

"My king," this elf began. He was seated down toward the other end of the table. He had dark hair, almost black. He had a short beard of the same hue. Whenever Reith had caught his eye, this elf had always glared back at him with greater intensity than any of the others. "What is to be done with your father, King Koinas?"

Romulus peered down at this elf lord for several seconds before answering.

"My father is no king," Romulus replied slowly. "Not anymore. And as for what is to be done with him, I do not know your meaning. He is held in comfortable quarters, and all his needs are met."

"And you will keep him there indefinitely?" the elf lord asked. "Surely that's not fair. And with no trial."

"He needs no trial, Dracus," Romulus declared. "He consorted with a Shadow to the detriment of the whole elven kingdom."

"So say you," Dracus said simply. "You who have everything to gain by usurping the throne." There were murmurs of assent up and down the table.

"I did what I did for the good of our kingdom," Romulus said softly. "My father recklessly sent our soldiers abroad. And what do we have to show for it? So many sent, so few returned."

"We would have Darren Shahr and the dwarves to show for it if you hadn't stopped that part of the plan," Dracus spat. "And maybe more if those soldiers had traveled north after their victory."

"Those dwarves and humans are no enemies of ours," Romulus replied, and he was greeted with exclamations of disgust up and down the table. Reith began to get nervous. He began to wish he hadn't left his sword upstairs in his room. This could turn ugly in a hurry.

"Let Koinas stand trial then," Dracus answered when the clamor had died down. "Let him stand trial and be judged fairly."

"And who shall judge him?" Romulus asked. "I have already found him unworthy."

"Your highness and the Lord Myon may sit in judgement,

as well as myself and four others. A court of seven will bring about justice."

"Who shall choose the other four?" Myon asked, interjecting himself into the conversation on Romulus' behalf. "Surely the four must be impartial, and it will be hard to find four such lords in the city who do not prefer Koinas or Romulus."

"Perhaps you choose two lords and I choose two lords," Dracus replied. "That would be fair."

"I shall think on it," Romulus answered carefully. "And you shall have my answer tomorrow evening."

With that, the dinner was adjourned, and each lord bowed and left. Soon, it was only Romulus, Myon, Reith, Remus, and Ellyn left.

"I sense a trap," Romulus said. "I am uneasy about this. I do not see how it benefits us to go through with this plan."

"It could have some benefit," Myon pointed out. "You could solidify your hold on the throne if your father is found guilty."

"And if somehow he is not?" Romulus asked. "I will be exiled or worse. The potential gains are small compared to the massive catastrophe if we lose."

"The numbers should still be on your side," Reith chimed in. "Four against three. Do you have lords you trust?"

"Remus would be a good addition," Romulus replied. "But I shall have to think on the other. Our position is precarious."

"I say we go through with it," Remus said. "As you say, we are in a precarious position. If we refuse, it will be whispered that we have not the courage to face our father over this matter, and your throne will be seen as less and less legitimate."

"I still don't like it," Romulus replied.

"Nor I," Myon answered, "But what else can we do? We are stuck between two unsavory outcomes."

"Myon, are there any lords you trust for such a task?" Romulus asked. "We must be sure that this lord will not betray us. If he were to side with my father, we are ruined."

"I have one or two in mind who would be loyal to you," Myon replied. "I think we can move forward in confidence."

"We can also agree to the trial, but delay its beginning," Remus pointed out. "Dracus wanted a trial, he didn't say when, though."

"There's wisdom in that," Myon answered. "And we need time to get our legal strategy together."

"A month?" Romulus suggested.

"No, longer," Myon said. "I would prefer a year, or even six months, but Dracus would accuse us of stalling. No, three months should do the trick. It gives us plenty of time."

And they all agreed with him.

The following evening, dinner was again served in the great hall. All who were in attendance the previous evening were back, as were a few more. News of the trial seemed to have spread like wildfire.

After dinner, Romulus stood up. "We will convene a trial in three months' time. Our tribunal's decision shall be law."

There was a tumult as various lords and ladies rose as one to speak. Reith looked over at Dracus and found the elf lord was wearing a sly smile, which made Reith very uneasy.

Four

T he trial of the deposed king was the talk of Sardis for the next few weeks. Reith heard whispered speculation and exuberant discussions of the matter as he walked through the city, shopped in the market, and visited the temples and libraries.

Ellyn was his constant guide, and she was just as enamored as he was with the great city. She had spent nearly all her life in Crain and found the sights and sounds of Sardis to be mesmerizing. First thing each morning, they went down to the stables to visit Aspen before going out and exploring a new part of the city. Each afternoon, they settled into a library to read, or they visited a temple. In the evenings, they dined with Romulus and Remus and whichever lords happened to be around.

Before he knew it, Reith had been in Sardis a month. He found himself thinking more and more of Dema. He was having a splendid time among the elves, how was her errand to the dwarves going? But mostly, he missed her simple presence and touch. But when would he see her again?

He asked Myon about the possibility of sending a letter to

Darren Shahr, but Myon shot the idea down, though he did it very kindly.

"No, Reith," he said gently, "I am afraid that right now, with this trial looming, we can't possibly send out envoys to the dwarves. But as soon as the trial is over, Romulus will, I am sure, waste no time in extending the hand of diplomacy to the dwarves."

Though the trial was on everyone else's mind, it wasn't much on Reith's. After all, he was a visiting ambassador for the humans, sent by King Calmon. In his professional capacity, it did not matter who was on the throne, only that he was able to maintain diplomatic ties. Personally, he hoped Romulus would remain in power, but even as an ambassador, he guessed his presence would not be welcome if Koinas were to come back into power. But he tried not to worry.

Instead, he poured great energy into researching his sword and his ring. He knew his sword was a key and that he needed to travel north, to the Temple of Ice. Onias, the High Priest of the Shrine of Antropa had told him a prophecy when he had visited the Free Isles.

"A thousand years hence, there shall be war. Shadows will rise and the key will be found. When hope seems lost, the key bearer shall travel due North, across the inland sea, and follow the frozen river. At the Temple of Ice, the key bearer shall present the key and encounter the power of restoration."

He had committed the lines to memory, and he puzzled over them. The part that perplexed him was "When hope seems lost." Right now, hope did not seem lost. Things were looking up for him and Terrasohnen. And he hadn't heard that voice in his head in a while, the one beckoning him to "Find me."

He held the key. But the time had not come. Not yet. But soon?

He fidgeted with the ring on his finger. Solzar had told

him the ring would lead him in the right direction when it was time to go. But when would be the right time? How would he know?

To find the answer to these questions, he pored over books and scrolls. The one thing he did not do was confide in any of the priests at the temples in Sardis, or in Ellyn. As a stranger in a foreign land, he thought it best to keep some of his secrets to himself.

His second month in Sardis involved less exploring and more research, but also more official visits with Romulus and his court. Formal meetings and dinners were arranged, and he began to meet with various lords and ladies of the city. Mostly, they asked him about what life among the humans was like and what he liked about Sardis. But most were guarded with the information that they shared with him. But still, after each meeting, he took notes of the interaction, and soon had thorough notes on each of the leading lords and ladies of the city. He thought King Calmon might be interested in such knowledge.

Dracus, he discovered, owned several mines to the east of Sardis, which produced iron, copper, tin, and gold. These had made him very wealthy, as well as powerful. Romulus was dependent on those metals to equip his armies.

Other lords and ladies were old families with old wealth, and large land holdings in the countryside. They employed villagers as farmers and controlled the supply of food in the kingdom. Still others owned ships and controlled trade around the kingdom and to the Free Isles. Or at least they used to trade with the Free Isles.

As his second month in Sardis came to an end, he noticed Romulus, Remus, and Myon were growing more and more stressed about the upcoming trial. If they had chosen another lord to sit on the tribunal, they kept that information to themselves. Dracus walked around the palace with a certain swagger that made Reith uneasy. Three days out from the trial, Reith asked Myon about their plans.

"We are uneasy, Reith," Myon said with a sigh. "It's hard to know who to trust. Politics is not a game for the fainthearted. Koinas has many allies still, and Romulus' hold on the government depends on the goodwill and support of various lords and ladies. Even if the trial ends in our favor, Sardis is still a dangerous place. You would do well to have an escape plan."

Reith visited Aspen a second time that afternoon, and from the stables, walked slowly to the north gate of the city. He wanted to know the way by heart if he needed to make a quick escape. He memorized each turn and mentally cataloged as many landmarks as he could. Once free of the city, he could follow the river all the way to Galismoor. *I hope it doesn't come to that.*

From then on, he vowed to always have on his person his pack with the essentials, just in case he needed to make a quick getaway.

The night before the trial was to begin, Reith went down to dinner as usual, and took his customary place at the table. Lords and ladies entered the hall, heralded on their arrival with their name and title. Reith paid little attention and instead focused on the tomato soup in front of him.

"May I present the Lady Ellamora, ambassador to the humans!"

Reith dropped his spoon with a clatter and a splash. Drops of soup splattered his tunic. He paid it no mind and rose to his feet to see Ellamora walking toward him, a huge smile on her face. She broke into a run, and he matched it, and they met in the middle of the hall in a passionate hug.

"What are you doing here?" Reith asked when they broke apart.

"Well, I'm an ambassador, reporting back to my king," Ellamora replied.

"I didn't expect you yet. Did something happen?" Reith asked.

"Not here," Ellamora said, looking over his shoulder. He turned and looked back at the table and saw the eyes of the whole hall on them. "I'll tell you, and Romulus later."

He escorted her to the table, where she greeted Romulus, Remus, and Myon. A new place was set for her beside Reith.

Reith was dying to ask a million questions, but he held his tongue until after the main course was served.

"What can you tell me?" he asked.

"Something big happened," was all Ellamora said in reply. "If I could, I would tell you right now, but there are too many ears around. But I can tell you that I bring new instructions from King Calmon." She slipped a scroll out from her sleeve and handed it to Reith. He broke the royal seal, unrolled it, and read.

Reith,

I trust that all is going well for you in Sardis. Keep an ear to the ground and use your best judgement. As long as it is safe to remain in Sardis, do so. I know you are there for diplomacy, but things are afoot in Terrasohnen that we cannot begin to know. Friends may become enemies; enemies may become friends. Remember where your loyalties lie. I trust that you will.

His Royal Highness,

King Calmon

Reith tried to parse why Ellamora was here in Sardis based on the note, but he couldn't come up with anything.

The rest of dinner was agonizingly slow. Ellamora chatted with Ellyn as Reith pondered his dessert pastry. Finally, after many farewells, the guests began to leave, and soon the great hall was nearly empty.

"Well, Ellamora," Romulus said, "I think it is time for your tale."

They retired to a secure side room, and Romulus gave explicit instructions that they were not to be disturbed. Ellamora stood in front of the fireplace while Romulus, Remus, Myon, Ellyn, and Reith took seats in comfortable cushioned chairs in a semicircle around her.

"If you will," Romulus said, and gestured to her with an open hand to begin.

"Kal-Epharion has declared independence from the humans and the rumor is, a Shadow is leading the rebellion."

Romulus swore. Remus gripped the arm of his chair tightly. Myon stood and began to pace. Ellyn nodded slowly, as if she had expected the news. Reith sat in shock, gaping at Ellamora.

"How did you come by this news?" Romulus asked.

"A few men loyal to King Calmon escaped from the city and rode with great haste to Galismoor."

"How did this coup take place?" Remus asked. "Surely one man could not overthrow a city, even if he were a Shadow."

"That's just the thing," Ellamora said. "From what we were told, the Shadow gained the hearts of the people through speeches and pamphlets. When she had enough support," and she paused here, letting the implications of "she" ring through the room. "When she had enough support, it was a simple matter to gain a vote of no confidence in the King appointed governor. The Shadow took power in a legal way, as far as the laws of the humans are concerned. But declaring independence, that's another matter."

"Did they say anything about the Shadow's intentions?" Myon asked.

"The escapees said as they were leaving the Shadow was mustering an army. Where it would march, we cannot say.

Galismoor is the simplest march, though it is a long way. Darren Shahr is closer, but there are mountains to deal with. An army from Kal-Epharion could not march to any elven city without encountering resistance from humans or dwarves."

"But surely Kal-Epharion cannot muster an army great enough on its own to challenge either of those cities?" Romulus asked.

"From what I know, Kal-Epharion is nearly as large as Galismoor," Reith said. "It could muster a large army that would have a chance against Galismoor, depending on how many troops the king had in the city."

"There has to be another angle here, something we are missing," Remus said. "It would be foolish for anyone to march out of Kal-Epharion with all their troops and none left behind. Say they march to Darren Shahr. King Calmon could march east and easily retake the city, then meet Kal-Epharion out in the wild, away from any retreat. They'd be caught between the king and the dwarves. Or if they marched to Galismoor, even a small force of dwarves could take the city for their own and increase their interests to the east."

"I agree, there has to be more," Myon replied. "Perhaps this new Shadow is looking for aid from another, yet unknown Shadow among the humans, dwarves, or even among our people."

"Is it possible Kal-Epharion has not heard of the fall of Solzar?" Romulus asked. "This Shadow could be expecting help from Solzar."

"You're forgetting the nature of a Shadow,' Ellyn said, entering the conversation after sitting quietly and pondering their words. "A Shadow is controlled by the Dark Powers, spiritual beings. They are not bound by space and time as we are. The moment Solzar fell, all the Dark Powers knew it. They have a communication advantage on us."

"So, they can communicate instantly across the continent,

and we are stuck responding to their moves?" Remus asked. "They will be several steps ahead of us."

"They are still limited by the humans in their control." Ellyn answered. "As far as we know, there is just one Shadow, with one army. If there were two, or even three, that would make our situation dangerous.

"So we have time to see how this plays out," Romulus mused.

"See how this plays out?" Reith asked. "A Shadow is marching on friends and allies. Would you not go to the aid of your new friends?"

"We can't split our force between Galismoor and Darren Shahr," Romulus pointed out. "That would leave us vulnerable. But I am not inclined to leave either of our friends out to dry. The elves will send aid, but we will not overextend ourselves."

"What will you do?" Ellamora asked.

"Nothing," Romulus said, and then quickly added when Reith shot him a look, "I mean nothing at the present. We need to see this trial through to the end. After that, I suppose we can send troops to Crain. From there, they march north or east."

"The trial should be over tomorrow," Myon added, trying to comfort Reith. "This time tomorrow, we can plan our response to this new Shadow."

The morning of the trial dawned in fog and rain. The trial itself was to take place in the throne room, heavy security provided by the palace guards. In addition to Remus, Romulus appointed an elf lord named Festus to the tribunal. Festus had been a general before retiring in comfort and luxury in Sardis. Myon emphatically vouched for him.

Dracus appointed his two lords, Valinus and Nerus, both of whom had been highly favored under Koinas' rule. Reith did not like the look of either of them. They would go with Dracus no matter what.

"As long as Festus remains on our side, we will be able to condemn my father," Romulus declared on the morning of the trial.

The trial convened. The seven sitting on the tribunal sat on a raised dais, while the rest of those assembled sat in chairs facing them. A small table was placed in front of the tribunal with a single chair.

Koinas was led out. He was well dressed and well cared for. He eyed the crowd with a mixture of disdain and apathy. He and Reith locked eyes for a long second before Koinas took his seat. Reith sat near the back with Ellyn and Ellamora. Romulus, Remus, and Myon, of course, were up at the front sitting among the seven. Romulus sat in the middle with Remus on his right, then Myon next to him, and Festus on the end. Dracus sat to Romulus' left, and Valinus and Nerus were on the other side of Dracus. Romulus started the whole affair.

"Koinas, formerly King Koinas and lord of this kingdom, you stand here today to face charges of dereliction of duty and high treason against this kingdom and this throne. Such a crime has never been committed by the kings and queens of our land, and this matter is being treated with the seriousness of the offense."

Romulus spent the next half hour going through the case against his father point by point. Romulus' case focused on Koinas abdicating responsibility to Solzar, the Shadow, and needlessly sending troops into harm's way and provoking their formerly peaceful neighbors in the Free Isles, Darren Shahr, and Galismoor. On several occasions, a statement by the king resulted in muttering around the hall. Reith grew uneasy about the sentiment in the room.

Romulus concluded his case and sat back down. Koinas rose to his feet and spoke. His voice was silky and smooth.

"My son, my son," Koinas began. "Your zeal for this throne and our house is admirable, to say the least. And it is for my own zeal that I am here today. I will admit that I took drastic action to send our troops in two different directions. But I saw an opportunity. Our foes were weak, and we were strong. We could have greatly expanded our territory and the riches of our land, had we been successful. And oh, were we nearly successful! And I will admit too, to accepting the advice and guidance, and military support, of a man you claim to be a Shadow. But we all know Shadows are but myths out of children's tales. No, this man was simply sympathetic to my aims at strengthening my kingdom and offered his help, which I accepted. Does that make me a traitor or a villain? Hardly."

There was another round of muttering in the hall.

"No, everything I did, I did with my kingdom in mind, our kingdom, for it would have become yours one day. But what of your part in this whole affair?"

"It is not I who am on trial," Romulus replied bluntly. "Speak to your own defense."

"As you wish, your highness," Koinas answered with a hiss. "You say I am on trial for dereliction of duty and high treason? Now that hardly seems fair. I worked hard so that all those gathered here today could live in prosperity."

There was yet another round of muttering, and lots of nodding of heads. The crowd was firmly on Koinas' side. Reith stood up and stood beside the door, a hand on his sword hilt. This could get messy.

"As king, my task was to strengthen this kingdom," Koinas continued. "We all want a strong kingdom, don't we? A strong kingdom keeps us safe from outside enemies and gives us the basis of a prosperous economy. And rumor had reached my ears that our enemies were too comfortable at our borders.

Humans had crossed into Crain and opposed our people there."

Several heads turned in Reith's direction at that comment, but he stood tall.

"Dwarves, well, you can never trust a dwarf," Koinas went on. "And the Free Isles have been in rebellion against this throne for years. They harbor the Red Fleet, which disrupts our trade and steals our profits. It was time to subdue them and bring them back under our banner. And my plans would have been successful, if my son hadn't taken off with human vagabonds and villains to thwart me."

There was more muttering and nods of agreement around the room.

"So, yes," Koinas continued, his tone noticeably harsher now. "I suppose I did exactly what you say I did. But it is up to this tribunal to decide if I did anything worth the horrific treatment I have received thus far at your hand. I appeal to the gentlemen of the tribunal, judge whether I have done anything against the laws of our land, or whether my son has wrongfully usurped my position before his time."

"It comes down to a vote then. All in favor of conviction ..." Romulus said, raising his own hand. Remus and Myon quickly shoved their hands into the air. But Festus wavered. He looked pale and sweaty, even from where Reith was standing. For several long seconds, his hands remained in his lap. Every eye in the hall was upon him.

And then he twitched as if to raise his hand, and triumph passed over the faces of Romulus, Remus, and Myon. But just as soon as it crossed their faces, it disappeared, as Festus resolutely stared straight ahead, and his arms were still down.

"And all in favor of acquittal ..." Dracus said with glee, rising to his feet, his hand proudly in the air. Valinus and Nerus shot their hands into the air, and for a fraction of a second that lasted an eternity, Festus remained unmoving. But then he too shot a hand in the air. Romulus slumped in his chair, and then someone screamed. It was pandemonium.

The crowd rose as one and several people were screaming. In the confusion, Reith tried to figure out what the cause of all the commotion was.

"Look!" Ellamora shouted to him over the din. He followed her finger which was pointing to the head of the room at Romulus. Reith had assumed he was slumped over in defeat, but now he saw the real cause. An arrow was sticking out of the side of Romulus' neck and the dead elf stared unseeingly across the room.

FIVE

"You have to get out of here!" Ellamora yelled. "It's not safe for you here."

Reith was stunned. The crowd was scattering. Dracus was leaving the hall at the other end with Koinas by his side. Remus and Myon tended to Romulus while the palace guards surrounded them to defend. Following the shaft of the arrow, Reith tried to determine its source, but now Ellamora had him by the shoulders and was shaking him.

"There's nothing you can do; we need to leave!"

Reith remembered his preparations.

"Come on," he beckoned to Ellamora and Ellyn. "To the stables."

They ran along with the panicking crowd, and blended in as much as they could. No one paid them any attention.

They rushed through passages, but at doorways, they had to wait for the surging crowd to press through. As they waited for one of the doorways to clear, Ellamora took the hands of Reith and Ellyn. "So we don't get separated."

Eventually, they freed themselves of the crowd and were able to jog down to the stables. Aspen was waiting for them.

Aspen's saddle and Reith's bow and quiver were nearby, and he quickly saddled her. Ellamora and Ellyn found two other horses and saddled them as well. Within five minutes, all three were mounted and ready to fly.

"Where to?" Ellamora asked.

"North," Reith replied. "Along the river to Galismoor."

They trotted out of the stables and into the street. Most people seemed to be going about their day, not aware that inside the palace, the whole world had been turned upside down.

Ellamora led the way with Ellyn behind her and Reith bringing up the rear. Aspen was a good follower, and this gave Reith the opportunity to keep an eye out for danger as well as think about what had just happened.

Romulus was dead. And worse, Koinas had been acquitted and set free. Who would rule? Remus was next in line after Romulus, but would Koinas take the throne again?

The ordinariness of the day suddenly shattered in a scream in the distance. Reith turned in his saddle and looked in the direction it had come, behind him and to his right. More screams rent the air. And it was clear to see why they were screaming. In the center of the city, the palace structure stood high above the rest. And it was engulfed in flame.

Suddenly, the previously peaceful street was a mass of confusion. Venders shut down their stalls in haste, shoppers fled away from the smoke rising high in the sky over Sardis. And guards from the walls came galloping back toward the center of the city, knowing that any danger from outside the walls could wait until the danger within was dealt with. Several companies rushed past Ellamora, Ellyn, and Reith, and luckily, the three of them escaped scrutiny.

Each time a company of guards passed, they were required to make for the edges of the street, often getting pressed up against the wall. The horses fared well despite these cramped quarters, though Ellyn's horse took a bite at the rear end of an elf who got a little too close.

Every minute or so, Reith looked back at the fire, which raged bigger and stronger, and smoke eventually hid the central tower from view.

Koinas' men must have lit fire to the palace as they escaped. I hope Remus and Myon are ok.

They had not gotten to say goodbye, and Reith feared he may never see Remus or Myon again. But Ellamora was right. They had to escape. They had to bring news of what had happened to King Calmon. They had to prepare.

But prepare for what? Kal-Epharion was independent and raising an army. The elven kingdom would soon be in the hands of Koinas, if it wasn't already. Were the dwarves similarly in peril? A shadow was falling over all Terrasohnen.

With the thought of the dwarves, Reith's mind went to Dema. She was fulfilling a similar duty to what he had been doing here in Sardis. Queen Kalis was a good ruler and had probably received Dema warmly. But could a Shadow rise among the dwarves? A pang of fear gripped Reith's heart. He had lost Kydar, Vereinen, and now Romulus, and perhaps Remus and Myon too. He couldn't stand to lose Dema as well. For one wild second, he thought of traveling east and riding to Darren Shahr to rescue her. But the moment passed as he realized the foolishness of such an errand.

They neared the city gate, the Northern Gate, through which they must pass. Ellamora led them around the final turn but then pulled up her horse and gasped. Ellyn and Reith reacted quickly to check their own mounts.

The gate was perhaps a hundred feet away. Crowds of villagers milled about the square wandering aimlessly. They had nowhere to go because the gate was shut.

Ellamora swore.

"Now what?" Ellyn asked, glancing back and forth from Ellamora to Reith.

"All the gates will be shut," Ellamora said. "All the guards are in the city center."

"Can we open it?" Reith asked. "All these people seem to want to get out too."

Ellamora pointed to the guard towers on either side of the gate. "We need at least four people to open the gate," she pointed out. "Two on each side. Maybe more."

"Can someone here help us?" Reith asked.

"We can ask," Ellamora replied, "But I'd better be the one asking. You're clearly not from around here."

Ellamora swung down from her saddle and walked cautiously toward a tall elf standing near a donkey and a cart of apples. Amid the hustle and bustle of the city, Reith could not make out her words, nor his, but they conversed for a minute or so, and the tall elf repeatedly shook his head.

This pattern repeated itself with three more elves that Ellamora approached. Each shook their heads no at the request to help with the gate.

"Come on," Reith said to Ellyn, impatient to get out of Sardis. They left their horses, who stood together watching them leave. Reith headed toward the left guard tower. He ascended the stairs and reached a locked door at the top. He jiggled the handle, and then gave the door a shoulder, which was enough force to break the weak locking mechanism. He and Ellyn slipped inside.

Inside the guard tower, there was a large wheel with spokes, like a ship's wheel, set on a platform in the center of the room. Looking down through the spokes, Reith saw chains which would open and shut the gate when the wheel was turned. He pushed at one of the spokes of the wheel in an experimental way to test how heavy it would be. It didn't budge, even when he was leaning most of his weight against it.

"Do we need to open both sides?" Ellyn asked. She was standing by the window looking across at the other guard tower. "Or will one side do?"

"I think one side would be enough," Reith answered. "But it's heavy."

"Another question," Ellyn began. "If we were to turn the wheel, would the gate stay open? Or would it slam shut the moment we stopped turning the wheel?"

"Good question," Reith replied, pondering the implications. "Give me a hand with it, we can see if it will open with the two of us."

Reith stood on one side of the wheel and Ellyn stood on the other, and they each faced opposite directions.

"On three then," Reith said. On three, they each put their full weight on the wheel and dug in their feet. For a long second, the wheel remained motionless. And then slowly, ever so slowly, it began to turn. Reith made it halfway around the circle, when he called for a stop.

"Can you see out the window?" he gasped as he strained to hold the wheel steady.

"The gate is open about a foot," Ellyn said, standing up on her toes, craning to see. "Another turn and a half should be enough."

"We need to secure the wheel when we do that," Reith grunted. "How do they normally do it? Is there a rope?" From where he stood, he couldn't see one.

"Oh, there, right behind you," Ellyn said, pointing to the wall. "It's looped on the end."

"Can you reach it when you come around to my side?" he asked.

"Let's try a quarter turn, and I'll reach."

Ellyn counted them off and they pushed the wheel until Ellyn was close to the wall with the rope.

"Almost there," Ellyn panted as she strained toward the wall with one hand still holding the wheel.

"Hurry."

"I can't reach," Ellyn said. "I'll have to let go. Can you hold it in place?"

"Possibly," Reith said. Already he was holding most of the weight as Ellyn was only pushing with her left hand.

"On three then?" Ellyn asked.

"Sure."

She counted off and let go. Suddenly, the full weight of the wheel hit him. His arms flopped uselessly, and the spoke struck him in the stomach. He fell back, landing in a heap on the floor gasping for air.

"Reith!" Ellyn exclaimed, and she dropped to her news by him.

Reith felt as if air would not enter his lungs. He took great shuddering breaths and felt his head spinning.

It took several minutes for his breathing to return to normal. He slowly sat up with a groan.

"Are you ok?" Ellyn asked.

"I've been better."

Soon, he was able to stand and then stood by the wheel again, ready to turn it.

Ellyn set the loop of the rope on a chair next to the wheel, in easy reach of whoever was nearest when it was time to stop turning the wheel.

"Two full turns?" she asked.

"Let's try for two and a half, maybe three," Reith suggested. He would hate to get down to street level only for the gate to not be open far enough for them and the horses.

Ellyn counted them off and they began pushing. The wheel turned ever so slowly at first, but by the time they had finished the first rotation, they were moving quickly.

"Three turns," Reith grunted as he pushed. At the end of the turn, Ellyn reached over and grabbed the rope.

"I think it needs to be on your side, to stretch it out." She handed him the rope across the wheel and Reith leaned his whole body on the wheel to take the rope in both hands and stretch it out as far as he could.

He strained forward and managed to loop the rope around the spoke.

"It's on. Let's see if it will hold."

He beckoned for Ellyn to step away. She let go and nothing happened. The rope held fast. Reith stepped to the side, away from the spokes, though he still held on. He did not want to get struck again. He let go with one hand, then the other, and the wheel stood in place.

"Let's go!" he exclaimed, and he and Ellyn turned toward the door.

"What are you doing here?"

Standing in the doorway was a single guard, armed with a spear and looking at them with shock.

"Well, someone had to open the gate," Ellyn said, immediately springing into a businesslike tone.

"The gate is supposed to remain shut," the guard said.

"Tell that to the king," Ellyn wildly made up on the spot. "I have an urgent message from the king that must reach the proper ears in a timely manner."

Reith wondered who the king was at that moment in time and who the guard thought was king. And whose side was he on?

Ellyn continued her wild bluff.

"Your men abandoned this gate," she said. "So we had to come up here ourselves. Oh, when the king finds out, he will be livid."

"But the palace is on fire," the guard protested feebly.

"Of course the palace is on fire. Congratulations, you

understand what it means when smoke rises from a building. Why else do you think the king was sending a message."

"Who is the message for?" the guard asked.

"Oh, so now you want to know the king's business? You're a nosy one, aren't you?" She stepped forward and was nearly nose to nose with him. He quivered in discomfort.

"Now, if you don't mind, my companion and I shall be off."

She stepped around him and headed for the door. Reith followed behind. The guard remained in the room, dumbfounded.

On the street, Reith whispered to Ellyn in awe.

"Well done."

She beamed.

Ellamora stood by the horses, and a look of relief crossed her face.

"I saw the guard go up the steps. How did you get away?"

"By Ellyn's sheer force of will," Reith said as he mounted Aspen. "We'll tell you later."

Within minutes, they were trailing north on the tree lined road that Reith had once taken to arrive at Sardis, what seemed like a lifetime ago.

———

They rode hard all day, stopping only to let the horses drink in the river that ran beside the road. On these brief stops, when they looked back, they could see faintly the smoke rising in the distance. Whether or not the fire was still burning, they could not tell.

When they passed others on the road, Ellamora took the lead, with Ellyn at the rear, and Reith between them. He kept his head down to avoid recognition as a human. They trusted Ellamora's official position as a diplomat to keep them out of trouble, though the uncertainty they left behind in Sardis would complicate that. Still, no one they would encounter heading north would have any idea that Romulus was dead. But they still didn't know whether news of Romulus' ascension had ever reached the outskirts of the nation. However, that day they had good fortune, and no one paid them any mind.

As the sun neared the horizon, they left the road and traveled inland about a quarter mile. There, in the trees, they could light a fire and avoid detection from the road, but they were still near enough to the river to get water.

In no time, the fire was kindled, and the horses were unsaddled. Reith leaned back against Aspen's saddle on the ground, letting the fire warm his legs as he stretched out. Ellamora and Ellyn mimicked him, and each was lost in their own thoughts.

Reith's mind replayed the events of the day. The trial. The arrow. The blood. The commotion. The fire. The gate. The road. Each came to mind, one after the other.

He allowed himself to mourn. Soon tears welled up in his eyes. He leaned forward and bent his head down, and the tears trickled into the grass.

He sniffled and wiped his eyes with the back of his hands. He looked up and saw the firelight glittering off Ellamora's tears.

"When can we stop running?" Ellamora asked. "Ever since I left Crain, I have been running non-stop. When will it be enough?"

"Shadows for the night," Ellyn replied quietly.

"Shadows," Reith said, nodding. "Exactly our problem."

Reith took the first watch that evening. He walked circles around the camp, keeping a silent vigil over Ellamora and Ellyn, but also over Romulus, Remus, and Myon. He stared into the starry sky and lost himself in the depths of space.

Pinpricks of light dotted the darkness, small beacons of hope in the universe full of shadow.

"Shadows for the night," he whispered quietly to himself. "But light at the dawn."

It was an old prayer of the elves that Ellyn had taught him when he first had arrived at Crain. How true was it now. It was nighttime, in more ways than one, and he wondered if now was the time when all hope seemed lost.

My time will come soon, he thought to himself as he spun the ring on his finger.

As he made another lap of the camp, he edged closer to where Ellamora and Ellyn lay. He couldn't hear their rhythmic breathing of sleep, and he realized he was not the only one still awake, lost in thought.

———

At dawn, the three riders and their horses found the road again and pressed onward to the north. They took it easier on the horses this day, as there was less danger of being followed by Sardis now, but also because this day would be a full day on the road, and there was no need to recklessly charge onward at a frantic pace. The slower pace allowed them to ride three abreast and talk to one another.

By unspoken agreement, they kept their distance from the events in Sardis the previous day and instead talked about Reith and Ellyn's experience in Sardis and Ellamora's experience in Galismoor.

"What sort of treatment can I expect in Galismoor?" Ellyn asked, rather nervously. Reith remembered that this would be her first time out of the land of the elves. He remembered what it was like when he first crossed the river and left the human country behind. He marveled at how much things had changed since then. He had been all over the elves' land, sailed to the Free Isles then to the Dwarven coast, and made his way to the Dwarven capital city before departing again for his homeland.

"You will be well received, especially as my guest and Reith's guest. Though you won't be given any official diplomatic treatment, you will be warmly welcomed, and a place will be made for you in the king's house. At the very least, you can stay with me, if there are not enough rooms free."

"I appreciate that," Ellyn replied. "What is King Calmon like?"

"He is a good king," Ellamora replied. "Very wise. The kind of king I think Romulus would have become, given time and freedom to rule as he wanted." She paused here, and the remembrance of the recently dead king washed over them like ice water. The moment soon passed, and they continued their conversation, silently agreeing to pass over this unfortunate bit.

By nightfall the next day, they reached the intersection of the Rammis River flowing down from the mountains in the east and the Great River, which flowed down from Galismoor in the north. Though they would have rather crossed the river and slept on human land, they were unable to find a ford sufficient for their needs in time, and instead had to search for a campsite in the gathering dusk.

In the morning, they traveled east up the Rammis River and eventually found a ford a few miles upstream, where the river was wide, flat, and gentle. They crossed with little difficulty.

As their horses stepped onto dry land, Reith breathed in a deep breath. *Home.*

They cut across country traveling north and west, angling to intersect the Great River and travel along it north.

The miles passed swiftly beneath the hooves of their

horses, and all three travelers felt much more relaxed now that they were out of elven territory.

They camped beside the river that evening, not bothering to leave its banks as they had in the elven lands. The gentle sounds of the river soothed them all to a quick and happy sleep. In the morning, at first light, they again took to the saddle and traveled north.

Across the river, to the west, the land was lush and green, and it wasn't until later that day that Reith noticed something odd about it.

"Hey!" He exclaimed. Ellamora and Ellyn turned to look at him. "The land across the river, it's green."

"Why shouldn't it be?" Ellyn asked.

"It's green on this side too," Ellamora pointed out, as if Reith's eyesight were an issue.

"It's not supposed to be green," Reith pointed out. "It's supposed to be black and gray and dead. We should be traveling alongside Dragonscar now."

Dragonscar was the western edge of Terrasohnen perpetually scarred by the fire of dragons in ages past. Reith had traveled through it at the onset of his adventures, traveling to Erador and back. The land was blackened and charred, and nothing grew.

Nothing except the grove of trees and the grass along the stream.

On his first visit to Dragonscar, he was surprised to find a grove of fruit trees and a stream, both of which had seemed to pop into existence recently. The fruit had proved magical, as anywhere its seeds fell, new trees grew unnaturally quickly.

"Are you sure we've reached Dragonscar?" Ellamora asked.

"I'm positive," Reith replied. "It began just north of where the Rammis and Great Rivers meet. We've traveled a long way since the intersection of those rivers. In fact, we should be getting close to where I crossed the river."

They continued, and it wasn't an hour more before Reith spotted the ford and the dilapidated old guard house that marked the place where he had camped and crossed.

Except now, he could just make out the old guard house. Another grove of fruit trees was dominating the landscape here. He saw peach, apple, pear, and orange trees, among others.

And across the river, Dragonscar was in full bloom.

Six

Mesmerized, Reith dismounted from Aspen and led her to the river's edge. Gone were the blackened and charred remains. Gone was the stench of lingering smoke. Gone too was the silence of a dead land. Even from across the river, Reith could hear birds and watched them swoop to and fro.

Ellamora and Ellyn joined him beside the water.

"That was Dragonscar?" Ellamora asked.

"Yes, this is where I crossed the river to go to Erador," Reith replied.

"This can't be," Ellyn said in wonder.

"It's the magic in the fruit," Reith replied. "It spreads quickly."

"What magic is this?" Ellamora replied. "What magic that can resurrect this land?"

"It's the God of Light," Ellyn said simply. "Light driving out shadow."

"I want to cross," Reith said. "It's not far from this bend in the river to Erador."

"We must get to Galismoor," Ellamora replied, though the longing in her voice betrayed her true feelings.

"We can travel to Erador, camp there for the evening, and then be on our way tomorrow," Reith answered. "Besides, I think the king will want a full account of Dragonscar."

It was decided. Reith remembered the river was not too deep, so they all mounted their horses again and rode across. The water nearly reached his knee, but got no higher, and they all were across safely in a matter of minutes.

Surprisingly, there was still a path through the newly grown forest. Reith guessed it followed the path he had tread to Erador all those months ago, though he was a bit shocked it had not grown over as well.

Erador is meant to be entered and traversed.

The air was sweet and warm but not too warm. The horses seemed to gain strength from the new forest, and galloped on at a fast pace, faster than they ordinarily could have sustained, and they did it all themselves, with little to no urging from the riders.

The riders, freed from their normal riding attentiveness, allowed their eyes to wander freely. They saw birds of all shapes, sizes and colors flitting among the branches. They saw rabbits and deer frolicking in and out among the trucks. When the birds and animals saw them, they did not stiffen with fear, but rather watched them with interest, or even awe and wonder, Reith thought. Not once did it occur to him to pull out his bow and take down one of these animals.

The fruit seemed to present itself to them as they rode. Each rider would see a juicy specimen from afar and as they drew nearer, its branch would lower so that the fruit was in easy reach. Even the horses were able to munch on fruit as they ran.

In no time at all, the sweet air of the forest mingled with

the salty air of the sea, and soon they were intoxicated with the mixture of sweet and salty.

Rounding a bend in the path, they gasped as a great lake stretched before them. It was perhaps a mile long and a half mile wide, and its waters were clearest blue. They all dismounted, and the horses, elves, and human all drank their fill. Reith had only tasted waters like these once before, and it was at the stream that flowed near Erador. Across the lake, he could see the stone ruins of the ancient city.

"This lake was the stream I saw when I was here last," he announced.

"There wasn't a lake here?" Ellyn asked with surprise.

"No, just a small stream," Reith answered. "And it flowed to the cliffs."

He looked across the lake and saw a small inlet jutting off toward Erador.

"There should be a waterfall over there," he said, pointing at his discovery.

They remounted their horses and were soon on the far side of the lake, near the river that flowed from the lake to the cliffs.

"There must be an underground spring feeding the lake and the river," Ellamora said. "It's flowing perpetually, but it's not shrinking."

For several minutes, they stood in silence, save for the sound of the waterfall, and they watched the water cascade over the edge of the world down to the sea below. Its droplets caught the sun just right and there was a rainbow. Erador, ruined yet beautiful, stood in the distance.

"The world is being made new," Ellyn said softly.

"But what does it all mean?" Ellamora asked. "Fruit trees are great and all, and a lake, and a waterfall, but what good does it do?"

"Good?" Ellyn replied. "What good does anything beautiful do? Beauty is not good because its useful, beauty is good because it was made to be beautiful. It's fulfilling its purpose. Wherever the God of Light's purposes are fulfilled, there will be beauty."

"But what about the Shadows?" Ellamora asked.

"Shadows eclipse the light," Ellyn explained. "But here, here we see the light. Here, everything is as it should be. Remember the birds and the animals? Their fear of us is gone. This is how things were meant to be. The world is becoming new. We can either join in on that, or we can stand in the way and block the light. And when the Shadows press in on us, we can remember this place. We have hope that the Shadows will be vanquished, dead lands can rise, and what's been ruined can be made new again."

They stood in silence for several more minutes. The birds and animals seemed to get closer to them than normal. And in his heart, Reith felt true and abiding peace, peace like he had never known before.

"Let's make camp by the lake," Reith suggested, finally breaking the silence.

———

He was soaring along on the back of some giant, winged creature. They flew over a vast body of water, an ocean or a large lake, he could not tell. The air grew colder on his face as they flew, but the creature was strangely warm beneath his touch.

On and on they flew, and Reith saw the opposite shore and knew that they were flying over a lake. Mountains loomed in the distance, covered with snow and ice. At their foothills, a vast forest of pine trees spread out from horizon to horizon.

The winged creature adjusted course slightly, and they were heading toward the northernmost edge of the lake, where two mountains stood as sentries. Between them ran a river. They soared between the mountains and followed the course of the river through valleys, over waterfalls, and deeper into the heart of the mountain range.

They began to descend, still following the river. With a thrill of fear, he thought the creature meant to land in the water. He braced for the icy splash of water, but it never came. The creature touched down and slid across the icy surface of the frozen river, before digging in its claws and bringing them to a stop. He slid down from the creature's back and jumped to the icy surface of the river below. He looked around and the creature, whatever it was, was gone. He was alone.

Beside the river stood a huge cathedral, a giant temple carved in ice. And then, from everywhere and nowhere at all, a voice spoke.

"The time is coming. Shadows have risen and the key has been found. When hope seems lost, the key bearer shall travel due North, across the inland sea, and follow the frozen river. At the Temple of Ice, the key bearer shall present the key and encounter the power of restoration."

"Is hope lost now?" he asked the voice. "How will I know?"

"Enemies will come to the great city, but do not be afraid. Hope is not yet lost."

"When should I come?" he asked desperately.

"You will come when I call, and I will come when you call."

"Who are you?"

"I am a mirror. I am smoke. I am water."

The scene began to change a shift, darkening as though a curtain were drawn in front of the light.

"Wait!" he cried. "Need I come alone?"

The darkening stopped but did not reverse.

"Only the worthy are permitted to enter the Temple of Ice."

And with that, the darkening began gathering again until he was left in dreamless darkness.

———

Reith awoke and lay there on the soft grass with his eyes still closed. The sounds and smells of Dragonscar overwhelmed his senses.

It needs a new name. It's no longer scarred.

He opened his eyes and saw that the sky was a lovely shade of blue. Sitting up, he saw that Ellamora and Ellyn were still asleep nearby. The horses grazed untethered.

He rose and washed his face in the lake. The water was cool and crisp and shocked him into full alertness. He drank his fill and surveyed the nearby trees for breakfast. He ate an apple and a pear, and each was as lovely as any such fruit he had had in his life.

As he was finishing, both women awoke and stretched into wakefulness.

"Good morning," he called cheerfully.

"Good morning," Ellyn and Ellamora replied sleepily. Ellamora even yawned.

The women washed in the lake and ate from the trees around them. Soon, they were back in the saddle.

"I wish we had time to explore Erador," Ellamora said longingly.

"One day," Reith answered. "One day, we'll come back."

In what seemed to be no time at all, they stood on the banks of the river again. They each took one last look at the land previously known as Dragonscar before urging their horses forward into the current. Soon, they were again on the eastern bank and their horses dripped water on the ground.

All day they followed the river north. On the other side, the lush lands continued with no hint that they had recently been dead.

"It's marvelous," Ellyn said that afternoon as the sun set over Dragonscar.

The light illuminated the world in golds, greens, reds, and oranges, as if the entire forest were made of rainbow.

Everything the light touched glowed with life and vibrance, including the three horses and their riders. Long after the sun set that evening, Reith, Ellyn, Ellamora, and the horses radiated with an afterglow.

They made no fire that evening, as the light they gave off was more than enough for them to see.

———

They traveled on for several more days, maintaining a course along the river. Soon, the land that was Dragonscar was replaced by normal plains and hills and trees. They passed through several small villages along the river, which Reith entered to get supplied while Ellyn and Ellamora rode well out of the way to circumvent the towns. Reith wished it were not so, but the arrangement kept them all out of trouble, which is exactly what they desired at this stretch of their journey.

The further north they went, the colder the air grew. After one particularly miserable night where the three of them stayed as close to the fire as they could without getting scorched, Reith swore to buy them coats, hats, and gloves in the next town. The addition of the cold weather clothing made all the difference for them.

In the distance, a great forest stretched away to the north and west.

"We're getting close to Galismoor," Ellamora declared. "That forest stretches north and grows on the western edge of the Inland Sea, which Galismoor sits at the southern edge of."

With the promise of a warm place to sleep ahead of them, they quickened their pace that day. By midafternoon, the towers of Galismoor appeared over the horizon. Reith kept anticipating the city to grow larger soon as they approached, but the towers remained a small blip on the horizon for a long time.

"Is it still that far away?" he asked Ellamora after a couple of hours with little change in the city's size on the edge of the world.

"Oh yes," Ellamora answered. "It's huge."

It was dusk before they finally arrived at the gates of the great city. True to Ellamora's word, it rose hundreds of feet above the plain and towered above them. Its walls were hewn of red sandstone, so it seemed to glow like fire in the twilight. Banners and flags waved in the wind above the city, and here and there along the wall, Reith could see small specks pass in front of the torches, which he took to be guards patrolling the wall.

The wall of the city itself was perhaps a hundred feet high, and various towers and buildings stretched ever higher above the city.

As they neared the gate, twenty armed knights on horseback trotted out to meet them.

"Hail, strangers!" their captain called to them. "Dismount and state your names and business at Galismoor."

Reith and the others pulled up their horses and dismounted. They even raised their hands to shoulder level to show they meant no harm.

"I am Reith, his majesty's ambassador to the Kingdom of the Elves. My companions are the Lady Ellamora, ambassador to King Calmon from the Elven Kingdom, and Ellyn, Lore Master of the elven city of Crain. They are my friends."

"Welcome, ambassador," the captain said. "I am Captain Tahor. Lady Ellamora, it is my pleasure to welcome you to Galismoor once more. And Lore Master Ellyn, welcome to our city. You shall be treated as an honored guest."

"Your welcome is most gracious," Ellamora replied, adopting her court manner.

"Come, let us find you lodgings and food," Captain Tahor beckoned. "You may ride behind me."

The three travelers mounted their horses once more and followed Tahor into the city. The remaining guards stopped just inside the gate, but Tahor rode onward, into the city itself.

Reith didn't really know what he expected from Galismoor. His entire life, Galismoor was a concept at the back of his mind, a city far away on a map. But he had never really stopped to consider what the city itself was like. From the outside, it seemed to combine the majesty of the elven capital, Sardis, with the fortress and battle readiness of the dwarven capital, Darren Shahr. But on the inside, it was simply different.

Though it was late, the streets bustled with activity. Pubs and taverns were hubs for activity. As doors to these establishments opened to the street, Reith could hear the merry voices of patrons as they passed. In many establishments, singing could be heard as well. These sorts of places in the other cities were less boisterous, and more likely to empty as darkness fell. Here in Galismoor, they seemed to grow more crowded.

"The streets of Galismoor are merrier than those in Sardis," Ellyn pointed out, evidently thinking along the same lines as Reith.

"The feasts of Galismoor are incredible," Ellamora replied. "They were my favorite parts of my stay here."

Tahor led them on a path that wound back and forth as they neared the center of the city. *This city would be hard to take,* Reith thought. *But that's exactly what someone's going to try and do.*

The thought of a Shadow led army from Kal-Epharion frightened him, but seeing the fortifications of Galismoor strengthened his resolve.

The shadows lengthened as they weaved their way through the city, and soon the only light was that of lanterns hanging on hooks along the walls or the light spilling out of open doors and windows of taverns, shops, and homes.

Presently, they reached a wide street which seemed to be circular, with a tall wall, perhaps fifty feet high, looming over them toward the center of the city.

"In the event the enemy breaches the outer wall, the city can fall back to the center and hold out again," Ellamora pointed out to him as though reading his mind.

Tahor brought them along to a large gate which stood open. Several soldiers came to attention as Tahor approached. He exchanged words with one of them, the one who seemed in charge, and they came to an understanding.

"Here is where I leave you," Tahor said to the three travelers. "Captain Simon will take you into the inner city where lodging adequate for your station will be provided." Tahor gave a slight bow to them, and they went back the way he had come.

"Follow me," Simon said, barely looking at Reith but staring in fascination at the two elves.

Simon had no horse, so the three travelers dismounted and led their horses along after him.

The gate opened into a large courtyard which seemed to be arrayed as a practice yard for city soldiers. Reith saw stacks of arrows and targets, barrels full of practice swords and spears, and a ring roped off for sparing. *I will have to come here and practice.*

Simon led them across the courtyard. At the other end, he called out, "Stable hands!"

A door burst open a few seconds later and a young man, or maybe he was a boy, perhaps Reith's own age, stepped out.

"Yes, captain?" he asked.

"Take these three horses to the stables. See that they are well cared for."

"Right away, sir," the boy replied, and took the reins from each in turn.

"They will be in good hands with Leo," Simon said. "He's young, but he knows horses."

Reith patted Aspen on the neck and sent her on with Leo, then followed Simon. Beside the door to the stables was another door, which Simon opened and led them through a stone passage lit with torches at regular intervals along the walls. After a few twists and turns, they found themselves at a staircase, which they ascended. The stairs opened into a large room that smelled of roasted meat and savory sauces. Several men and women were either cooking or cleaning. It was a large kitchen with several ovens and stoves. To the side, a door was propped open to a pantry that Reith could see was well stocked.

"Someone fetch the steward," Simon called out. One of the women dropped her dish rag and promptly scurried from the room, returning a minute later with an older man, with neatly combed black hair that was thinning on top. He was a stout man, acquainted to life at court. When he saw the three travelers he broke into a smile. Reith liked him right away.

"Guests, welcome, welcome," he said heartily. "Ellamora, it is good to see you again." She offered him her hand, which he stooped to kiss.

"I am Mr. Bateson, steward of the halls of the king. And you are?" he asked.

"I am Ellyn, Lore Master of the elven city of Crain, and friend and companion of Ellamora and Reith."

"And I'm Reith, King Calmon's ambassador to the Kingdom of the Elves."

"It is a pleasure to meet you both," Mr. Bateson said warmly, shaking their hands. "As Ellamora can tell you, we take good care of guests here in Galismoor. If there is anything either of you need, no matter what time of day or night, please do not hesitate to ask. We are here to serve. After a long journey, can we interest you in a hot meal?"

Soon the travelers were situated in a room off the kitchen with several tables and chairs.

"Ordinarily, this is where the staff eats their meals," Mr. Bateson explained. "As it's late, this is the perfect spot for you to eat this evening."

Soon, large bowls of steaming beef and vegetable soup were placed in front of them, and a platter with a loaf of warm bread, butter, and several types of cheese was placed in the center of the table. They dug in and ate happily. When they were done, Mr. Bateson returned.

"I have left a note for the king's chamberlain that the three of you have arrived. I am sure he will want to see you tomorrow. When his daily schedule is made, someone will come to tell you what time your audience is so you may make yourself ready for court."

Mr. Bateson showed them down yet another hallway, up another flight of stairs, and onto a wide indoor balcony that overlooked the lower floor, from which there were several doors.

"Lady Ellyn, this is where you will stay." He opened one of the doors, and Reith caught sight of a large bed and a tub before Ellyn stepped forward to enter her room. "If you need anything, there is a bell on the bedside table."

"Good night," Ellyn said, and then gave a big yawn. "I didn't realize how tired I was."

Ellamora and Reith wished her a good night and then Ellyn shut her door.

The next room was Ellamora's, and she wished Reith goodnight as well. The last room was Reith's.

"Here you go, Mr. Reith," Mr. Bateson said with a flourish as he opened the door to Reith's room. Like the other rooms, this one, too, had a large bed. In the corner stood a large tub.

"I shall have clothes sent up for you in the morning," Mr. Bateson said. "They will be hanging on the outside of your door when you wake. If you need anything this evening, just give that bell a tinkle. Goodnight, sir."

"Good night," Reith said sleepily.

He closed the door, then turned to survey the room. Beside the bed, on either side, were two tables. Both had lit candles and one had a small silver bell. Across from the bed stood a wooden chest of doors. Then he noticed that across from the door he had just entered was another door. He walked across and opened it slowly and as quietly as he could. What was beyond it took his breath away.

He stepped out onto a small balcony that seemed to run the length of his room. There was a small table and two chairs. There was a small stone wall that prevented him from walking straight out into space. He rested his arms on the wall and stared out over the great city of Galismoor. Here and there, firelight flickered and illuminated small parts of the city. He couldn't make out much detail beyond the sheer enormity and greatness of the city. Above, the moon glowed white as a small sliver in the sky. Stars twinkled merrily. If he wasn't so tired from his journey, he would have stayed there all night long.

SEVEN

The next morning, true to Mr. Bateson's word, several new items of clothing were hanging on Reith's door. He tried them on and found they fit reasonably well. Along with the clothing, he found a note in meticulously neat writing.

Your audience with the king will occur at midday. Someone will fetch you and bring you to the throne room. In the meantime, if you are hungry, breakfast is served in the great hall. Yours sincerely, Mr. Bateson

He found his way to the great hall with the help of a couple of servants who pointed him in the right direction. He found that the hall was mostly empty, except for a few people who seemed to pay him no mind. He spotted Ellyn across the room sitting alone.

"Good morning," he said, helping himself to the platter of eggs and bacon before him. "How did you sleep?"

"Well, thank you," Ellyn replied. "It was good to be indoors again."

"My thoughts exactly," Reith said as he devoured his

breakfast hungrily. A servant came around and offered him a cup of water, which he gratefully accepted.

"Ellamora still sleeping?" he asked in between mouthfuls.

"It appears so," Ellyn answered. "I should wish to be as well."

A few minutes later, just as Reith was finishing his breakfast, Ellamora wandered in sleepily.

"G'morning," she yawned.

"Good morning," Ellyn said with a smile.

"Help yourself," Reith said, but Ellamora was slower to wake up than he was and didn't take the food just yet.

"I slept like the dead," Ellamora said finally. "From the second I hit the pillow, I was out. I didn't even blow out the candles. I don't think I even moved all night long."

"Do your rooms have balconies?" Reith asked the women.

"Honestly, I didn't even look," Ellamora replied with a chuckle.

"Mine does," Ellyn answered. "It is lovely. I can't wait to go up there again."

"I meant to check it out this morning, I only went out last night," Reith said.

"It was a great place for morning prayers," Ellyn added.

After Ellamora had eaten, which didn't take very long as her appetite wasn't very big this morning, Mr. Bateson sought them out.

"I trust you all had a good night's sleep?"

"Oh yes, wonderful," they chimed in.

"Splendid," he said, and Reith could tell he really meant it. Affection swelled inside him for this very hospitable man he had just met. *So much different than anyone who welcomed me elsewhere on my travels,* he mused.

"Now, you all received my notes?" he asked, and they nodded. "Your time is yours to spend as you will. Tea will be available all morning if you should desire it. You are welcome to explore the city or remain in your rooms. You have a few hours until you are expected in the throne room."

"Thank you, Mr. Bateson," Reith replied.

Mr. Bateson bowed to them and walked away, attending to other guests in the hall.

"Well, what shall we do?" Ellyn asked.

"I want to go to the practice range," Reith answered.

"I wouldn't mind going there," Ellamora replied.

"I am not much for sport or fighting," Ellyn said. "I shall see if Mr. Bateson can procure for me any reading material. It should be a splendid morning for tea and a book on my balcony."

And with that, she was off, leaving Reith and Ellamora.

"Come on," Ellamora said, and she led the way out of the hall.

They soon found themselves on the practice field. Several men were firing arrows at distant targets across the lawn. Several others were hurling spears at sacks of hay. And a few were in full armor, sparring in the ring with practice swords.

"Shall we shoot?" Reith asked.

"I'll teach you a thing or two," Ellamora said with a smirk.

They crossed the lawn and found a barrel with several weather-beaten bows. Reith selected one that looked to be about the size of his own and tested the tension of the strong. Ellamora likewise selected a bow. They went to the edge of the target range and set up in front of a target no one else was using. There were a few arrows in a bucket, from which Reith plucked one.

"Closest to the center wins?" he asked.

"You're on."

He settled into his stance and took a deep breath. He raised the bow and pulled the string back, testing it. Satisfied with how it felt in his hands, he notched the arrow and drew it back by his ear. He sighted along the line and steadied his heart beat and breathing. *Everything together,* he reminded himself. The target was fifty feet away. He exhaled and released the arrow. It sped forward and buried itself in the target about a handset breadth from dead center.

"Not bad," Ellamora said. "For a beginner." He scowled while she grinned mischievously.

She took her place and pulled her own arrow back to her ear. After a few breaths, she loosed her arrow toward the target. It struck hard, buried a couple of inches nearer than Reith's arrow.

"Well done," he remarked. "But I'll get better. New bow."

"It's a poor worker who blames his tools," Ellamora quipped.

They took turns shooting, each trying to best the other. By the time their bucket of arrows was empty, their competition was a tie and the target looked like a porcupine.

"How about swords next?" Ellamora suggested. Sword fighting was where she had a definite advantage on Reith, having been taught by Laneras many years ago in Crain. Reith hadn't picked up a sword until he found the key sword in the library of Erador, though he had picked up quite a few tips from Ellamora during their journeys and made up for inexperience by being slightly bigger than her.

They headed toward the ring. They attracted attention from some of the men as they crossed the lawn, but no one said anything.

They reached a barrel of practice swords. Several were wooden, and a few were metal with clearly dulled edges. All would hurt if a direct strike were to be made, but none would do lasting damage.

"Wood or steel?" Reith asked, knowing in his heart which Ellamora would go for.

"Steel, of course," she said, confirming his suspicion. He picked up a sword in each hand and hefted them, feeling their weight and balance. The one in his left hand felt friendlier, so he put the other back. Ellamora did not like either of the two swords she picked up and instead took up Reith's recently discarded weapon. The ring was open, so they clamored inside.

"Ready?" she asked, eyeing him with ferocity in her eyes.

"I guess," he said, taking a ready position. He eyed her posture and knew she would spring forward immediately at the beginning of the match, and he readied himself for the quick attack.

"One ... two ... three!" Ellamora called and was lunging at him before three was even completely off her lips. He was ready and blocked the blow and spun off to the side, and he swiped at her exposed side. She easily parried this blow, and the duel was on. Around and around they went, each feeling out the other's weaknesses and vulnerabilities. Reith hadn't practiced with the sword in weeks, but then again, neither had Ellamora. But after a few minutes, all the rust was shaken off and they were sparring with speed and power. Reith pressed and unleashed a flurry of blows at Ellamora, which she blocked. But even still, he managed to drive her back to the edge of the ring.

But then the momentum of the fight shifted, and Ellamora fluidly went from defense to attack, her sword a whirlwind in front of her. She wasted no motion, and soon Reith was gasping for air at the effort of keeping her at bay.

With one last flourish of her sword, she struck his hilt in such a way that forced him to drop his sword in surprise, and the next thing he knew, her sword was an inch from her heart.

"Do you yield?" she asked calmly, hardly breathing fast at all.

"I yield," he replied.

There was a round of applause and some cheering from

several of the men that had assembled near the ring to watch their fight.

"Good one, elf!" one of the men called out.

———

After a bath and a change into fresh clothes, Mr. Bateson retrieved Reith from his room for his audience with the king. Mr. Bateson knocked politely on Ellyn's room, then Ellamora's room and the two women joined them.

"I hear you made quite the impression down at the sparring ring," Mr. Bateson said proudly to Ellamora.

"It was nothing," she answered, looking down at her feet.

"It doesn't sound like it was nothing," Mr. Bateson replied. "'Best swordplay I've ever seen,' came from several lips."

He led them through the palace, and they found themselves in a large room with magnificent wooden doors inlaid with gold on one side, and magnificent wooden doors inlaid with steel on the other. The steel doors led outside, while Mr. Bateson led them to the gold inlaid ones.

"Through here is the king's throne room," he explained. "When you enter, traverse the whole hall to the other end, where the king is seated on his throne. Bow and present yourselves. You will do great. I will see you at dinner."

"Thank you, Mr. Bateson," Reith said graciously.

A couple of attendants pulled the double doors open simultaneously. Reith and Ellyn audibly gasped at their first sight of King Calmon's throne room.

It was a large room, as big and as tall as a cathedral. Huge windows lined the walls and let in copious amounts of natural light. Giant pillars of white marble lined the halls, and between each pair of pillars, a guard in ornamental armor stood at attention. The floor was tiled in white marble as well, with the occasional granite square set in regular patterns to break up the monotony. A red carpet ran from where they stood all the way up the room to a raised platform on the far wall, on which rested two chairs. One chair was empty, while the other was King Calmon. Before the throne stood several attendants and government officials. At the sound of the doors opening, all eyes turned to look at the three newcomers.

"Come on," Ellamora whispered to the other two. Reith and Ellyn were awed by the splendor of the room, but Ellamora had been in here several times on her own visit and was not nearly as overwhelmed.

Ellamora led the way down the carpeted track with Reith to her left and Ellyn to her right, each a half step behind her, willing to let her take the lead in this intimidating throne room.

As they approached, Calmon rose and descended from the platform to greet them.

"Greetings, weary travelers," he called to them cheerily while they were still a dozen paces away. "Welcome to my court."

After a few more steps, Ellamora stopped and curtsied in the elven fashion. Ellyn mimicked her a second later, and Reith simply bowed.

"Welcome back to court, Lady Ellamora. I was not expecting to see you so soon, having sent you back to your own people. I am sure there is a story there, and we will get to it soon. Welcome, Ambassador Reith. I look forward to hearing your report of your time in Sardis. And who might this be?"

"I am Ellyn, Lore Master of the elven city of Crain, and companion of Reith and Ellamora," Ellyn replied, and bowed slightly as she said it.

"Any companion of Reith and Ellamora is welcome in my court, Lady Ellyn," Calmon answered. "Come, friends, we have much to discuss. Would you dine with me?" He beckoned to the attendants, who pulled out a square wooden table that had been sitting behind the pillars at the side of the room. Chairs were brought out as well, and the four of them sat down, one on each side with Reith to Calmon's right, Ellamora to his left, and Ellyn across from the king. Golden goblets were placed before each, and wine was offered and poured. "To your long life and good health," the king said, raising his cup to them. They raised their cups as well, and each sipped. The wine was the best wine Reith had ever tried.

"Now, to business," the king said, placing his goblet on the table. "What is your tale, Reith? How was your assignment among the elves and what befell you there?"

Reith told Calmon of the journey to Crain and Pryderus' removal from power. He told of his and Ellyn's travels to Sardis, and the court intrigue there. As he spoke, attendants brought out food for them, and Reith had to interrupt his story several times to take a bite. The trial of King Koinas intrigued Calmon, and when Reith told of the attack on Romulus at the trial, the king shook his head.

"So much darkness in these lands," he said with a sigh.

"And that is why we all came here," Ellamora said. "The darkness is spreading. I could not stay among my people, for we don't even know who the king is anymore."

"This is unwelcome news. I rejoiced to have an ally in King Romulus and Prince Remus to the south. But if they have fallen, and their father is on the throne again, it can only mean ill fortune for us. Ellamora told you about Kal-Epharion?"

"Yes," Reith answered. "All we know is that they are in rebellion and are amassing an army."

"Very true," Calmon replied. "It is so far from here, that we are not able to keep an eye out for them. But I have my swiftest horsemen lined up across the continent to speed to

Galismoor with news, should an army come marching toward us."

"So we should have fair warning, if we are attacked," Ellamora pointed out.

"What of the dwarves?" Reith asked, anxious for any news about Dema. "Has Dema sent any messages?"

"No, not yet," Calmon said, "Though that is hardly surprising. No, we know nothing of what is going on in the dwarven lands. I have patrols in the south and east who can bring us news in haste, but as of yet, we have heard nothing. These are ill tidings you bring me."

"Is there to be war?"

"So much remains to be seen," Calmon replied, scratching his chin thoughtfully. "Are the elves our friends or our enemies? Is Kal-Epharion going to attack us, attack the dwarves, or will they simply remain put? Are the dwarves inclined to be our allies in the event of an attack from either of our potential enemies? If we were secure in our alliances with the dwarves and elves, I would send the might of my army to Kal-Epharion to claim what is rightfully ours and put down those rebels. But now, I cannot stretch my hand out if I have not guaranteed that I can draw it back again if the need arises. So we wait. We cannot make the first move. But I feel that war is coming to this city one way or another. It's in the air. The ravens are gathering for a feast that is promised."

"Is there nothing we can do?" Reith asked. "Should we send a messenger to Dema? Or spies to the elves?"

"I shall think on it," Calmon answered. "But for now, enjoy Galismoor and enjoy your rest. I hear that you two made quite the impression on the training ground today," he said to Ellamora and Reith. "Keep up the training. Your swords will be needed before long, though I wish it were not so. Ellyn, whatever your heart finds for you to do, do it. Our city is open to you. If any man harasses you, let me know and he will be dealt with. Now, I have other business today. I shall call for you if I have need of you."

With the dismissal, the three of them rose and walked back down the hall toward the doors, which opened before them. Ellamora led them straight through the doors, through the atrium, and out the other doors. They stood blinking in the light of the street outside.

"What did you think of King Calmon?" Ellamora asked Ellyn.

"He was very kind," Ellyn replied after a thoughtful second. "Kindness is the best trait in a king."

"I want to go the dwarves," Reith said. "I need to see if Dema is alright."

"I don't think you should go," Ellamora replied. "Soon, it will be time for you to go north. That's what the voice has been telling you, right?"

"Yeah, I guess."

"If you want to help Dema, you will go north when you are summoned," Ellyn pointed out reasonably.

———

The following days passed swiftly for Reith. He and Ellamora spent many hours on the training grounds, honing their warcraft. His archery was as sharp as it had ever been, and he was much better at swordplay. He even fought some of the king's soldiers on occasion and more than held his own.

But the greatest pleasure of Reith's days came when he left the city walls and rode Aspen along the shore of the Inland Sea, a giant lake that was hundreds of miles long. It reminded him of the true sea, except there was no smell of salt in the air here.

Galismoor was built on the southern edge of the Inland Sea, where the Great River flowed south toward Sardis and the ocean. Here at the southern edge of the lake were sandy beaches, which city dwellers took advantage of on nice days. Further up the coast, the shore became rockier, with cliffs overlooking the lake. He managed to ride to the top of some of these cliffs to see out further, but all he could see on the horizon was more water.

Ellamora and Ellyn occasionally joined him, but he appreciated the ability to ride with Aspen alone. His eyes gazed ever north, wondering when it would be time to head for the Temple of Ice. *When hope seems lost,* he kept reminding himself.

One day, about two weeks after they arrived in Galismoor, he was out again by the shore of the Inland Sea, standing on the cliffs overlooking the water. To his left, Galismoor stood gleaming in the sun. As he looked, a single rider on horseback was galloping toward him. As the rider drew near, he realized it was Ellamora. He mounted Aspen and rode down to the beach to meet her.

"Reith!" she yelled out to him when she was close enough.

"What's going on?" he asked. She looked excited or anxious, he couldn't tell for sure.

"Scouts have arrived, from three directions at once," she said. "Kal-Epharion is marching to Galismoor, with a Shadow at their command." She paused to let him take this in. "Scouts from the south brought news that an elven army is massing at the border, looking ready to march." She paused again.

"And the third direction?" Reith asked, knowing already from what direction it had come.

"Some scouts arrived from the southwest with news that a dwarven army is marching toward Galismoor as well. And Dema is here!"

PART TWO
DEMA

EIGHT

The waters of Lake Banu stretched endlessly before Dema and the dwarves. Mountains rose in great jagged peaks covered with ice and snow. Dema shivered in the frigid breeze along the surface of the lake.

Beside her, nearly a score of dwarves settled into make camp. Firewood was procured and soon three raging fires bowed brightly in the gloom of dusk.

It was the third day after Dema and the dwarves had left Palander to go to Darren Shahr. Reith had traveled south to Crain on his way to Sardis. Ellamora remained behind in Palander and would go north to Galismoor. And here she was, alone in the southeast, the only human in who knew how many miles, and her only company was a band of dwarves.

Tears rolled slowly down her cheeks as she gazed out over the water, which rippled gently with small waves. The dying sunlight danced on the lake's surface. In that moment, all she wanted was to mount her horse and ride to meet Reith in Crain.

But she didn't. The scroll in her bag with instructions from King Calmon made her a girl on a mission, a royal mission. To leave now would mean forsaking her duty and the trust given to her. So she sniffled and then wiped the tears from her eyes.

This won't be forever.

She kept telling herself that, each mile that passed beneath her. Eventually she and Reith would be reunited. Everything would turn out for the best. But now ... now was horrible.

She hadn't given much thought to being the only human on this trip to Darren Shahr before she had left. But that first day on the road, it hit her just how alone she was. The dwarves talked and joked amongst themselves. They were polite and kind to her, but she could tell they had very little idea of what to do with her.

As she looked over the seemingly endless expanse of water, her future seemed to stretch out before her as well. She was commissioned to be ambassador to the dwarves, and really had no idea how long that would leave her in Darren Shahr. Queen Kalis would be a familiar face at Darren Shahr, but she could hardly be counted as a companion or friend. What she really missed was her family.

Kydar's face flashed before her eyes, and then it went away in a flash of fire as she remembered the funeral pyre engulfed in flames, with Kydar's body taken away by the God of Light. At least that's what Romulus had declared.

She had seen many wild and wonderful things in her travels, but she was not sure if she had seen anything to confirm the existence of the God of Light. Sure, many people she knew and had met believed, but what proof was there?

But deep down, she was skeptical because of what happened to Kydar. If there was a powerful God of Light, why did Shadows run wild? Why did Kydar have to die? It didn't make sense to her.

Suddenly, she felt even more alone than before, and in her

aloneness, she felt small. She shivered, but it had nothing to do with the cold.

————

They finally arrived at Darren Shahr after several more days of travel, near dusk. The river led right to the gates of the fortress city, and Dema could see that the scars of battle still marred the land near the walls. Stumps of the trees that had been felled near the city were plentiful. Remnants of the elven camp littered the forest. Fortunately, nearly all traces of the dead had been removed, though by dwarf or animal, she could not tell.

A cheer went up from the wall as the group approached. The gate was thrown open and for a few minutes, Dema was lost in the shuffle. Dwarves of the city swarmed the returning dwarves and there was a lot of loud talking and storytelling and clapping on the back. Dema allowed herself to be taken by the flow of the crowd and soon found herself with her back to the wall inside the city.

It was as she remembered. She hadn't been gone long, just a few weeks, but already that felt like a lifetime ago.

After the dwarves had greeted one other and the glamour died down, Dema was finally noticed.

"Oy! Who're you?" one of the city watchmen said, pointing a finger at her.

She took a second to compose herself, but before she could respond, one of the dwarves she had been traveling with responded.

"That's Dema, you idiot. She was here with us just a few weeks ago."

"Well, what's she doing back here?" the first dwarf responded defensively. "She should be with her own kind."

Dema cleared her throat and they all turned toward her.

"My king has commissioned me to be here as an

ambassador of goodwill. He would like to strengthen the ties between humans and dwarves."

"How very noble of him," said a new voice.

At the sound of this new voice, the dwarves parted, and many of them bowed toward the path they created. Through the crowd, Dema saw Queen Kalis who was striding toward her with two servants in her wake.

"Greetings, Dema," Queen Kalis said when she had drawn near. "Welcome back to Darren Shahr."

"It is my pleasure to be here, your majesty," Dema replied with a respectful nod of her head. "I hope that my presence here is welcome."

"You are welcome," Queen Kalis replied. "Darren Shahr has not seen an ambassador from the humans or the elves in quite a long time. Come, let us find you quarters worthy of your station."

The queen beckoned Dema to walk in step with her, and the queen's two servants followed behind them.

"Tell me of your travels," the queen suggested as they walked.

Dema told Kalis of their trip from Darren Shahr to the land of the humans and their fight with the giant snow spider on the shores of Lake Banu. She went on to talk about the battle against the forces of the Shadow, Solzar, and how it ended with Vereinen laying down his life and Solzar's transformation back into a normal man, though blind.

"And King Calmon commissioned me to be ambassador to the dwarves and Reith to be ambassador to the elves. And we accepted the jobs."

"You've had a busy few weeks," the queen noted.

"How have things been in the city since we left and since the elven army departed?" Dema asked.

"Not too well, I'm afraid," the queen said with a sigh. "We lost a lot of men. There is a lot of damage to our walls and to our city buildings. We have been hard at work clearing the rubble, fixing what we can, and rebuilding what we need to rebuild. But it is slow and hard work, and the men begrudge the long hours required. In their minds, they put in long days for the war effort. Now they want to rest and be with their families. But the war effort is not over when the enemy lays down his arms. The effects of war are carried by the survivors."

"Well, I am here to help, however your people need. If I need to pick up a hammer, I can do that."

"I appreciate the offer, Dema," the queen answered. "But that will not be necessary. I will think on how you can be of best use here in Darren Shahr for your mission. Shall we meet tomorrow to discuss what ambassadorship looks like here?"

With that plan agreed to, Kalis turned Dema over to one of the servants who had been following them. She instructed the servant to put her in the finest room available and to tend to her needs. Then she bid farewell and left to attend to other duties. Dema followed the servant to her quarters.

Dema's room had a small window overlooking a courtyard, a comfortable bed, a table, a chair, and a small wardrobe. Before she was allowed to turn in for the night, the servant took her measurements and promised that clothes would be brought for her. When the door shut behind the servant, Dema blew out the candles and collapsed onto the bed, where she fell asleep almost immediately.

That night, she dreamed of creeping things hiding in the shadows, things that remained just out of sight.

———

In the morning, a servant was sent to Dema's room to rouse her and take her down to breakfast in the palace. There she ate alone. Several dwarves were in the dining hall but other than inquisitive glances, no one paid her any mind.

When she finished eating, she looked around and tried to decide what to do next. She had no agenda, no schedule to follow, just the vague promise from Queen Kalis that the two of them should meet. Eventually, she rose, and went back to her room. She found several items of clothing laid out for her on her bed. There were tunics of red, green, and gray. A couple of pairs of pants in gray and blue lay beside those. She chose an outfit at random and placed the remaining items in the wardrobe for future use. She dressed in her new clothes and found they fit her rather well.

And now, dressed and ready for the day, she found that she had no idea what an ambassador was supposed to do. She was to establish diplomatic relations with the dwarves, but beyond that, she did not know much of what she needed to do.

I wonder what Reith is doing.

At the thought of Reith, jealousy rose within her that he was on a mission to the elves where he would be with Romulus, who had traveled from Sardis to Darren Shahr with them and was a friend on the road. And here she was, and who did she have?

The loneliness washed over, and she lay back on the bed, completely drained and defeated. How long she lay there, she had no idea. At times tears made tracks down her cheeks to the bed below. Finally, she willed herself to sit up and do something. She decided she needed a plan. If she was going to be an ambassador, she was going to be the best ambassador she could be, and to do that, she needed a plan with goals, strategies, and achievable actions.

She poked her head out into the hall and looked around for a servant, but she could not see any. She wandered the halls for a few minutes before she found a servant to convey her request to, and a few minutes later, she was back in her room with a quill, ink, and paper.

For the rest of the morning, she wrote down every thought

that came to her head about being an ambassador and what she thought she should be doing in Darren Shahr. She nearly filled up one page with notes and ideas. As she worked, the ideas began to gain clarity in her head, so she knew not only what she needed to do, but how she needed to do it. At last, she placed her quill down and knew she was onto something. And that made her smile, the first smile that had graced her face since she said goodbye to Reith.

A servant returned to fetch her for the noonday meal, and relayed to her that she would meet with the queen in the middle of the afternoon that day. Dema ate swiftly and then returned to her room, where she took out a fresh page and jotted down some notes for her meeting with the queen, some ideas and suggestions regarding her role and place in court. Satisfied, she simply waited in her room looking out the window and watching the dwarves in the courtyard move about.

There was a knock at the door. A servant had arrived to escort her to the queen. And she was ready.

———

It turned out, Kalis did not have many original ideas regarding Dema's place in court. Kalis suggested a weekly meeting, just the two of them, to talk about whatever it was that Dema found compelling to talk about. Kalis was amenable to Dema's suggestions that Dema be allowed free reign of the city to explore and mingle with the dwarves in the city. Dema suggested that a dwarf servant be assigned to her as a liaison of sorts, who would show Dema around and act as a guide for her during her stay in Darren Shahr. Kalis thought this was a good idea and promised to appoint someone to that role within a few days.

Dema felt good about the meeting when she left and was

glad she had done so much preparation for the meeting that morning. With a kingdom to run, Kalis was not going to be organized enough to bring and set an agenda, and Dema was happy to do that work. After all, this was her only job. Queen Kalis had to balance ruling the kingdom, rebuilding parts of the city, and dealing with a new ambassador.

The next day, Dema began exploring Darren Shahr in earnest. There was still so much of the fortress city she had not seen when she had last been in the city, having arrived under imminent threat of invasion with an elven horde close behind.

The thing she decided to go and visit first was the river port. The dwarves relied on the rivers to ship goods around their kingdom, and the port had been shut down the last time she was here because of the invading elves. She wanted to see it in action.

To the north, the river widened considerably as it approached the waterfall. The narrow waterfall acted as a sort of natural damn, causing a backup of water behind it, which the dwarves used to great effect as an inland port. There were docks that stretched out from the city walls themselves, and in between were docked dozens of barges, some reloading, some unloading. Dema walked along the parapet on top of the wall and surveyed all the hustle and bustle below.

She knew that the river ran east here, out to the eastern lands, which she knew little about. She supposed there must be other dwarven cities, perhaps on the eastern coast of Terrasohnen. It was another thing she didn't know, but something Reith may have known.

She spent several hours watching the activity at the river's edge, and she began to take note of the sorts of cargo that arrived to Darren Shahr. There was a lot of ore that passed through, loaded on barges. There were crops of fruit, vegetables, and grains that came in as well. On one barge, she saw large rolls of fabric.

Dema's stomach growled so she left to find something to eat. She returned to the palace complex and found her way to the dining room, where she loaded a plate and then sat near the hearth, and the firelight danced across her face, and she wanted the flames to flicker and jump.

There was an empty chair by the fire, and Dema wished that someone, anyone would occupy it. Her eyes began to water, but she breathed deeply and kept the tears at bay.

God of Light, she pleaded in her mind as she watched the fire devour the logs.

For a few minutes, she contemplated simply rising, taking a horse and some supplies, and riding for Sardis. She could be with Reith and Romulus and plot her next move. In Sardis, she would be safe from King Calmon, who would surely be angry that she abandoned her post.

She was deep into this daydream and didn't even notice the approaching footsteps.

"Dema?" a soft voice startled her into alertness. She started to rise from her seat.

"No, don't get up," the voice said again, and Dema saw a young dwarven woman standing before her. The dwarf's arm was extended toward Dema with the palm down.

"I'm Yaz," she said, and she smiled at Dema. "Queen Kalis appointed me to be your guide and helper for the duration of your stay in Darren Shahr."

"Oh, wonderful," Dema replied. "You don't know how happy that makes me."

"Do you mind if I sit?" Yaz asked.

"No, of course not," Dema answered and gestured for Yaz to sit.

"I thought we could spend the rest of the day getting to know each other," Yaz suggested. "I can tell you about me, and then you can tell me about you."

"That sounds great," Dema said, and silently thanked the God of Light.

"Well, I'm Yaz," she repeated with a sheepish grin. "I was born and raised here in Darren Shahr. I'm something like a third cousin to the queen's children, but I didn't grow up royal or anything like that."

"Oh, interesting," Dema replied.

"Not as interesting as you'd think," answered Yaz. "My father is a merchant with a fleet of barges. My mother has always been in poor health and remains home most of the time."

"How old are you?" Dema asked, thinking Yaz to not be much older than her.

"I'm twenty-two," said Yaz.

"What do you do? Are you married? Got a boyfriend?"

"I work in the palace, as a page. I get sent around with messages and basically help wherever I can. Not married, no boyfriend. My parents are disappointed, but they'll get over it."

"Do you have any siblings?" Dema asked.

"No, it's just me," Yaz answered. "What else do you want to know?"

"I can't really think of anything else at the moment. But I think we'll have plenty of time to get to know each other over the coming months."

"Very true," Yaz said. "So tell me about you. How did you come to be here?"

"How long do you have?" Dema replied with a chuckle. "It's a long story."

"I'm all yours," said Yaz.

"Well, it all started when the Gray Man attacked my village."

For the next half hour, Yaz listened with rapt attention as Dema relayed the story of all her misfortunes, travels, adventures, battles, and triumphs. Yaz was surprisingly well informed, having been around the edges when Dema, Reith, and the others had been in Darren Shahr. Yaz was a good listener, very observant, and asked good questions at the right times. Despite sharing about Kydar's death and her separation from Reith, Yaz was encouraging and Dema did not feel herself drifting toward despair.

"And now you're a teenage ambassador," Yaz said with wonder when Dema had finished her tale.

"And I have no idea what I'm doing," Dema answered.

"Well, we can figure it out together," Yaz replied cheerily.

The two of them spent the rest of the day together until nightfall, when Dema excused herself to go to her room and wind down for the night. They made plans to meet at breakfast the next morning.

As Dema lay in her bed, she smiled to herself. Yaz was exactly who she needed. And she didn't feel as lonely anymore.

NINE

Over the following weeks, Yaz showed Dema nearly all of Darren Shahr. She got to witness craftsmen and smiths at work creating the wonderful goods of the dwarves. From the smiths, she purchased for herself a small, ornately figured dagger. It rarely was not at her side as she went about her days in the city.

Yaz also took Dema to some dwarven temples. They were not as grand as the temple of Sardis, or even the small temple in Crain, but there was still an unmistakable air of sacredness. Male and female dwarves led the prayers and the chants, and though it wasn't really Dema's thing, she enjoyed the experience and knew Reith would have enjoyed it too.

The more she plunged herself into her work, the more she was able to keep from her mind her loneliness. She missed Reith, of course, but she found that in the company of Yaz, she was relaxed and comfortable in Darren Shahr.

More than a guide, more than an assistant, Yaz was a friend. And Dema needed a friend. The two became inseparable, often spending their time outside of normal working hours together.

Dema was invited to Yaz's house one evening to have dinner with Yaz and her parents. Yaz's parents took to Dema almost as quickly as Yaz had taken to her, and that night they spent hours talking and playing some dwarven games that involved dice. It became a weekly rhythm for Dema to go home with Yaz for dinner and games.

On the work front, Dema was making great strides. Her first order of business was to establish a postal system. With Yaz's help and the queen's blessing, she managed to hire half a dozen messengers. She studied maps and determined the optimal way of travel from Darren Shahr to Sardis and to Galismoor. Within a month, three messengers would go to Sardis with official communication from Queen Kalis to King Romulus (as well as letters from Dema to Reith, which she had already started working on) and three other messengers would go to Galismoor, again with letters from the queen and from Dema. The thought of communicating with Reith and Dema again, even if just in letters, was a real pick me up for Dema.

Despite all the new-found fortune in Darren Shahr, she still felt like an outsider. The Lords Tabriz, Sahand, and Mengar, with whom she had sat on war councils during her first visit to Darren Shahr, treated her with utter indifference. She saw them on occasion as their paths crossed regularly in the palace complex. At first, she had tried to greet them, but when she received no reply, she gave up. They treated her as if she did not exist, and she returned the favor. There was not much she could do about them, though she worried what they may say about her behind closed doors to Queen Kalis.

The queen herself did not have much time for Dema, simply an hour a week, during which they mostly exchanged pleasantries. Once official channels of communication were open to the other kingdoms, Dema was sure their topics of conversation would increase.

One day, she was sitting in a courtyard with Yaz and enjoying the nice weather. The sky was perfectly blue without a cloud to mar it. The sun warmed the skin pleasantly.

"Tell me about the Gray Man," Yaz said.

"What about him?" Dema asked, wondering where this line of thinking was coming from.

"Well," Yaz began, "He sort of started all this, you know? He's the reason you're here now. I'd like to understand my enemy."

"Well, you know he's a Shadow, right? Or at least, he was a Shadow."

"But what exactly is a Shadow?" Yaz asked. "And what do you mean, 'he was a Shadow'? Is he not anymore?"

"Reith could tell you more about Shadows," Dema replied, "But I will try my best. A Shadow is someone who has given themselves over to the evil of the Dark Powers. They let spiritual forces of evil take over them. The Gray Man, Solzar is his real name, he gave himself over to the Dark Powers. They came into him, changed him, that's why we call him the Gray Man. But he's not that anymore. At the battle, Vereinen, that older man, jumped in front of a sword meant for Solzar, which killed him. Solzar's color returned to him, and the Dark Powers left him. But he's blind now."

"Oh, wow," Yaz said in amazement.

"I don't think he's our enemy anymore," Dema explained. "He's different. Something changed inside of him."

"Are there other Shadows then?"

"Who's to say?" Dema replied. "It's possible. The Dark Powers can't be happy that Solzar switched sides."

"What was Solzar like as a Shadow?"

"Evil and insane," said Dema. "It seemed he tried to inflict maximum pain and suffering on others. He even seemed dreadful to his followers."

"I just hope there aren't any more Shadows," Yaz said with a shudder."

"Me too."

———

About a week before the new postal service workers were going to be sent on their first mission, Dema fell ill. She woke up one morning shivering cold. She felt her own forehead and it burned with fever. She remained in bed and drifted in and out of feverish dreams. Yaz was there, sometimes, but other times she was alone.

Nightmares and waking mixed and merged in her subconscious. Monsters seemed to be lurking around every corner. Yaz would morph into a giant bird of prey. When Dema tried to cry out, she felt like she was falling down an endless hole in the earth, forever falling, falling, falling.

The dread and the anxiety were a physical presence pinning her to the bed. The covers felt like they were made of lead.

She did not know how many days and nights passed, but one morning, she awoke, and her sheets were sopping wet from sweat. Her fever was gone.

She rose, dressed, and went to get some food. She was starving. In the hall, she met Yaz, who was coming to check on her.

"Oh, good, you're up!" Yaz exclaimed, and she hugged Dema. "I was so worried about you. Feeling better?"

"Much better," Dema said. "How long was I sick?"

"Three days, three nights," Yaz replied.

"That long?" Dema asked. "I don't really remember."

"I visited you a few times a day, checked on you, tried to get you to drink something, that sort of thing. But you were pretty out of it."

"What did I miss?" Dema asked.

"Only one thing: Darren Shahr has received a sorcerer from the Eastern Wilds."

"WHAT?"

"Yeah, she arrived yesterday," Yaz said with the air of someone untroubled by the news.

"A sorcerer?"

"Are there not sorcerers where you're from?" Yaz asked, confused.

"No!"

"Oh," Yaz replied. "There are dozens of sorcerers in the dwarven kingdom. They mostly keep to themselves, but occasionally, they turn up."

"What does a sorcerer do?" Dema asked.

"Well, magic," Yaz explained. "They can do things by magic. Probably why they stay to themselves. Easier to get on with life that way."

"What kind of magic?" Dema asked.

"Healings, miracles, that sort of thing. Like I said, they keep to themselves."

"So why is this one here?"

"Well, I don't really know," Yaz said. "I've tried to find out, but all I know so far is that she wants to meet with the queen."

"Hmmm, that's interesting," Dema mused.

"I'm sure you'll get a chance to meet her soon," Yaz said.

———

Soon came the very next day. Dema was summoned to meet with the queen, as their weekly meeting was scheduled to have occurred during Dema's illness. Dema presented herself to the queen, and found an older woman cloaked in gray standing beside the queen.

That must be the sorcerer.

"Good morning, your highness," Dema said with a small bow as she approached.

"Dema, it is good to see you," the queen replied. "Are you feeling well?"

"Yes, I am, thank you for asking."

"Dema, allow me to introduce Malowe," the queen said, "And she is here as one of my advisors." She gestured to the older woman, and Dema took her first good look at her.

As Dema had noticed earlier, she was older and wore a long gray cloak that hid her features underneath. The bottom of the cloak rested on the ground, and Dema could see the toes of her shoes sticking out. Her face showed she was older than Kalis, though Dema had no idea how old this woman actually was. Her hair was white and long and her skin was similarly white, as if she never saw the light of day. Her eyes were dark, almost black. And Dema sensed that the woman did not like her.

"I am pleased to meet you, Malowe," Dema said, and offered her hand to shake. Malowe ignored the gesture with a cold gaze, and Dema dropped her hand to her side again, stung by the greeting.

"Why are you here, child?" Malowe asked in a soft, cold voice.

Dema bristled at the 'child' comment but shook it off.

"I am here as an ambassador from King Calmon," Dema replied, wondering where this line of questioning was going. Queen Kalis knew about her ambassadorship, so why was Malowe questioning her?

"The human king? He sent you?" Malowe asked.

"Of course," Dema answered, still confused.

"How interesting," Malowe answered simply.

"I'm sorry, I don't really understand why you are asking," Dema blurted out.

"I am simply looking out for my people, my dear,"

Malowe answered. "Queen Kalis values my opinion, and I wanted to meet the foreigner in our city."

"Anyone who the queen values is a friend of mine," Dema said, attempting once again to keep the peace.

Malowe said nothing to this declaration. After a pause, the queen spoke.

"Thank you for meeting with us, Dema," the queen said gracefully. "You may return to your quarters."

Dema bowed and left the throne room, thoroughly perplexed by what had just happened.

I need to talk to Yaz.

————

"How very odd," Yaz replied, when Dema had finished telling her all about meeting with Malowe and the queen.

"I'm not crazy, then?" Dema asked. She had been worried she was reading into things too much.

"No, you're spot on," Yaz answered. "Your gut feeling was right. There's something odd here, and we're missing it."

"Malowe certainly seems to hate humans."

"Well, yeah," Yaz said. "Many dwarves are prejudiced toward humans and elves. We've stayed to ourselves for so long, it's the default position to be suspicious."

"You're not," Dema pointed out.

"I try hard not to be," Yaz replied. "I try to see the best in people, regardless of where they're from."

"I appreciate that, Yaz."

"I think we're all on the same side," Yaz said. "I'm on the side of peace and prosperity for all Terrasohnen. I think that's what the queen wants, too, and I know that's what you want. It looks like you'll have to spend some time winning over Malowe too. Remember, she wasn't here when you were here the first time. She doesn't know about all you've done for us already."

"True," Dema said, and she resolved to try her best to see the best in Malowe and to win her over.

———

The next day, Dema met with the teams of dwarves who were going to travel to Sardis and Galismoor as the first workers of the intercontinental postal service. At this stage in the process, they were simply crossing some t's and dotting some i's. Supply lists had been double and triple checked, and were lying on the table, official papers had been drawn up and stamped with the queen's own seal, and inventories of letters were sorted and packed away in special bags. Maps, too, lay strewn about the table, showing the routes the travelers would take.

"Take tomorrow off," Dema explained, "And enjoy the time with your families, and rest up. We will meet by the city gate an hour after sunrise the day after."

The dwarves chatted merrily together as they left the room, and Dema and Yaz were left to check over the logistics of supplies being delivered on time to the city gate. Their heads were down, so they did not see anyone approach.

"Greetings," came a voice from the doorway, and Dema and Yaz both jumped. "No need to be frightened," Malowe said as she entered the room. "Unless of course you have something to hide."

"Of course not," Dema said coolly. "As always, I work for the good of all Terrasohnen, for my people and for yours."

"And yet," Malowe said slowly, as her fingers drifted lazily over the papers on the table, "It would appear that you and I have a different opinion of what is good for my people. Undoubtedly, you are sending reports to your king about the strategic weaknesses of our city and our people. You aim to give Darren Shahr into his hand."

"I have no such aim," Dema shot back angrily. "I am no spy, Malowe." In truth, her report did contain details of Darren Shahr, particularly about their rebuilding efforts after the elven assault. To the malicious eye, those words could be interpreted as spying, but that was hardly Dema's aim.

Malowe's eyes darted around as she peered at the contents of the table.

"Then you will have no problem," she said, raising her hand, "with me reading this?"

At the word, "this," Dema's report for King Calmon leapt into the air and soared into Malowe's outstretched hand.

"That is privileged communication between an ambassador and her king," Dema stated with all the authority she could muster.

"But I thought you have nothing to hide?" Malowe said, eyeing Dema suspiciously.

"She doesn't have anything to hide!" Yaz interjected. "And it's not for you to decide. Queen Kalis trusts her."

"A development, I fear, that is most unwise," Malowe replied slowly. Her voice hissed on the last syllable of "unwise." She still held Dema's report.

"I do not know what to tell you that will cause you to trust me," Dema said. "Like I have already told you, I am here on a diplomatic mission from my king to establish official ties to the Dwarven kingdom. My friend Reith is doing the same among the elves at the moment."

"The same elves who attacked this city not so long ago?" Malowe asked. "My, my, why is your king reaching out to a kingdom who so recently was an aggressor to my people?"

"It is not the same kingdom," Dema pointed out. "Romulus is king now, not Koinas. Romulus and Remus stopped the attack."

"But still your king seeks their hand in friendship. They will receive no consequence for what they did to us."

"I am here to extend the hand of friendship to Queen Kalis and her people," Dema said sharply. "The past must be buried. We went centuries without official contact between the kingdoms, and that was shattered by attack and war. We must have peace and we must work together toward it." She stuck out her hand. "And I would appreciate it if you returned that report to me."

Malowe contemplated the request for a long moment before slowly dropping it into Dema's outstretched hand.

"We're all on the same side," Yaz said softly.

Malowe turned to leave, but at the door, she turned back and spoke. "I don't think so."

———

That afternoon, Dema and Yaz were summoned to the throne room.

"Why me?" Yaz asked.

"I assume it's because of this morning," Deme replied.

"I hope I wasn't talking out of turn," Yaz said nervously.

"No, you were brilliant," Dema encouraged.

Queen Kalis was seated on her throne and Malowe was standing beside her. For a second, Dema was reminded strongly of King Koinas and Solzar. She shook the image away.

"Good afternoon, Dema, Yaz," Kalis said, but her tone did not convey anything close to goodness. Her voice was sharp and cold.

"Your majesty," Dema and Yaz replied, and each bowed.

"Dema," the queen began, "Malowe brought me a serious accusation today. She accuses you of spying for your king. She accuses you of plotting to overthrow the dwarven kingdom."

She let the accusations hang in the air like smoke for a few moments.

"I am doing no such thing," Dema replied when she was sure the queen was done speaking. "Your majesty knows that I am commissioned here as an ambassador, a diplomat charged to renew the relationship between our people."

"A worthy goal, I am sure," Queen Kalis said dismissively. "But what proof do you have of your claims?"

"I have a letter of commissioning from my king," Dema replied. "It is in my chambers."

"Yaz, go and retrieve this letter," the queen ordered. "You know where it is?"

"Yes, your majesty," Yaz said with a bow, and she hastily departed.

"You will pardon me for being so distrustful," the queen said to Dema when Yaz had gone. "But I must be certain. My husband died because of the treachery of another race. I cannot fall in the same way."

"This is why I am here," Dema explained. "If we have good relationships, we can have peace."

There was silence in the hall until Yaz brought back the letter from Calmon. Kalis read it to herself and then handed it to Malowe to read.

"It all seems in order," Kalis said, shaking her head.

"But we do not know if this is all the communication from King Calmon to Dema," Malowe pointed out. "What of verbal instruction? Or another, secret, letter?"

"It's unknowable," Kalis sighed.

"No it isn't. The postal service messengers are departing the morning after tomorrow."

"I am not going to read official diplomatic mail," Kalis replied firmly. "I have no official reason to be suspicious of Dema, beyond what you are telling me. Dema, Yaz, you may leave. Continue your preparations. I am sorry to have dragged you in here like that."

"You are simply being thorough," Dema answered sympathetically. As she turned to leave, she noticed Malowe looked deflated, and she took great pleasure in it.

When they were well clear of the throne room, Dema turned to Yaz.

"What was that about?"

"I have no idea," Yaz said with a shrug.

"It's trouble, that's what it is. The sooner the postal messengers can leave, the better I'll sleep. Malowe seems to want to stop that communication."

"She does, but why?"

"That is the question," Dema said.

"They leave first thing the day after tomorrow," Yaz pointed out.

"That's still a long time for Malowe to do something."

———

Dema slept fitfully that night. She had trouble falling asleep, and even when she did drift off, she awoke a little while later. All in all, she was glad when the morning went from black to gray so she could get out of bed, even though she was dead tired.

She found her way to the outer walls of the city to watch the sun rise. Long shadows were cast by the sun, and the world filled with yellows, oranges, and reds, and the ever-lightening blue of the sky. Alone with her thoughts in the chilly morning air, Dema pondered all the recent developments. Who exactly was Malowe? What did she want? Why was she so opposed to Dema?

As she watched, clouds poured over the eastern horizon and soon the sun was hidden in shadow. A chilly breeze sprung up and it bit at Dema's exposed skin. She shivered and rose. *Inside is the place to be.*

She wandered the halls and made her way back to her quarters. It was a busy day today, and she knew she must get ready for it.

Tomorrow, the messengers would depart, and she wanted their first trips to go smoothly. This felt like the first big test of her ambassadorship, and she wanted it to go off without a hitch. She went over her checklists and notes again and again, and even sent Yaz to run some errands to check on supplies.

Around midmorning, rain began to fall and lashed at the windows and percussively beat on the roof. The wind howled, and Dema hoped the weather would clear by the morning.

In the middle of the afternoon, while the rain still poured down, Dema and Yaz went to the stables to check on the horses. The stable master showed them the horses he had selected for the journey, and relieved Dema's fears by showing her where the saddles and other things for the horses were stacked, ready to go in the morning.

As Dema was petting the nose of one of the horses, she heard a chuckle from a shadowy corner of the stables.

Dema whirled around to see who it was. She moved so fast, she startled the horse she was petting, which backed away from her, swinging his head back and forth and snorting.

Out of the gloom stepped Malowe.

"What do you want?" Dema asked with a note of defiance in her voice. Yaz stepped close to Dema in solidarity, her body tense and ready for action.

"I want you to go back to where you came from, dirty human," spat Malowe.

"Don't talk to her like that," Yaz said, stepping forward.

Malowe made a motion as if she were tossing a small pebble to Yaz, and Yaz staggered backward as if struck by charging bull. She sprawled to the ground and Dema dropped to her knees beside her to see if she was alright. Yaz was breathing heavily and wincing.

"Do I have your attention now?" Malowe asked silently. She took a step nearer.

"What did you do to her?" Dema demanded.

"Just a little spell," Malowe said dismissively. "I can do far more." She held up her hand again threateningly. "Do you understand?"

Dema nodded.

"Good," Malowe said, her voice dripping with malice. "Now, as I was saying, I want you to leave. Go back to where you came from."

"Why?" Dema asked. "And really, I can't."

"Why? Why?" Malowe asked incredulously. "Because my king is dead, and you and your friends are to blame. And the dwarves can never mingle with humans. It's not right, it's not natural."

"Says who?" Yaz asked, gritting her teeth through the pain that was still in her chest.

"Says me," Malowe said simply. "And my friends."

"Who cares what you think?" Dema spat.

"The queen does, my dear, the queen does. So like I said; leave. Go. Flee. Run. Whatever it takes, get out of here. Or else."

"Or else what?"

"Or else things will get even more unpleasant for you."

And with that, Malowe swept out of the stables, leaving a very shaken Yaz and Dema in her wake.

———

That evening, Dema decided to take dinner in her room, rather than be in public in the dining hall. Yaz stayed with her. Occasionally, Yaz would wince in pain.

"It feels like she broke a rib," Yaz said, gently rubbing her left side.

"I am so sorry that happened," Dema said apologetically. "It's my fault."

"Nah, it's not your fault," Yaz replied, leaning back gingerly in her chair. "It's Malowe's fault and her bigotry. Bunch a dung, that bit about humans and dwarves never mingling."

"I'm glad you don't think it's unnatural to be with me," Dema said gratefully.

"It's the most natural thing in the world."

There was silence for a few moments, as each of them got lost in her own thoughts.

"You're not thinking of leaving, are you?" Yaz asked, breaking the silence.

"Of course not," Dema replied, shaking her head. "How could I explain that to King Calmon? 'A scary woman threatened me, and I left.' No thanks, that's not a conversation I want to have."

"Still, you need to be careful," Yaz replied. "I didn't like the sound of her threat. And she can do some serious damage with magic if she wants to." She rubbed her side again and grimaced.

"What did she mean by things will be more unpleasant if I don't leave?" Dema asked.

"I don't want to find out."

"But what can we do about her?" Dema asked. "If I stay, it will only mean trouble."

"I wish there was a way to get rid of her," Yaz said, looking off into the distance in thought.

"Well, it needs to happen quickly," Dema answered.

"Could you talk to the queen?" Yaz suggested half-heartedly.

"Perhaps," Dema replied. "But Malowe is like a spider tugging at webs that she has spun around the queen."

"Are there other allies you could talk to?" Yaz wondered. "Another lord or lady, someone sympathetic, someone who knows you? They could interject."

"I don't really know anyone except Tabriz, Sahand, and Mengar," Dema said with a dark chuckle. "And I can't picture them helping me out, can you?"

"No, you're right," Yaz said. "Well, there's always assassination."

"Yaz!" Dema exclaimed, shocked, even though she knew Yaz was only joking.

"What?" Yaz said with a devilish grin. "A girl can dream."

"I think I'm going to write another letter to King Calmon," Dema said. "I'll tell him about Malowe. Maybe we can get a response as to how he would like me to deal with her."

"That's a good idea," agreed Yaz. "What about Reith?"

"Oh, you're right, I should send another one to him too."

"But be careful," Yaz said. "I wouldn't put it past Malowe to have read all the letters being sent. Don't give these letters over until the last minute."

"Good point," Dema said, and she sat down and began to write out her letters. A short time later, she sealed them with her wax and seal. She hid them among her clothes in the dresser.

"Let's get some sleep," Yaz suggested. "It's a big day tomorrow."

TEN

It was still dark when Yaz returned to wake Dema. Dema had slept poorly, and her dreams were full of shadowy monsters chasing her through the dark. When Yaz gently prodded her, she started and nearly struck Yaz.

"Sorry," Dema said a few seconds later after she realized what she had almost done."

"No problem," Yaz said, her fists held in front of her in a faux fighting stance. "Ready for today?"

"I'll be more ready when the messengers are gone."

"We meet them in about two hours," Yaz said, looking out the window to ascertain the darkness of the pre-dawn sky.

Dema dressed quickly and slipped her two new letters into her pockets before leaving her room with Yaz.

As promised, all the supplies the messengers would need were stacked neatly in an empty corner of the stables, ready to leave.

"Thank you so much," Dema said to the stable master.

"It is my pleasure," the stable master replied.

"Is there anything else we need to do before we send them off?" Yaz asked Dema.

"I don't think so," Dema said, consulting her list. "I think we've done it all."

"Then let's go get a celebratory breakfast!" Yaz declared.

With assurances to the stable master that they would be back soon, Dema and Yaz departed for the dining hall. Even in the early morning, Dema was surprised to see so much activity in the castle. Dwarves in larger quantities than normal for this hour were rushing here and there, and they all had strange looks for Dema and Yaz.

"What's going on?" Dema asked.

"I don't really know," Yaz replied, looking at the back of one dwarf who had shot them both a dirty look.

"Come on," Dema said, hurrying along.

They went on for another minute or two and received a few more nasty glances. At last they turned and found themselves in a vacant corridor.

They rushed along toward the door at the other end. When they were about halfway there, the door opened, and out stepped Malowe, with a dozen guards behind her.

"Stop right there," she commanded.

Dema's first impulse was to flee. She had no idea what Malowe wanted, but it couldn't be anything good.

She turned and saw with dismay that a company of armed dwarves were marching toward them from the direction they had just come.

"What do you want?" demanded Yaz bravely.

"Arrest the human," Malowe ordered calmly, as though she hadn't heard Yaz.

Guards from both ends of the corridor rushed at Dema, and she froze. But just as hands clenched her upper arms, her reflexes took over and she whirled around and lashed out at those guards who had reached her first. She managed to drop them both with quick punches. The victory was short lived, as more and more dwarven guards swarmed her. They were rough and harsh with her, striking her repeatedly until she slumped in submission.

They dropped her to the ground, and she lay there with the cold of the stone soothing her aching body. She opened her eyes a fraction of an inch and saw feet in front of her eyes.

"Search her," came a cold voice from above her. Guards stooped down and rummaged through her pockets.

"We found something," one of the guards said excitedly. The two letters had been extracted from her pockets.

"No, you can't," Dema groaned as she tried to rise. A swift kick to her ribcage sent her crashing back to the floor.

There was a rustling of paper and a satisfied, "Ah ha!"

"Guards," Malowe said triumphantly. "Take the ambassador back to her chambers. Lock the door and set a guard."

"You can't do that!" Yaz shouted at her.

"Of course I can," Malowe replied. "And the queen will see things my way when I show her these letters."

"Those were diplomatically privileged letters," Yaz said defiantly.

"That's neither here nor there. What matters is stopping a human plot from taking over our kingdom. The dwarves must be for the dwarves, don't you think Yaz?"

"No one wants to take over the dwarves," Yaz retorted. "That's not what's in those letters."

"You're a silly girl," Malowe replied with a wicked grin. "Now, guards, take Dema away."

Dema felt strong arms pulling her upright, but she refused to cooperate. So the guards ended up dragging her, and the toes of her boots scrapped the ground behind as she was pulled along, twisting and turning around the passages. At her room, they wrenched open the door and threw her in unceremoniously. She crashed to the ground and bit her tongue. The taste of blood welled up inside her mouth, and as she rolled into a sitting position, she heard the click of the lock.

And the tears she had been holding in fell in torrents.

———

Morning turned to afternoon and afternoon turned to evening. The room darkened as the sun set, and all day, no one had come to Dema's room. No meals, no Yaz, no Malowe or guards to take her away. For the first few hours of her incarceration, Dema was on edge, ready to fight or flee if someone arrived at her door. But the silence stretched on and on.

She decided to take stock of her room and everything that could potentially help her in a fight or to escape. She looked around and realized with a sinking feeling in her stomach that her room had been cleared while she was out that morning. Her documents were gone, her weapons were gone, all her personal possessions were gone. All that was left in the room were the bare minimum comforts of the bed, an empty dresser, and her desk. She walked to the window and peered out. It was perhaps twenty feet down to the ground. Even if she dropped down, chances were she would be hurt in the attempt.

At dusk, she heard footsteps in the hall. She crept over to beside the door, wondering if this would give her an opportunity to escape. There was a sharp rap at the door and a guard called out.

"I have your evening meal. Back away from the door! Failure to comply will mean no food for two days."

Reluctantly, Dema backed away from the door and stood by the bed. She wasn't desperate enough yet to attempt to escape. *I'll size this guy up.*

She heard the key enter the lock, and with a click, the door swung open. The guard stepped forward quickly, placed a tray on the ground, and shut the door behind him. The lock clicked again, and footsteps retreated down the hall. From lock click to lock click, only about ten seconds had passed.

Only one guard, Dema noted to herself. *That could work in my favor.* She walked over to the tray, hopeful for a fork or a knife, but she was disappointed. There was a hunk of bread and a clay goblet of water.

I supposed if I let the bread go stale and harden, it could be used as stone she thought to herself with no real conviction. Hunger won the day. She eagerly dove into the bread, which was gone much too soon. With her meal gone, she returned to the window to watch what was left of the sunlight disappear into darkness.

———

Shortly after dawn, while Dema was still lying in bed, she again heard footsteps and then a knock.

"Stay away from the door!" came the same voice as the night before. The door opened, and the routine of entering, putting the food down, retreating, and locking the door was repeated. Dema yawned and stretched. It had been good to slip away into the nothingness of sleep. It was an escape of sorts. But in the cold light of dawn, her situation pressed on her heart with even more gravity than the previous evening.

The food, she could see from her bed, was the same as last night's: bread and water. She wasn't yet hungry, so she let it sit for now. She surveyed the room and thought of how to best occupy her time.

Eventually, she deduced, if King Calmon did not hear from her, he would surely send a small group to check on her. But such a small force couldn't possibly fight through to rescue her. So she would need to wait for them to return to Galismoor and return with an army. But, she thought with a sinking feeling in the pit of her stomach, the king would hardly send an army for the sake of one ambassador.

It's up to me.

Strangely, this thought gave her a measure of confidence and hope. If she could not rely on the outside world, then everything she needed was inside her room already. The thought gave her a renewal of purpose and motivation.

She stretched, and then climbed out of bed. Ignoring the meal, she instead turned her attention to the door. It was solid wood, and likely not to budge if she attacked it with her shoulder. But she noted the hinges were on her side of the door. *If I can remove those, I could get out of the door.*

She filed the thought away and inspected the lock mechanism. It was a simple lock, but strong and sturdy. From the outside, a key could be inserted and turned so that a bolt would go into a hole in the door frame. But there was also a keyhole on her side.

It might be possible to turn the lock, if I could fashion some sort of key.

With two potential avenues of escape giving her hope, the morning light seemed brighter, more inviting. She realized she was in fact hungry and made quick work of her breakfast.

While she ate, she pondered her situation. There was one question that puzzled her. *Why am I in my own quarters? Why am I not in the dungeon?*

She thought back to her time in Sardis and the horrible time they spent in the dungeon while Solzar, then a Shadow, was whispering in the ear of King Koinas of the elves. It was cold, and dark, and without hope.

When Remus was here, he was in the dungeon.

Remus, the younger brother of Romulus, had come to

Darren Shahr as an assassin. He had come to kill the king of the dwarves. When he failed, he was imprisoned, left for dead, until Romulus had come, though Romulus had not known his brother was here. Remus was treated as a dog, yet Dema was still being treated relatively kindly, her incarceration notwithstanding.

Perhaps it is because I am an ambassador. Maybe that still has some weight. Perhaps they fear King Calmon's retribution if I am mistreated.

She remembered the elven force before the walls of Darren Shahr and how close they had come to breaching the city and winning. Perhaps Calmon could wage a successful siege.

The dwarves are weak.

While all three of the races were weakened through battle, it was the dwarves who had taken the heaviest losses. Their port city of Balkh had been destroyed, and their capital, Darren Shahr, had nearly fallen. Their king fell in battle, leaving an inexperienced queen on the throne. And the queen was looking for help and guidance in all the wrong places, it seemed.

Malowe. It all came back to Malowe. Dema was sure by now that Malowe was a Shadow, or at least well on her way to becoming one. Clearly, she was selling some form of dwarven exclusivism to Queen Kalis, sowing seeds of fear regarding the elves and the humans. But Solzar's purpose had been conquest. Malowe's seems to be isolation.

She sipped her water thoughtfully. When finished, she placed the cup on the floor and stood up. As she did, her foot hit the cup and sent it clattering across the floor under the bed. Dema groaned and stooped down on all fours to look under her bed. Of course, the cup was under the very center of the bed, equally difficult to reach from all sides.

Dema dropped to her stomach and reached as far as she could. Her fingers brushed the cup and sent it rolling away from her toward the wall. Cursing to herself, she crawled around to the side of the bed and once more reached under to take the cup.

Dema looked and saw that the cup was resting against a floorboard that was slightly raised above its brethren. Frowning, she retrieved the cup, but did not rise. Her fingers traced the edge of the board, which was raised enough that she could feel the side edge with her fingertips. She pressed on the board, and it creaked and gave just a little, but when she removed the pressure, it remained up as before. On the far edge of the board, she dug her fingers in and tried to pull it up. Her fingers slipped off at first, but on her second try, she dug her nails into it and pulled up again. Slowly that edge of the board lifted, and she sifted her hand to put her fingers under it and found that it came out easily now that most of one side was free. She carefully set aside the board, making sure to make as little noise as possible. In the darkness under the bed, she couldn't see inside the hole where the board just sat, but she could tell it was a hollowed-out space, the perfect place to hide ... what?

Wondering who knew about this and what they could possibly have put there, she reached in and groped around. Her hand brushed something hard and slender. She picked it up and pulled it out. It was a short dagger. Its blade was perhaps as long as her hand and the handle was nearly as long. It gleamed in the sunlight. Her heart pounded with the possibilities this new tool brought her. Hope blazed inside her, an unquenchable fire now. She was Dema the invincible.

She reached in again, wondering if anything else was hidden in the recess below her bed. She felt around and found a small piece of paper which had been folded once in half. She pulled it out and sat up with her back against her bed. Unfolding the paper, she saw the familiar handwriting of Yaz.

Just in case.

With the dagger safely back underneath the bed, Dema plotted her next move. She vowed to keep the knife hidden until she was sure she was ready to use it. It would be too much of a risk to keep it out. Clearly, only she and Yaz knew about the secret compartment underneath the floorboard. And she planned to use that knowledge, and the weapon it contained, to her gain.

Dema decided to rest as much as possible that day so she could stay awake late into the night and survey the activity near her room. Footsteps on the floor in the hall were easily heard, so she could work on the lock or the hinges quietly in the middle of the night without much fear of being overheard.

But deciding and doing were two very different things. She found it hard to rest, let alone fall asleep during the day. Her mind raced with the possibilities that her newfound dagger gave her, and she had a hard time quieting her thoughts.

The day dragged on and on, easily feeling longer than any other day Dema had ever experienced in her life. Finally, the evening meal came. She decided to push her luck a little bit and stand nearer to the door than she had yet tried, to see what reaction it would attract, and to see if any advantage could be gained going forward. She decided to sit against the wall to the left of the door. She'd be out of reach of the guard, even when he stepped in and dropped the food. Her seated position afforded her a slight element of surprise, as she would be out of his natural line of sight. Sitting also conveyed that she was not a threat, and she hoped her little maneuver would not result in any harsh treatment. But even if it did, she thought it worth the risk.

Footsteps echoed down the hallway, and Dema got into position.

"Stay away from the door!"

The lock clicked and the door swung open. Dema's hunch was spot on. It took the guard a couple of seconds to notice her.

"Hey, what do you think you're doing?" the guard asked, angry from the delay in spotting his charge.

"I'm just sitting," Dema replied casually.

"That's too close to the door," the guard stated.

"What? You're afraid that I'll do something to you, while seated?" Dema asked mockingly. "I'm good, but I'm not that good. Or maybe you're just that bad."

The verbal barb seemed to strike a nerve with the guard, who turned red and blustered at her.

"Next time I come, you'd better not be there, or there will be consequences."

"Yes, sir," Dema answered, and rolled her eyes dramatically for effect. The guard stormed out of the room and slammed the door behind him. The lock clicked and his hasty footsteps retreated down the hall.

Next time, his first glance will be to where I was sitting. I could use that to my advantage in the morning. Or would it be better to remain in that spot for a few more meals?

She puzzled over this conundrum, wondering how best to use her new knowledge to aid in her escape, while she mindlessly ate her bread.

She took another bite, and instead of simple bread, her teeth met something that crackled in her mouth. She spit it out and saw that there was a piece of paper folded up twice in the bread. She pulled it out and unfolded it. There were words written on it, and she had a hard time making them out at first, most likely because it had been baked inside a loaf of bread.

Night after next, be ready to run.

Despite the smudges that the baking process had

introduced to the note, she could tell that it was Yaz's handwriting.

That girl is a life saver.

Eleven

The next day, Dema was surprised when she heard footsteps in the hall around midday. She had been lying on her bed staring straight up at the ceiling, plotting her escape, but she hastily sat up, wondering who was coming at this hour.

There was no announcement, just a key inserted into the lock, which clicked open. In stepped Malowe.

"You are wanted," Malowe stated, "in the throne room."

"Why?" Dema asked.

"Because the queen would like a word," Malowe replied, rolling her eyes.

Possibilities raced through Dema's mind. *What does the queen want with me now?* She thought longingly of her knife under her bed which could aid her in an escape.

As if reading her mind, Malowe spoke. "Don't even think about trying to escape."

For the time being, Dema decided to see what may come of this new meeting, but ever mindful of opportunities to flee.

Malowe stepped out into the hall and held her arm out, indicating that Dema was to take the lead.

Smart. She can keep an eye on me.

Dema walked the familiar path to the throne room, and when she reached the atrium, she paused, waiting for Malowe to tell her what next. For her trouble, she received a shove in her back which sent her crashing to the floor.

"Did I tell you to stop?" Malowe asked.

Dema did not reply, but merely groaned as she lay sprawled out on the floor.

"Get up, you useless girl!"

The breath was forced from Dema's lungs as Malowe's shoe made contact with her stomach. She wheezed on all fours, trying to catch her breath, but it felt like her lungs were refusing to inflate. She felt panic rising in her as she struggled to draw breath, but just then, her breathing began normally again.

Dema struggled to her feet, still breathing heavily.

"You shouldn't have done that," she said, glaring at Malowe with as much animosity and spite she could muster. "I may be a prisoner, but I am still an ambassador of the king. You will pay for what you have done."

"Unlikely," Malowe replied dismissively. "Now open the doors, and walk in. And do show proper respect for her majesty."

Dema opened the great door and stepped inside. She did not, however, hold it open for Malowe, and she saw with great satisfaction that the woman had to spring forward to catch the door before it crashed shut. Dema smirked as they turned toward the room and began to walk toward Queen Kalis, who sat on the throne, with three dwarves beside her. Dema saw instantly that these three were the lords Tabriz, Sahand, and Mengar.

This can't be good.

She approached the throne and gave a small bow, the

smallest she could manage without being incredibly rude. *Ambassadors still must be diplomatic.*

"Ambassador Dema," Queen Kalis began. "Thank you for joining us."

"Your majesty," Dema replied, "I do not think I had a choice."

"No, no you didn't," Kalis agreed.

"Why am I being held prisoner?" Dema asked. "It can't be standard practice to imprison diplomats."

"You are being held because you are a threat to the sovereignty of the dwarves," Malowe answered dismissively.

"Peace, Malowe," Kalis said, holding up a hand to silence the woman.

"You have been held in protective custody while we sort out what is going on and what we are going to do with you," Kalis explained.

"And how would you feel if one of your dwarves was held similarly in Galismoor?" Dema asked.

"That is beside the point."

"No, I think that's really the whole point," Dema retorted.

"Lady Dema," Sahand spoke up, "We would appreciate your cooperation in these proceedings."

"I would appreciate your respecting of my diplomatic office while we're at it," Dema replied.

"It is because of your diplomatic office that you are being treated as you are," Kalis answered.

"Imprisoned? Only two meals of bread and water a day?"

"You could spend some time in the dungeon with one meal a day," Malowe answered spitefully. Dema did not respond to the threat.

"What we are debating here, is not your accommodations," said the queen. "We are debating what must be done with you."

"You are a security risk in our city," Tabriz interjected.

"How am I a security risk to you. My friends and I came and warned you of the coming elven attack. We helped you. We fought for you. I am here as an ambassador to strengthen the ties between our two nations."

"So you say," Malowe said.

"You've seen my official commission," Dema said to Kalis. The three dwarf lords and Malowe were all very much opposed to her, and she decided that Kalis alone may yet be a friend to her in this place. "I am blameless of what they are accusing me."

"That's what must be decided," Kalis answered. "I have read your correspondence that you meant to send out the other day. I do not think you can remain as an ambassador here."

"Then send me away," Dema demanded. Already, she had hope that this may all soon be behind her, if she could play her cards right. "Send me away, banish me. Give me my horse and my possessions and send me on my way to Galismoor."

"I told you she would ask for that," Malowe said with a sneer. "She wants to run along and share our weaknesses with her king."

"I most certainly do not," Dema answered angrily. "My first priority is to establish diplomatic ties between our nations. As that seems unlikely at best, I simply would like to return to my homeland. I have not been spying. My king has no intention of attacking the dwarves."

Queen Kalis frowned, and the dwarves sighed incredulously.

"You see, your majesty," Malowe began slowly, "We already know that she has been spying. She has been all over the city. She lies." The last word trailed off in a serpentine hiss, and it made Dema's blood run cold.

"I'm not lying!" Dema answered, her voice rising in anger and frustration.

"Queen Kalis, you see now that I have been right all along," said Malowe. "We know the elves are not to be trusted, and we now know that those who consort with elves are not to be trusted. They are a blight on our land, and they must be eliminated."

At the word "eliminated," Dema's heart sunk.

"Let her speak once more in her own defense, and then we may decide," said the queen. "Dema, you may begin."

Dema's mind raced looking for something, anything she thought she could say that would get her out of this situation. She looked from face to face, looking for any sort of weakness that could be exploited. The dwarf lords' faces were hard and cruel. Malowe's face was darkened by shadow. *Shadow!*

As she looked at Malowe, the truth of it all came crashing down on Dema. Malowe was a Shadow. Though not exactly like Solzar with his gray appearance, Malowe had a cloak of darkness around her that was able to be pierced by neither the light of the sun nor the light of fire. Something had seemed off about Malowe to Dema since they had met. Having met Solzar, she thought she knew all about Shadows, but apparently, there was so much more to know. She decided that this was her best card to play.

"Queen Kalis," Dema began slowly, taking great care to pick her words carefully. "You know that I was driven from my home by a Shadow. He attacked my home, killed my friends and family, and destroyed the village." She paused slightly to glance at Malowe, but her face was an unreadable mask.

"I journeyed across the river to the land of the elves and sojourned among them. We were greatly mistreated and fled to Sardis to plead for mercy from their king. But we were not the first to arrive in Sardis. That Shadow, Solzar, arrived first. And he whispered evil into the ear of the king of the elves. The king of the elves became so bitter and hateful that he imprisoned my friends and I and ordered an attack on your kingdom and on mine. We escaped and fled before the wave of the king's fury, traveling to the Free Isles, and when the Free Isles fell, to Balkh. From there we brought word to you and your husband. After sending the elves on their way, we traveled back to our homeland and encountered the Shadow again. There we bested him in battle, and through a heroic sacrifice, we unmade the Shadow, and he is but a man again." Again Dema paused, and she saw hate in Malowe's eyes, as well as something else. *Could it be sadness?*

"Upon our victory, my king commissioned me here again to serve as ambassador. But I am afraid that history is repeating itself. There is a Shadow in Darren Shahr."

"You can't possibly be accusing me of being a Shadow," the queen interrupted, aghast.

"No, your majesty. I mean Malowe." For dramatic effect, Dema pointed her finger at Malowe, who gasped in shock.

"I am no Shadow," Malowe said to the queen. "Really, your highness, is this the best she can do? Turn the finger of blame from herself onto another? It's pathetic."

"Dema, how do you know?" Kalis asked. "I thought the other Shadow was all gray. You called him the Gray Man when you first came here, did you not?"

"Look at her!" Dema urged. "Look at the darkness shrouding her despite the light of day!"

The queen and the three lords leaned closer to Malowe to inspect her.

"I see nothing," Mengar said.

"Nor I," added Tabriz.

"The human is grasping at straws," Sahand chimed in dismissively.

"See, there is nothing at all to her tale," Malowe said,

smiling at Dema as if Dema were a confused child woken up from a nightmare. "Fairy tales and stories, that's all she has."

"Yes, very true," Kalis answered, and Dema's heart sank. "I expected better of you, Dema."

"If that is all she can bring in her own defense, accusations against another, then I think our meeting is at an end," Tabriz said.

"Call some guards to send her back to her room," Kalis said to Malowe.

"Her room?" Malowe asked. "Would it not be safer, better, to lock her in the dungeon while we settle the matter?"

"No," Kalis replied. "As long as she lives in Darren Shahr, she is an ambassador, and ambassadors are owed a certain level of comfort."

"As you wish, my lady," Malowe said, and she left the room to summon guards.

"My lords," the queen said, "We shall convene again tomorrow to weigh the evidence and decide on the fate of Dema." She dismissed the lords with a wave, and they bowed and departed. Malowe returned with two armed guards, and Dema was handed over to them.

The guards marched her from the room. The door shut behind them and the guards turned in the opposite direction of her room.

"That's not the way to my room," Dema protested.

"We have special instructions regarding your room," one of the guards replied. "We have been told to put you in the finest cell of the dungeon."

"But the queen!"

"Shut up!" the other guard shouted.

"Malowe said you'd protest, but our instructions will be heeded. It's the dungeon for you."

Dema began to struggle, and each guard got a couple of

punches in, before she gave up and hung limply between them as they dragged her down to the dark, dank dungeon.

———

Dema did not sleep. There was nothing in her cell besides four walls and an iron door. The only light came from a torch on the wall down the hall from her cell, by which she could see only dimly. She spent her time pacing or sitting in the corner of the cell, her head resting on her knees. She was too angry to cry. She just wanted to break something.

In the darkness, Dema lost all concept of time. She did not know if she had been there for hours or minutes. The time slipped away all the same, and she despaired.

For the first time since her involuntary incarceration in her room, Dema now came to terms with never being able to leave. Always there had been the spark of hope. But now, even that spark was extinguished and all was ashes.

Dema's mind drifted to thoughts of Reith. Where was he? What was he doing? Did he yearn for her with the longing she was feeling for him right now? What she would give for one last kiss ...

She remembered Kydar, slain as they fled from Sardis, after they had been trapped in a dungeon like this one. At least there, she had not been alone. She mourned for her brother and the time stolen from them.

She thought of her parents, killed by Solzar when the Shadow had attacked. It felt like another lifetime. So much had changed in the months since that moment. She had changed. No longer was she the scared girl running away. She was a warrior. She was an ambassador. But now, all she had become was slipping away. The scared girl had been there all along. And now she was all alone.

Eventually, the tears did come, slowly at first, and then

with huge, shuddering sobs. She lay on the floor in the fetal position, her back to the door.

I'm going to die here.

She thought it, and in that moment, she accepted it. This was her fate. She was done fighting, done running. She was so tired. Death would be a relief.

I'll be with Kydar again. And mom and dad.

The thought warmed her heart. It wasn't a hopeful thought, but it reignited the spark within her, the spark of love.

Gradually, the tears stopped flowing, and Dema realized she was incredibly thirsty. There was no water in her cell, and she had not heard a guard to whom she could call.

The thirst drove every other concern from Dema's mind. She grew angry with herself for wasting precious water on tears. She stood and shook the bars of her cell and called for a guard until her voice was hoarse, but no one came. Eventually, she slumped back against the wall, defeated.

She tried to sleep, but sleep eluded her. She didn't know if it was evening or morning, and her body clock was all out of sorts. She could feel the weariness in her bones but could not access the blissful unconsciousness of the world of dreams. Something seemed to be blocking her from crossing sleep's threshold.

The only way Dema could feel the passing of time was through the beats of her own heart. Each thump within her chest marked a second slipping away. She wondered, morbidly, just how many heartbeats she had left. She assumed Malowe and the dwarf lords would arrange for her execution. She hoped it wouldn't hurt.

Dema retreated into herself, until all that remained was her heartbeat and her thirst. It wasn't sleep, but it was nearly as unconscious. Her body continued the normal functions of life to keep her alive, the heart beating, breathing, and the like, while her mind retreated to a corner of her being, like a cell of sorts inside her personality. Only her lingering thirst managed to penetrate this inner sanctuary, reminding her, as though someone were yelling from a great distance, that she was still part of the land of the living.

It was in this inner darkness that a blinding light shone.

Salvation.

She came to herself, knowing that the light was casting out all darkness. She was free. The God of Light had come for her, as the Light had come for Kydar when he had perished.

"Get up!"

It was not the gentle voice she was expecting. This voice was harsh and rough. Confused, Dema blinked at the light, trying to peer toward its source to see who had come for her.

"I said get up!"

Something crashed against the bars of Dema's cell, startling her into full wakefulness.

It was a guard. A common, dwarven guard. Not a friend, not a savior, certainly not a God, just a guard. And enemy.

And just like that, the hope that she had been repressing shattered into a million pieces and Dema shattered along with it. She fell to the ground as great sobs rolled over her body. She cried as she hadn't since Kydar's death. There was nothing left inside of her to make tears, but she cried all the same. She was broken. She was lost. She was ashes.

Dema neither knew nor cared that the door to the cell was opened and that strong arms pulled her up and dragged her along. Her sobbing continued. The dam had fallen before the strong tide.

Voices tried to break into her consciousness, but she ignored them. What did they matter to one so damaged, one so alone?

Gradually, she realized that the strong hands had let her go several minutes ago and her cheek was pressed against a cold, tiled floor. She ignored the impulse to open her eyes and instead used her other senses to determine her new situation.

She was vaguely aware of two people in conversation near her, but she had no idea if they were alone or if silent watchers were nearby. She decided against jumping to her feet and fleeing or fighting.

"We cannot send her back in this state," said Malowe. It was the first sentence that made any sense in Dema's ears.

"No, she's insane," replied the other. *Kalis*, Dema determined. "It was not my wish that she spend the night in the dungeon."

"But you see how dangerous this girl is," Malowe pointed out. "One night in the dungeon caused her to completely breakdown. Imagine what she would have done if she had been free?"

"I hate to think what might have happened," the queen replied.

"It is as I have told you," Malowe continued. "These humans are all the same. They want to expand their territory at our expense. She would have killed you."

"How could you say that?" Dema asked, pushing herself up to a seated position. "I have only ever helped Queen Kalis."

"You have manipulated the queen at every turn," Malowe snapped. "You and your friends created a fake invasion of elves and managed to kill the king. But when you needed to, you called off the attack. And then you returned as an ambassador. More like a spy!"

"You have no proof," Dema retorted.

"Proof? We have all the proof we need," Malowe replied. And her eyes gleamed red and she smiled wide in triumph. And Dema saw what was about to happen right before it did.

Kalis was looking down on Dema with a concerned, stern expression. She was unaware of what Malowe was doing beside her. Malowe pulled a dagger from a sheath hidden in her robes and raised the knife up. It gleamed in the torchlight, and Dema called out a warning.

"No!" she yelled, but it was too late. The knife plunged down, stabbing through flesh, ripping, tearing, killing.

And Queen Kalis fell dead to the floor.

TWELVE

Dema stared in horror at the lifeless figure on the ground, blood pooled around the dead queen, and the knife remained lodged in her. Finally, Dema's rage helped her find her voice.

"How could you?" she screamed at Malowe. "You monster!"

"Oh, it was easy," Malowe said, with the air of someone commenting on a trivial task.

"Why?" Dema demanded.

"Because I wanted to. Why else does anyone do anything?"

"I meant why would you want to do something like that!"

"Well, surely you can't believe that when the guards come in that they will think I had anything to do with this?" Malowe asked innocently.

And then it dawned on Dema.

"You're going to blame me."

"Of course," Malowe replied, beaming at Dema as if Dema were her student and had answered a tricky question correctly. "Look closely at the knife."

Dema looked down at the body and the knife standing straight up out of the back. It was the dagger that Yaz had left for her in her room.

"It's too easy," Malowe went on. "This is your dagger. It's in our queen's back. It's obvious what happened here. Somehow you had the dagger on your person when you were brought in to her. Perhaps a friend slipped it to you. But you used it to assassinate our queen."

"But you were already going to be getting rid of me," Dema said slowly, still trying to work out why Malowe did this horrible thing.

"Blaming the queen's death on you is only one of the many perks of this fun twist of fate," Malowe explained. "With the queen gone, and her children too small to take the throne, of course someone will be needed to lead the dwarves. Someone whom the queen trusted. Someone who will seek vengeance for the queen."

"So I'm to be executed," Dema said, seething.

"That was already going to happen," Malowe said. "No, I mean vengeance on a grander scale. Vengeance that matches the betrayal. An ambassador sent here specifically to murder our queen? This will mean war."

And now the puzzle was complete. Malowe was always aiming toward this end. War between the dwarves and the humans.

"You won't win."

"And what are you going to do about it?"

Dema seized her chance. Throwing caution to the winds, she ran for it. Behind her, she heard Malowe's started shriek, and then Malowe's scream.

"Guards! Quick! She murdered the queen!"

Within seconds, her chance of escape vanished. From all sides, guards poured into the throne room, heavily armed and all running toward her. She turned left, then right, trying to find an escape, but it was useless. She was grabbed and subdued and dragged back to Malowe.

"This ambassador was an assassin the whole time," Malowe explained to the guards. "She came here to spy on us and learn all she could. But we were on to her. So she took this dagger and murdered the queen in cold blood!"

Several guards drew their swords as if to run her through right then and there.

"No!" Malowe yelled. "We are not savages. We are a proud people. She must be executed by the queen's executioner. You two," and she pointed to two of the guards, "take her to the executioner. I want her head back here when he is finished."

The two guards took Dema and dragged her away. She struggled and fought, but they were too strong. As they left the throne room, Dema could hear snatches of Malowe's war cries and the men's enthusiastic response.

They'll be marching by morning, and I'll be dead in a few minutes.

The thought made her struggle even more, trying to get free. The guards simply gripped her arms tighter.

She had no idea where they were taking her, and she was being dragged backwards. They took her down several halls and down a flight of stairs.

"Where are you taking that prisoner?" a commanding voice called out from somewhere behind her. Dema thought the voice was familiar.

"To be executed," one of the guards explained. "She murdered the queen."

"There will be no execution today," the voice replied, and to her surprise, Dema found that she had been released. She fell to the floor with a crash and pushed herself up to her knees just in time to see one of the guards fall dead beside her and the other guard facing off against a lone warrior. Yaz!

Dema took the sword of the fallen guard and rose to join

the fight. The remaining guard was too focused on Yaz and did not even know that Dema had joined the fight. He fell right beside his comrade.

"Yaz! I am so happy to see you!" Dema exclaimed, and the two girls embraced.

"I am so glad you're still alive," Yaz replied. "I've been trying to figure out what happened to you since yesterday. I knew something bad was going to happen today. Is the queen really dead?"

"Yes," Dema replied sadly. "Malowe stabbed her and blamed it on me. She even used the dagger you left me."

"That witch!" Yaz cursed.

"We need to get out of here," Dema said. "She's expecting my head back in the throne room any minute."

"Come on, I made preparations."

Yaz and Dema rushed through the city toward the docks. As they ran, Yaz explained the plan.

"I knew we'd need a getaway plan. I have horses and supplies waiting for us across the river. There is a small boat nearby that we can row across. If we can't get to that, we'll have to swim. You can swim, right?" She looked at Dema with worry.

"Yes, I can," Dema answered.

"Thank God."

They kept going, and came across a few people, who simply looked on them with surprise as they rushed past. News of the queen's death and Dema's alleged part in it had not spread.

At the docks, Yaz led the way toward the very end. There, under a sheet which Yaz pulled away with a flourish, was a small rowboat. Dema stepped in and took one of the oars while Yaz untied the boat and pushed them out, jumping nimbly in beside her. The two of them rowed hard, not daring to look back. Out in the river, the current took them down river a good hundred yards or so while they rowed to the opposite bank. Yaz steered them toward a grassy bank near the forest's edge. They ran the boat aground and they both stepped out and waded the remaining distance to the shore.

"We need to set the boat adrift," Yaz explained. "If we leave it here, I will alert someone that we crossed this way, and I'd like that information to remain a secret. Setting it adrift will send it over the waterfall, and it will be a mystery how we got away." They pushed the boat out into the current and they stepped into the shadow of the trees to watch it slowly work its way toward the waterfall.

"That's good enough," Yaz said. "Let's go."

Yaz led Dema upriver. They stayed away from the shoreline under the cover of the trees. They could not be seen from the river or the city, but they also could not see the river or the city. Dema's imagination ran wild with images of the dwarves mobilizing for war and crossing the river intent on her blood.

At last, they came to a small clearing. Four horses were tied to trees. Two were saddled, and the other two were bearing large bundles.

"One for each of us, and a pack horse," Explained Yaz. "We need all the supplies we can get for this journey."

"You're coming with me?" Dema asked, not daring to believe it.

"Of course!" Yaz exclaimed with surprise. "I can't stay here. I just killed a guard and freed the queen's killer!"

"Oh, Yaz!" Dema said, overcome with emotion. Yaz was leaving everything, friends, family, a job, for her.

"What are friends for? Now come on! It's time to go."

The two friends untied the horses and loosely tied the pack horses behind the riding horses. Then they took to the saddle and set off at a brisk trot, intent on putting as much distance between them and Darren Shahr as they could.

Not even an hour ago, Dema had despaired that she was going to die in Darren Shahr, but now she was free and riding home with a friend at her side.

———

During a break later in the day, Dema gave Yaz the full story of what had transpired in the throne room.

"She's going to war with the humans?" Yaz asked. "That was her plan the whole time?"

"It seems so. She tried to discredit me and make everyone suspicious of me, so it wouldn't seem so crazy that I killed the queen."

"But the dwarves aren't ready for war," Yaz pondered.

"Not on their own," Dema agreed. "But maybe Malowe is expecting allies in the fight?"

"Who though?" Yaz asked. "The Shadow you met, Solzar, he's not a Shadow, so he won't help."

"I've been wondering about that as we've been riding," Dema replied. "Maybe she thinks a surprise attack will be effective. It would be a surprise. But Galismoor is so far away from the border, King Calmon would have ages to get his army sorted and ready to defend the city."

"Maybe the elves are sending an army?" Yaz asked.

"Romulus is king there. There's no help for Malowe unless something goes horribly wrong in Sardis. And I hope nothing has gone wrong there."

"Either way, we need to make sure we go faster than the dwarven army," Yaz said. "That shouldn't be too hard for us. It's only us two on horseback. Most of the army will be marching."

"We should go as fast as the horses will allow," Dema said.

"Speaking of that," Yaz replied, "What route do you want to go? We've been following the river that leads up to Lake Banu, which is how you've traveled to and from Darren Shahr."

"That's a dangerous way," Dema said, remembering the snow spider that had attacked their company, as well as the tales of bears, wolves, and ghost leopards that prowled the area around the lake. "Is there no other option? I thought the mountains were impregnable."

"Oh, there's always a way," Yaz said. "I agree that the lake route is dangerous. We could turn north and go around the mountains, perhaps up toward the human city of Kal-Epharion if my geographic memory is correct. I think we'd have to contend with the desert."

"And that's a long way from Galismoor," Dema pointed out. "Will the dwarves march by the lake?"

"Most likely. Even if we're ahead of them though, we'd have to be careful about fires. They could see those and send scouts."

"What about to the west?" Dema asked.

"That's a possibility," Yaz answered. "There are some low passes that wouldn't be too treacherous to cross, and there are ancient trading routes along the sea. We'd essentially be walking with the mountains to our right and the sea to our left until we reached the plains of the Rammis River."

"Is it any quicker?"

"It's hard to say," replied Yaz. "All things considered, it's probably about the same. But perhaps a tiny bit less dangerous."

"I don't think the two of us could go by the lake," Dema said. "We'd be easy targets for anything that wanted to hurt us."

"Let's go west then! We probably should get going now."

They packed up the few things they had taken out of the packs and mounted their horses again. Their first order of business was to find a ford to cross the river. Otherwise, they'd have to just keep following the river up to Lake Banu, which is exactly what they wanted to avoid.

They had to go for several miles before the river widened out considerably with easy banks on either side to attempt a crossing.

"I'll go first, with these two horses," said Yaz. "If I get swept away, do not come in after me."

"No! Of course, I'll try to save you."

"What good are two dead people?" Yaz asked. "One of us needs to continue with word of the attack. Promise me you won't follow me in."

Dema hesitated for several long moments.

"Dema, please," Yaz said sternly.

"Okay, fine, I promise."

"Wish me luck then."

"Good luck," Dema said, as Yaz turned her horse to face the stream. She urged the creature in slowly and soon they were well out into the river. The flow wasn't very strong, and the horses had an easy time of it. The water eventually rose to Yaz's shin, but no higher. When both horses were safely on the far bank, Yaz turned and waved for Dema to follow. Dema managed to cross without incident, and the two girls and four horses turned away from the river and rode west, toward a gap in the mountains they could see in the distance.

That evening, they found a clearing in the forest to set up camp. The horses were tethered to trees all around the camp, thereby giving them some warning if anything or anyone were to approach. They set up a small campfire, and Yaz took the first watch of the night.

Dema fell asleep almost as soon as she lay down. She

hadn't realized how tired she was. But then she remembered that she hadn't slept at all in her cell in the dungeon and had been in there overnight. She slept soundly with no dreams.

When she awoke, the sunlight was gently caressing her face. The world felt damp, and as she opened her eyes, saw the light sparkling on the dew. Yaz was asleep on the other side of the fire. It took Dema a minute to realize what was wrong.

"Yaz!" she called out.

Yaz stirred and then grunt, "What?"

"Yaz, it's morning!"

Yaz rubbed her eyes and then slowly sat up. Her hair was disheveled, and her eyes blinked rapidly as she hid her face from the sunlight.

"You were supposed to wake me up!" Dema scolded.

"Slept well, did you?" Yaz asked. "And we're still alive I assume."

"Well, yeah," Dema acknowledged.

"Then what are you so made about?"

"Someone or something could have killed us!"

"But they didn't," Yaz pointed out.

"That's not the point."

"You take first watch then."

"I will, and I'll be sure to wake you up."

They ate and drank and then packed up their belongings and re-situated the horses. Then it was back in the saddle for more travel.

The next day, Dema and Yaz reached the shores of the sea. To their left, the sea gleamed blue, endless to the horizon. Dema hadn't seen the sea since she had left Balkh. To their right, the mountains towered above them as a wall.

"Now we go due west until the mountains begin to fade away, and we'll turn back north," Yaz explained.

The next few days found the two of them navigating this strange world at the intersection of mountain and sea. They tried to find level ground where they could, but often they found themselves traversing along the edge of a hill, and the horses had to go slowly. Every so often, the water pierced the land in a narrow valley, which Yaz called a fjord. Each time they came across one, they had to turn further inland, which meant going into the mountains.

At the largest fjord they had yet come across, they had to travel well away from the sea proper. Dema was getting frustrated that they had to do so much zig-zagging. She felt that they were losing their time advantage on the dwarven army.

This fjord, however, turned out to be a blessing. As they neared the point furthest from the sea, Dema noticed something weird in the rock wall above them.

"Yaz, look at that," she said, pointing to a strangely flat section for the wall.

"That looks carved," Yaz replied. "Let's check it out."

They continued a short way, and soon found a gentle slope that led up toward the flat section of the rock.

"Aha!" Yaz exclaimed, as she was in the lead.

"What? What is it?" Dema asked excitedly.

"It's the road!"

And a road it was. Carved into the side of the mountain was a road wide enough for two horses to ride abreast. It was flat and smooth, easy to traverse. To the right, the mountain cliffs offered protection. To the left, a drop down to empty space, and a beautiful view of the fjord.

"I knew we'd find it!" Yaz called out, and then she gave out a joyful laugh. "We must have missed the start of the road by coming too far to the south."

"This will speed things up," Dema said. "If, of course, the way is clear."

"This road should take us all the way to the edge of the

mountains. And from there, it will be easy riding across the country."

Dema and Yaz were quite thrilled with their discovery, and even the horses seemed to have a little bit extra energy now that their footing was sure. The miles flew by the rest of that day. They found that at each fjord, a ramp of sorts had been carved, leading to the valley below. It was on one of these that they managed to gain access to the road. These ramps allowed them to find food for the horses in the lush valleys below the mountains, as well as springs and runoff ponds for fresh water.

On the second day after they had found the road, Dema brought her horses to a halt. Yaz almost ran into the back of Dema's pack horse, and there was a lot of stamping of hooves as the horses settled to a stop.

"What is it?" Yaz asked.

"It's a huge boulder," Dema said as she hopped down from her saddle. "It's blocking the way."

Yaz followed her, and soon the two girls were standing beside the boulder. It was perhaps five feet high and six feet across. Beneath it, they could tell that the road was cracked. Looking up, they saw a huge cliff looming over them.

"It must have fallen," Dema pointed out.

"We can't get the horses by it," Yaz said. And it was true. There was about a foot of space on either side of the boulder between the rock and the wall and the rock and the fall to their left.

"Can we get behind it and push?" Dema asked.

"We have to try," Yaz said. The two girls slipped behind the rock. Dema leaned her shoulder into the boulder experimentally and gave it a shove, but it didn't move.

"Together, on three," Yaz said. "As hard as you can push." They leaned their shoulders into the boulder, Yaz counted to three, and they both struggled and strained against the rock.

But it wouldn't budge. After several long seconds of tremendous effort, both girls pulled away, panting.

"That went well," Dema said.

"Quite," Yaz said, staring at the boulder as if it were a difficult math problem that just needed the right solution.

"Could the horses pull it out of the way somehow?" Dema asked, thinking it was unlikely even as she asked.

"We have a little bit of rope in the packs, but not nearly enough to tie around this boulder and the horses in a way that would make any difference. And really, all the horses could do would be drag it back the way we came. And it's miles to the last fjord we passed."

They remained silent for several minutes. Occasionally, one of them would approach the boulder or the cliff wall, poking and prodding, looking for some stroke of inspiration.

"What if we put our backs to the cliff and pushed with our legs," Yaz suggested eventually. "I think we'll have better leverage that way."

"We can try it," Dema agreed. "We need to be higher up on the wall, at least half as high as the boulder is tall."

They got into position, standing with their backs to the wall. Dema pressed her left foot against the boulder while keeping her right on the ground. Her knee was almost in her chest, but she had enough weight on the wall that could draw up her right leg and remain suspended between the boulder and the cliff. Beside her, Yaz assumed a similar position.

"On three then?" Dema asked.

"I'm ready when you are."

This time Dema counted. On two, she raised her right foot and planted it on the boulder and on three she pushed back against the cliff, straining all her muscles as she pushed with her legs. For several long seconds, nothing happened. And then the boulder began to lean ever so slightly away from them. Dema kept pushing with everything she had, and slowly, ever so slowly, the boulder began to roll away from them. She gave one last push and had to drop her feet to the ground to avoid crashing down.

"Keep it going!" Dema shouted and rushed forward and connoted pushing with her shoulder and arms. With the boulder already slowly moving, she was able to keep it going. Yaz joined her, and the two of them pushed and pushed to the very edge. Then the boulder began to fall to the forest below. Yaz stumbled, thrown off by the boulder's fall, and she herself fell forward behind it. At the last second, Dema grabbed her hand, and Yaz came to a stop, her torso leaning over the side of the cliff. Dema pulled her back to safety and hugged her tightly. From below, they could hear crashes as the boulder tumbled through the forest. Flocks of birds took to the sky at the disturbance.

"That was close," Yaz panted.

"Too close," replied Dema, also panting.

———

After that, their going was smooth. The road was clear and easily traversed. The mountains dwindled in size around them, and they saw the curve of the land around the sea. At this point, they left the road, which began to head further to the south, and instead followed the course of a small river which flowed down from the edge of the mountains to the sea. The land was open, with no towns or villages that they could see. In the distance to the southwest, Dema could see the desert she, Reith, and the others had crossed while fleeing from Sardis to Amisos. The river they followed was narrow and swift, with sections of rapids that would have made any sort of boating dangerous.

They continued for several days, traveling northwest along the path of the river. The mountains remained to their right, but instead of the sea to their left, it was a great grassland which stretched out to the horizon, with gently rolling hills colored in greens, golds, and browns. At the first chance they got, they crossed the river, finding a place where the river was smooth and the current not so quick.

The days passed quickly, and the miles with them. Before she knew it, Dema was gazing at the Rammis River, the dividing line between the land of the humans and the elves. She took Yaz to the ford just south of Suthrond, and as they crossed, Dema began weeping. She had never imagined she would be back here when she was locked up in Darren Shahr. But here she was again, home.

She and Yaz spent only the one evening in Suthrond, determined to continue their way to Galismoor. She enjoyed tearful reunions with Heth and the rest of her countrymen. She told them all that had befallen her in Darren Shahr, and she warned them that once again, a Shadow was marching in their direction. Heth promised to increase a guard rotation to keep an eye on things. For the first time in days, Dema was able to sleep on a soft bed with a stomach full of delicious food. Suthrond was thriving, and she was content.

At dawn the next day, she was awoken by Yaz, and the two of them prepared to depart. She promised to return to Suthrond, but she could not put a date on her return, as she knew not what lay before her in Galismoor. Leaving that morning was one of the hardest things she had ever done. As she and Yaz rode north, she wiped tears on her sleeves, and the tears did not stop falling for several minutes.

Now, for the first time, she looked forward to going to Galismoor. Ellamora would be there, fulfilling her ambassadorial duties, which Dema was sure were going much better than her own ambassadorship had gone. King Calmon certainly wouldn't lock Dema up. She hoped for a respite, a break, time to sit, think, and be. Time to plan out her next move. Maybe after a few weeks, she could travel south to Sardis to be with Reith. *That would be wonderful.*

At the thought of Reith, she felt an ache in her chest, and realized just how much she missed him. She missed his voice. She missed his charming smile. She missed his humor, his passion, and his intellect. She missed his arms, and she missed his lips on hers.

But for now, she had a job to do. Her ambassador job would not be over until she told the king all that had happened to her in Darren Shahr and warned him of the coming invasion.

A couple of days later, they encountered a company of half a dozen riders. They turned out to be scouts for the king, keeping an eye on lands to the east in the south of Galismoor. They had heard of Dema and her errand to the dwarves, and they were dismayed to find out that a dwarven army was marching on them.

"This is grave news," their captain remarked, shaking his head. "War, war, and more war."

"Has something else happened?" Dema asked, wondering if there was something she was missing.

"Kal-Epharion has rebelled against the king," the captain replied. "With the desert in between, the human kingdom is essentially split in two, east and west."

"That is terrible news," Dema said. She had assumed that the king would be able to call for help from other areas of the kingdom when the attack came, but now, the kingdom was half the size it once was.

"Have you heard anything from the elven realm?" Dema asked.

"No, my lady," the captain answered. "We left Galismoor a fortnight ago and have heard no news from the south."

"No news is good news," Yaz said, shrugging.

"Would you ladies appreciate a guard for your journey to

Galismoor?" the captain asked. "I can spare two men to accompany you. They will guide you and offer protection."

"That is very kind," Dema said, "And we would be delighted."

Two of the soldiers were selected, young men by the names of Boris and Dain. The captain instructed them to give a report to King Calmon personally before turning back and returning to their base camp.

With many words of thanks, Dema and Yaz set off again with Boris and Dain. Dema found them to be exemplary companions, quick-witted and playful, with smiles never far from their faces. The four traded stories of where they had grown up, adventures they had had, and all the sorts of things you talk about when you meet someone new who you immediately get on well with. They were especially interested in Yaz, and her upbringing among the dwarves.

Their last days on the road passed swiftly and easily, accompanied with much conversation and joy. At last, the city of Galismoor loomed above the plains.

"We're here!" Dain declared. "Small city, hardly worth visiting. Perhaps, you'd rather continue?"

"I think Galismoor will suit us just fine," Dema replied with a laugh.

At the gate they parted company with the two soldiers, who went to give their report to the king. The steward, Mr. Bateson, assured Dema that she and Yaz would be granted an audience the next day with the king, but for now they were to go to their chambers and rest from the long, wearisome trip.

"There are certain persons here in the city who will be delighted that you have arrived," he said cryptically. When pressed by Dema as to the identity of these strange people, he simply shook his head and said, "You'll see."

The steward showed Dema and Yaz to magnificent rooms that made her lodgings in Darren Shahr, even when she was in the favor of the queen, look unimpressive in comparison. She took a long, hot bath, and found a wonderfully soft robe lying on her bed, which she put on. Her clothes had been taken to the laundry, but a suitable replacement set was in her chest of drawers. She lay down on the bed, ready to take a nap, when there was a knock at the door.

PART THREE
REITH

THIRTEEN

Reith stood excitedly waiting after rapping on the door three times with his knuckles. Beside him stood Ellamora and Ellyn. The door slowly opened, and the next thing Reith knew, he was enveloped in a tight hug and Dema was kissing him and crying.

"Dema?" Reith asked hesitantly.

"Sorry, sorry," Dema said, pulling away and wiping her eyes on her sleeve.

"Good to see you, too," Ellamora said sarcastically with a wry smile.

"Ellamora! And Ellyn!" Dema exclaimed, seeing the other two for the first time. She hugged them both at the same time, and Ellamora patted her back awkwardly during the three-way squeeze.

"How are you and Ellyn here?" Dema asked Reith as she pulled away.

"That," Reith began, "is quite the long story."

"Hold on," Dema said. "Let me get dressed. Is there somewhere we can go to share stories?"

"Of course," Reith said.

A few minutes later, Dema was dressed and back in the hall, ready to go.

"I brought a friend," Dema said. "She'll want to hear your story too."

She knocked on Yaz's door and explained the situation. Reith had the feeling that Yaz was eyeing him especially closely. Yaz was already dressed and ready to go, so Reith led the way to a courtyard that had a few tables and chairs.

"You go first," Reith and Dema said at the exact same time when all five of them were finally seated. Then they both laughed, and their friends chuckled along with them.

"Fine, I'll go first," Dema said. For the next half hour, Dema recounted all that had befallen her, from her travels to Darren Shahr, her initial loneliness, becoming friends with Yaz, the wickedness of Malowe, her imprisonment, the assassination of Queen Kalis, and her and Yaz's escape.

Reith, Ellamora, and Ellyn were good listeners, gasping at the appropriate times, cursing Malowe when required (which was nearly every sentence), and getting visibly angry on behalf of Dema for her treatment.

"That's awful," Ellyn said quietly when Dema had finished. "I am so sorry that happened to you."

"I want to get my sword into Malowe," Reith growled.

"And Malowe is leading an army here?" Ellamora asked.

"I think so," Dema replied. "She wants 'revenge' for my assassinating the queen."

"Which of course is nonsense," Yaz chimed in.

"It's clear to me that she is another Shadow," Reith said thoughtfully. *That's at least two Shadows we must deal with.*

"Another?" Dema asked. "You mean a second Solzar, or someone else?"

"Did you hear that Kal-Epharion rebelled?" he asked.

"Yeah, what of it?" Dema asked.

"Rumor has it a Shadow is behind that. And that Shadow is raising an army."

It took a few seconds for those words to sink in with Dema and Yaz.

"Another Shadow? And another army?" Yaz asked, a sickened expression on her face.

"We beat Malowe here, and we can be ready for a weakened dwarven army. But a second army from Kal-Epharion? Can we withstand that?"

"It's actually three armies," Reith continued.

Dema swore loudly, startling a couple of nearby pigeons.

"You'd better start telling your story," Dema demanded.

Reith recounted for her his travels to Crain, Pryderus' deposal, the trip to Sardis, and all that happened there, including Dracus and his treachery and Koinas' trial. Dema began to cry when Reith told her that Romulus was dead and that they had no idea about Remus or Myon.

"And then we traveled north to Galismoor," Reith continued. "And we saw the craziest thing. You know Dragonscar?"

"Yeah, the western edge of Terrasohnen, permanently scarred by the dragons," Dema replied.

"It's alive again. Green grass, trees, animals, birds, it's teaming with life once again!"

"That's impossible," Dema said. "You were just there, and it was all black!"

"It's a miracle only the God of Light can be behind," Ellyn said with a smile. "Rebirth from the ashes."

"And then we came here. And we just received word that you had arrived, and that a dwarf army was behind you. And Kal-Epharion is marching this way. And an elven army is massing at our southern border."

"So two Shadows?" Dema asked.

"Maybe three," Reith said. "Koinas or Dracus might be one, we're not sure."

"But why attack Galismoor?" Dema asked. "This seems coordinated."

"We're sure it is," Ellamora agreed. "Two assassinations and a revolt? And now all three places are marching toward us?"

"The Dark Powers are ever at work fighting the Light," Ellyn replied. "But this is the greatest attempt since Erador a thousand years ago."

"King Calmon is mustering the troops," Ellamora said. "And tomorrow there is to be a war council. Dema, you'll be asked to give an account of the dwarves, their capabilities, their new leader, and their aims."

"I'll be ready," Dema said.

"War will be on our doorstep soon," Ellyn said. "We must all be ready for it when it comes."

———

That evening, Reith and Dema enjoyed each other's company. Reith took Dema to the walls of the city, where they walked and watched the sunset.

"I missed you," Reith said, as they walked, holding hands.

"I missed you too," Dema said. "I didn't think I would ever see you again when I was in that cell."

"There were moments I wondered if I would make it out of Sardis," Reith admitted.

"What a mess we have landed ourselves in."

"We didn't start this," Reith pointed out. "We didn't attack Coeden and Suthrond. We didn't send armies across the world seeking to conquer and destroy. Others are the wind; we are simply being driven along by it."

"You minimize the part we are playing in this story," Dema said.

"It's a story, is it?" Reith asked pointedly.

"You know what I mean," Dema said. "All of history can be told as a story. You of all people should know that."

"But is this a good story or a bad one?" Reith asked. From his studies with Vereinen, he knew that history wasn't entirely full of happy endings.

"There's something more at play here," Dema said. "There are parts we need to play before this is all over."

"You're very optimistic."

"Don't forget your sword. And your ring."

"The ring is still cold," Reith said. "And the Voice hasn't told me to 'find me' yet."

"I have a feeling the time is coming soon," Dema said. "Do you know who you should talk to about this?"

"Who?"

"Solzar."

"What? No," Reith said, anger rising within him. "I don't want to talk to him." *If it wasn't for him, Vereinen would still be alive. If it wasn't for Solzar, Reith would be living in Coeden with Vereinen, continuing his studies.*

"I know you hate him," Dema said.

"I don't hate him," Reith replied sharply. "I do not care whether he lives or dies. I just don't want to have to see him. I want to stay far away from him."

"Just think about it," Dema said gently. "He's here, right?"

"Yes, he's not in the dungeon, but he is under guard. He's being treated well."

"So it should be easy for you to go see him, when the time comes."

"Ha, we'll see about that."

The next day, Reith, Ellamora, Ellyn, Dema, and Yaz were fetched by Mr. Bateson to appear before King Calmon.

The king met them in his private study, a room that resembled a library more than anything else. Shelves lined the walls, filled with leather-bound books. In the center of the room was a large wooden desk, intricately carved and magnificent. Behind the desk sat King Calmon, scrolls and parchments spread out across its surface so that hardly any of the wood could be seen. Behind the king was a set of double doors that were thrown open to reveal an outdoor balcony overlooking the city square. Sunlight flooded the room through the open doors, and a gentle breeze caused the papers to rustle, making the office feel as if it were outside. Upon their entry, King Calmon rose and shut the balcony doors, and the outdoor feel temporarily subsided, though the light was still bright.

"Dema," the King called out joyfully. "It is so good to see you! I am glad that you have returned safe and sound, though I am troubled by the tidings your arrival brings. I have spoken to my scouts, and they tell me that you have quite the adventure to tell. Please, spare no detail."

Dema launched into her story, focusing more on her official duties as ambassador. During the telling, Reith let his mind wander to the books on the shelves, and he read the titles on their spines out of the corners of his eyes. *I would live in this room.*

That got his imagination going. He began to envision himself as king, with this as his study, where he could read to his heart's content. He imagined himself giving speeches from the balcony to the citizens gathered below in the square. So totally did he lose himself in his daydream that he completely missed when Dema had finished her story. Seemingly aware that his mind was elsewhere, Ellamora discreetly stomped on his foot, which brought him back to reality.

"Your story fills me with rage," said Calmon, shaking his head. "That the dwarves would treat an ambassador like that, it's against goodness, it's against decency! We would never treat any ambassador as such, even if he or she were sent by our greatest adversaries. Of greater concern now though, are the armies marching for Galismoor. In peace time, we might rectify the situation of your treatment through a show of force, but it is of no matter now. Tell me, Dema, of our enemy's army."

"The dwarves were greatly weakened by attack of the elves," she explained. "As your majesty is already aware, the elves nearly succeeded in conquering Darren Shahr, and that's after they already destroyed Balkh. Queen Kalis would never have sent an army while portions of her city were still being repaired and everyone was still mourning the dead. That's why Malowe killed her. Now the dwarves march with the anger of revenge. As to their size, I do not know for sure, but they cannot have brought a large force. They lost many in the war with the elves."

"A small force with fire in their bellies is a greater foe than a large force largely indifferent on the aims of their general," the king replied.

"Your highness, if I may," Yaz began, and the king nodded to her to continue. "The dwarven force numbers perhaps only 3,000 or so."

"You're Yaz, right?" Calmon asked.

"Yes, I am." Yaz blushed at the pleasure that the king knew her name.

"It was very brave of you to save Dema. We are in your debt. Thank you for your service."

"I was only trying to do the right thing."

"If only more in Terrasohnen would try to do the right

thing," the king answered. "Now, tell me why you think the dwarves number so few."

"As we have already discussed, the dwarves suffered heavy casualties in the war. But before Dema arrived, a large portion of the dwarven army was sent by Queen Kalis to Balkh to see if there was any salvaging of the city, its fleet, and to search for survivors and refugees. It is my understanding that that force remains in Balkh, hard at work rebuilding the city. That leaves a small remnant of their forces."

"That is good intelligence," the king said, "and helps us in our planning. A dwarven force of 10,000, or more, surely would have given us more difficulties. Reith, Dema, could you give us any insight you may have gained as to the purposes of these armies marching for our gate? Do they want us to surrender? Or do they want us destroyed?"

"All three armies seem to be under Shadow control," Reith said. "Therefore, they must all be aligned in purpose. What is it that Shadows want?"

"Can I jump in?" Ellyn asked.

"Of course, Ellyn," King Calmon replied. "Any insight you can provide would be greatly appreciated."

"Shadows want to block out the light and spread darkness. I should think they want us to surrender and submit to a Shadow kingdom. If we refuse, then they shall attempt to destroy us."

"We will never bend the knee to a Shadow," King Calmon growled.

"No, of course not," Ellyn said. "Then they will fight to destroy."

"And we fight to defend," the king replied. "Thank you all for your service to this kingdom and your service to peace in Terrasohnen. We will use this information to plan our defense."

And with that, the king dismissed them all.

The following day, King Calmon took to his balcony and announced to the city that foes were marching on Galismoor. The people of the city sprang into action. Villagers from nearby regions were evacuated into the city and placed in temporary housing in the streets. All available food supplies in the area were gathered in, inventoried, and stored for a potentially long siege. Every able-bodied soldier was armed and enrolled into a unit. Smiths and carpenters set about making and sharpening weapons. Fletchers made arrows. The gates were shut on the morning of the second day, and gravel and sand were piled up behind them to make them impregnable.

Amid all the war preparations, Reith found he had a great amount of free time, which of course, he spent with Dema. With the city preparing for war, there wasn't much to do. Libraries were closed, and any venture outside the gates was prohibited. So they spent a lot of time on the walls, sitting quietly in a corner where they were out of the way of the soldiers.

"I still think you should see Solzar," Dema said. "I think he can help you."

Reith fidgeted with the ring on his finger but said nothing.

"Have you heard from the Voice again?" Dema asked, changing tact.

"No," Reith said honestly. "But I can't imagine it will be much longer. Three armies are marching on us. If hope is not yet gone, it might be soon."

"What's the voice waiting for?" Dema asked. "Already, the gates are shut. It would be nearly impossible to get away from the city now."

"I don't know," Reith answered thoughtfully. He had wondered about that same thing too. For months, the Voice would chime in and give him a bit of guidance, leading him across Terrasohnen to help and fight for people in the way of the Shadow. *Shadows,* he corrected himself. But now, silence. And it confused him. If he had it his way, he would leave right that moment to go north and seek the source of the Voice and find out once and for all what his ring and sword were meant for.

"You're sure the ring hasn't grown warm?" Dema asked.

"It hasn't," Reith answered. The ring was supposed to grow warm when he was on the right path. At least that's what Solzar said. Even thinking about Solzar caused Reith's heart to race and rage to bubble up inside of him. In these quiet moments with Dema before war, he realized that anger had been simmering inside of him since Vereinen's death. It was eating away at him from the inside out.

Reith didn't know what it was, but there was some sort of wall in front of him, blocking him from his next move. It was blocking the voice, blocking the ring, blocking his decision-making process. He felt lost. He felt torn in two. He felt double-minded. No course of action seemed right.

"As long as I've known you, you have never hesitated to act," Dema said softly. "You've always known the right thing to do and when to do it. I've admired that about you."

"But?" Reith asked, sensing that there was more Dema wanted to say.

"I think, deep down, you know what you need to do right now, you just don't want to do it."

"I don't know what to do," Reith said, defensively. "I don't know if I should stay or if I should leave and seek the voice."

"That's not the next thing you're supposed to do," Dema said. "And please don't take this in the wrong way. When we left each other, after the battle, after Vereinen... you know, we were all so raw. And you especially. I've lived my grief since Kydar died. I don't think you lived your grief."

Reith started to protest, but Dema held up her hand to silence him.

"I said don't take this the wrong way," she continued. "Don't be defensive. I'm trying to help. I think Kydar's death affected you. I think the deaths of everyone in Coeden affected you. But I think you never really let that grief in. And it's been sitting there, inside you, this whole time. When Vereinen died, and you were sent to the elves, you left that grief behind you. Sure, you carried it with you some, but your heart remained on the Fields of Palander."

Dema paused to let those words sink in. He weighed them in his mind, took each as if in his hand and measured it against the others, before placing it back in line, and taking another word to weigh and measure.

"You know I love you," she whispered to him.

"I know," he said. He did love Dema. And he had loved Vereinen. And Kydar. In his mind's eye, he watched a parade of all the people he ever loved walking by. And they were nearly all dead. And at that moment, he realized something. In all his travels across Terrasohnen, he was running toward people to help, to fight, to save, but he was also running away. Running away from Coeden, running away from Erador, running away from Suthrond, running away from Crain, running away from Sardis, running away, running away, running away. Always running away from something. The Shadow, yes, but something else. Dema was right. *I've been running away from my grief.*

So much had happened to him in so little time. So much loss, so much pain. The constant traveling had been a relief from it, a respite, even though he was on the run for his life. It was those moments that he was still that his grief seemed to haunt him in greater measure. Like right now.

Tears began to fall, slow at first, but then more steadily. Dema reached across and took him in her arms. She wrapped him close, and he lost himself in her tender embrace. The softness of her skin, her scent, her warmth all caused him to sink into her, melting. For a long time, they remained like that. And for a moment, Reith knew he could stop running. He didn't have to be the strong one all the time. He could trust Dema.

Finally, he said, "I'm ready to go see Solzar."

Fourteen

Despite her protests, Reith insisted he go to Solzar alone. He didn't know why exactly, but he thought Solzar might be a bit forthcoming with him if it were just him. Dema escorted him as far as the end of the hall where Solzar was kept. Reith was surprised to find Solzar was not being kept in the dungeon, but was living in a nice room, though with constant supervision and a guard on duty around the clock. The guard knocked, unlocked the door, and announced Reith. He stepped in, the guard stepped out, and the door clicked shut. He heard the bolt slide into place, locking him in with the former Shadow.

Solzar's room was much like Reith's own. The only difference was Solzar's room felt much more lived in, which made sense as he had been here several weeks while Reith was in Crain and Sardis.

"Hello, Reith," Solzar said in a pleasant voice. He was kneeling on a small carpet laid out under the window, his face turned toward the light. He got to his feet, and turned his unseeing eyes toward Reith. Solzar took a seat at the desk and turned his chair to face the room He pointed toward another chair by the wall, and Reith sat down. The room was clearly set up for its inhabitant to have company, which Reith found odd for a prisoner. *Well, I'm here, so it's not that crazy.*

"Solzar," Reith acknowledged as he took his seat. He studied the former Shadow closely. As he had noticed at Palander after Solzar's conversion, the color had returned to Solzar's hair, eyes, and skin. He looked healthier now, better fed, and seemed to have more energy as well. All told, this life was treating Solzar well.

"To what do I owe the pleasure?" Solzar asked.

"The king seems to be treating you well," Reith pointed out.

"It's more than I deserve, I'll admit to that," Solzar agreed. "I have my creature comforts. The only thing I lack is my freedom of movement, but I am told I still have enemies who wish me dead for things that I did before." He hung his head, clearly ashamed of his past actions. "It's for my safety, and for that I am grateful."

Part of Reith reared up inside of him and wanted to strike Solzar dead right then and there, but he quieted that aspect of himself.

"I am glad that you are well taken care of," Reith said.

"Reith," Solzar said slowly, with sorrow in his eyes, "I don't know if I can ever convey just how sorry I am to you. I'm sorry about Vereinen. I'm sorry about Suthrond. I'm sorry about Coeden. I'm sorry about putting you in prison in Sardis. I'm sorry for it all."

And Reith found that he believed the former Shadow. For a long moment, Reith hung on the edge. Two choices lay before him. One led to bitterness and despair. The other would open those wounds of grief, but healing would begin. And he knew what he must do.

"I forgive you."

Instantly, a weight lifted from Reith's shoulders that he

had not noticed before. His heart felt lighter, and he sat up straighter, no longer bound by the anger that had come to define him. And most shocking, he felt his ring warm on his finger.

"Now that," Solzar replied, "Is infinitely more than I deserve."

Reith sat staring at his former adversary. Whatever Solzar was to him now, even if he wasn't a friend, he was no longer an enemy. Reith's forgiveness eliminated that possibility.

Reith held up his hand and inspected the ring. It looked the same as it always did, but he touched it with his other hand and it was warm to the touch, warmer than simple skin contact to do.

"The ring is warm," Reith said. "What does it mean?"

"It means the time is near for you to depart Galismoor."

"What will I find?"

"I don't know," Solzar said. "The ring never burned for me."

"They say there are three Shadows marching on Galismoor," Reith said, changing the subject.

"So I've heard."

"Is there any hope?"

"As long as the Light yet shines, there is hope," Solzar said gravely.

"What will you do during the battle?" Reith asked.

"I will stay in my room and do what I can," Solzar answered simply. "They will not trust me with weapons, so I cannot fight in that sense, but I still have one thing left to me here."

"And what is that?"

"I can pray," Solzar replied. "I can pray to the God of Light. When I was a Shadow, I knew about the God of Light, and I despised him. I hated him with every ounce of my being.

But now, I know him as a Father and a Friend. He is merciful and forgiving. And so I pray."

Reith was surprised at first, but the more he thought about it, the more it made sense. Solzar wasn't just changed from a Shadow to a man, he was transformed into a new man, a man who sought the God of Light. There was a newness, a freshness to Solzar that was beyond simply ceasing to be a Shadow. The darkness inside was replaced with light.

"And Reith," Solzar added, as Reith stood to leave. "Take Dema with you. You should not be alone on this journey."

Reith knocked on the door and the guard came and let him out. As he crossed the threshold, the Voice came back to him again.

Find me.

———

Through Mr. Bateson, Reith requested an audience with the king straight away.

"It's urgent," he told the steward.

Toward evening, Mr. Bateson retrieved him and took him back to the king's study.

"Reith, welcome," King Calmon said distractedly as Reith entered. His desk was covered with papers, charts, and maps. "We are in the final stages of our preparations. Mr. Bateson said you wished to see me with an urgent matter."

"It is urgent, sire," Reith said, twisting the ring on his finger. It was still quite warm. "I have to go north." Reith explained as best he could about his sword, his ring, and the prophecies regarding what he may find at the end of his journey.

"This is the moment when hope seems lost. The Voice is asking me to come. My ring is warm."

He took it off and handed it to the king to touch, and the king was surprised at its unnatural warmth.

"With your leave, your highness," Reith continued, "I ask that you allow me to travel north out of Galismoor on this new adventure, and to come back with all haste to help in the defense of the city. And if the king allows, I wish to travel with Dema."

"It's true, Reith," the king answered sadly, "It's true that this is the moment where hope seems lost. Our scouts have informed us that the armies marching toward us are bigger than we anticipated. We will be stuck in this city, waiting for them to breach our defenses. So my answer is yes. I do not know if there will be any hope outside of our walls, but the chance of hope is a chance we must take. But I would amend your request. If you find that there is no hope, save yourself. Do not try to come back into the city and so doom yourself. Now, what do you need for your journey?"

"We require food and warm clothing. And gear for camping. We need horses if we are to travel beside the water, a boat if we are to travel by it."

"It would be better to sail," the king said. "The winds at this time of year are favorable for northward travel. I can spare a small vessel and a man to sail it. You and Dema have experience on ships?"

"Yes, we do."

"Then you should be able to make a small craft work for you. I will issue the order for these things to be made ready. When will you leave?"

"If possible, by first light," Reith said.

"Then it shall be arranged. There is a small gate that allows water into the city on the north side. You will be there at sunrise, and I will have someone there to greet you and send you on your way."

"Thank you, King Calmon."

"Farewell, Reith. I wish you all possible haste and pray that the winds are favorable for your journey."

———

Reith went straight to Dema and the others to tell them the news. He found Dema, Ellamora, Ellyn, and Yaz sitting in a courtyard in the palace complex.

"King Calmon said we can go," he announced. "We leave tomorrow at first light."

"We?" Ellamora asked.

"Just me and Dema," Reith said apologetically. "Sorry."

"I guess I'll just wait here for the Shadows to fall on me," Ellamora said, rolling her eyes.

"Who knows what we'll face on this trip," Dema said. "You might be glad to be inside Galismoor, especially when we are freezing our butts of far to the north."

"True, true," Ellamora agreed.

"May the God of light go with you," Ellyn said.

"I'll miss you, Dema," Yaz added.

"I'll miss you all," Dema replied.

There were tearful goodbyes that evening, as they said their farewells. Danger was encroaching on the city, but Reith and Dema were journeying off into the unknown. It was hard to say who faced more danger.

Reith slept poorly that night. He drifted in and out of dreams, and unseen monsters lingered at the corner of waking and sleeping. Shadowy figures prowled just out of sight. A sense of foreboding weighed heavy on him.

Just before dawn, he was awoken by a soft knock on the door. A servant had been sent to wake him and take him to the water gate. His bag was already packed from the evening before, and he was ready to go in minutes. The servant did not try to make conversation as they walked, and Reith was grateful. He yawned profusely as he walked through the city.

He arrived at the gate and found a middle-aged man waiting. Dema had not arrived yet.

"Good morning," the man said pleasantly, holding out his hand to shake. "I'm Morris."

"Nice to meet you, Morris," Reith said. "I'm Reith."

"The pleasure is all mine," Morris replied. "Ah, here's the young lady."

Dema arrived with a servant repeating the greetings that Reith had shared with Morris. She gave Reith a hug as well.

"Well, are we ready to go?" Morris asked. Reith and Dema nodded, and the servants were dismissed.

"Follow me," Morris said.

Morris led them down a staircase. The sound of rushing water grew louder the further they descended. The stairway opened to a man-made cave like structure. The river was flowing into the city from the lake, which could be seen in the distance. A metal grate was blocking the entrance to the cave from the outside, but a single file walkway brought them right to the edge of the grate.

"You don't mind getting a little wet, do you?" Morris asked. Neither Reith nor Dema protested.

"We have to go under the grate," Morris explained. "The water is only three or four feet deep, and the grate extends to about a foot below the surface of the water. That means there's a lot of space under it, but not enough space to make this place vulnerable to large scale attack. Hand me my bag through the grate after I make it."

Morris stepped into the river and plunged under and resurfaced on the other side seconds later.

"Easy!" he said, as water dripped down his hair and beard. "I'll stay right here to help you clear the grate. Hand me my bag, then your own."

Reith went first. He passed Morris his and Morris' bags, and his sword, and bow. The water was cold, and he had to force himself to plunge under, but he felt Morris' hand and was soon across. Water flowed down his face, and he found he was instantly much more awake. Dema followed, and soon the three of them were back on the bank walking toward a dock set in between the river and the city, where a small, single sailboat was docked, perhaps fifteen feet long.

"We'll get cozy on here," Morris said. "Welcome aboard *Lake Ranger*."

There was a small cabin built into the ship and Reith found it was filled with supplies, as well as three hammocks. In hardly any time, they were floating out into the river. Reith and Dema rowed from each side of the ship while Morris steered and began to unfurl the sail. The wind was slight, but steady from the south, and they soon left the river behind and entered the lake. Morris told them to put their oars down.

The lake was like an inland ocean, and there was only blue along the northern horizon. Waves gently rocked the *Lake Ranger* as the wind propelled it along. The sun was beginning to rise in the east, giving light to the whole world.

Suddenly, Reith's vision went dark. He cried out, but then an image began to form in his mind. He saw himself, Dema, and Morris from above on the deck of the *Lake Ranger*. But then his perspective zoomed up and away. He followed the coastline, past numerous fishing villages, on and on along the endless lake.

In the distance, he saw mountains, and from the mountains, a river flowing down into the lake. It was frozen. From far away, he felt his ring glow warmly on his hand.

Find me.

And then his vision went black again before gradually refocusing onto the worried face of Dema.

"What's wrong?" she asked.

He blinked and shook his head to clear the remnants of the vision.

"We're on the right track," he said.

"What's that supposed to mean?"

"I had a vision," he explained. "We are to travel north to the frozen river."

"That's a long journey, lad," Morris said. "But I'll get you where you need to go."

"How long will it take to get to the north end of the lake?" Reith asked.

"In this wind, perhaps a week," Morris replied. "We'll only be able to sail by day; the wind dies down at night."

"Will we spend each night on the ship?" Dema asked.

"Only if we're a bit unlucky," Morris answered. "There are several fishing villages along the coast. I aim to stop at one each night, if it lines up with our travel. We can't keep going through the nights. One, I'll be tired and need sleep. Two, you two wouldn't know the first thing about sailing. And three," he added when they were about to protest. "There are a thousand bloody rocks out there waiting to tear this ship to bits."

As the morning wore on, Reith and Dema helped Morris with the sailing duties, and proved his second aspersion wrong.

"Well I'll be shark food," Morris exclaimed. "You two aren't half bad." Coming from Morris, that was a mighty fine compliment.

"Tell us about yourself, Morris," Dema asked that afternoon.

"They say old Morris was born on this lake," Morris began with the air of master storyteller. "My father was the waves, and my mother was the wind."

"Really?" Reith asked, and Dema elbowed him in the side.

"It's a story," she hissed, rolling her eyes.

"My father was a fisherman on this lake all his life. My mother was the prettiest, kindest woman one would ever hope to meet. We lived in a small village far to the north. As soon as I was old enough, I went out with my father to fish. We'd leave early in the morning, hours before sunrise."

"Did you have any siblings?" Dema asked.

"Aye," Morris replied. "A sister. Mariana. She was 8 years younger than me. Flu took her and my mum when I was fourteen."

"That's awful," Dema said softly.

Reith tried to place himself in Morris' shoes, and then realized with a jolt that Dema knew exactly what that felt like. He put his hand comfortingly on her shoulder.

"It was just me and dad then," Morris continued. "He did the best he could. It's a hard life, fishing. We were up early, worked hard. But we had enough. It's a good life."

"How did you end up in Galismoor?" Reith asked.

"Quite by accident," Morris said. "A few years ago, dad died. Well, by then, I was already doing most of the work on the boat. So I carried on. I came to Galismoor because I wanted to check on the fish markets here, and to see if they had any gear I could use. And I never left! A fisherman offered me a job on a bigger boat, and I took him up on it. I still have my place up the lake, and he's good to let me have some time off every now and again to take it easy and travel home. But I've been in Galismoor for six years now. I know this lake better than most, and that's why I was hired on for your adventure."

"Well, we're glad you're with us," Reith said.

"It'll be the smoothest voyage you've ever had," Morris replied.

"Good," Dema answered, "Because the last one had a sea monster!"

"Goodness gracious!" Morris exclaimed. "You must tell me the story!"

For the next few minutes, Reith and Dema told Morris of their voyage from Amisos to the Free Isles, where they had briefly been chased and captured by the Red Fleet. Then they told of their flight from the Free Isles to Balkh and the sea monster that had attacked them on the journey.

Morris was a lively listener, gasping at all the right places, exclaiming where that was called for.

"As far as I know, there are no pirates or sea monsters in this lake."

FIFTEEN

That evening, Morris guided the *Lake Ranger* to the docks beside a small fishing village. There were a couple of other fishing boats bobbing gently at the docks. The village was a simple cluster of buildings on either side of a single street which led away from the lake. From what Reith could tell in the twilight, there were about two dozen houses, a tavern, and a small chapel. The tavern doubled as a market and had three or four bedrooms for out of town guests.

The tavern keeper supplied them with fried fish and potatoes, which Reith and Dema devoured hungrily. Morris seemed to know the tavern keeper as well as the other patrons of the tavern. He was the center of attention, telling stories, laughing loudly, and once even leading everyone in the singing of a shanty. Reith and Dema stayed off to the side, preferring to let Morris be the center of attention, while they observed.

Soon, it was time to retire to their rooms. No one else was staying at the tavern, and the keeper allowed them each their own room. Reith's bed was comfortable, and he fell right to sleep, almost as soon as his head hit the pillow. His dreams that night were of seas and heroes and monsters.

In the morning, Reith awoke to the first traces of dawn lighting up the world to the east. He dressed, retrieved his few possessions, and went downstairs, where a pot of coffee and a hot breakfast of eggs and toast were waiting for him, along with the indefatigable Morris, who was quite chipper.

"Good morning, Reith!" he called out cheerily.

"Morning," Reith replied, with a hoarse grunt.

"Fine weather we'll have today, I reckon," Morris exclaimed, looking out the window at the sunlight. "Yes sir, it'll be a good day on the water."

After a cup of coffee, Reith was more ready to talk, and Dema had finally arisen.

"Good morning," Reith said, trying to be as chipper as Morris.

Dema echoed his previous grunt and sat down to her plate.

"The wind is still coming from the south at a good clip," Morris observed. "We'll make good progress today."

"How long until we reach your village?" Reith asked the sailor.

"With this wind, oh, perhaps three days," Morris guessed. "We'll bunk at my house that night, whenever we pass by. Even if we get there and it's only midday, it'll be worth spending the night."

"What is the village like?" Reith asked.

"It's a lot like this one," Morris answered. "A couple dozen houses, a general store, a butcher shop, a builder, a smith, and a chapel make up the buildings."

"What's the chapel like? Is there a priest?"

"The chapel is a small building with a few rows of benches for seating. It's got big, huge windows that let in so much light you feel like you're outside. As for a priest, well, my village hasn't had a regular one in a long time. There's one that comes into town once a month or so and leads services, but he's a traveling priest, see. He has about four chapels he oversees."

"What are the services like?" Reith asked. "My friend Ellyn, she's an elf, and she was the lore master of the elven city of Crain, and I worked with her in the temple for a time when I lived there."

"You worked in an elven temple?" Morris said with surprise. "Well I'll be. I never would have thought. Times are changing in Terrasohnen. What was that like?"

"I loved it," Reith said. "Ellyn let me read lots of books, and we had a lot of discussions about the God of Light. My daily duties involved candle lighting and keeping the temple open for prayer."

"People don't really go to the chapel other than the first day of the week," Morris said. "The priest will lead some singing, read some sacred writings, say a few prayers, and give a short message of encouragement for the faithful."

By this time, Dema was finishing up with her breakfast. When she drained the last of her cup of coffee, she nodded to the other two, and as one, they rose and departed. Soon they were on deck again, and the *Lake Ranger* was pushed out from the docks into the open lake. Morris pointed the ship the right way, then unfurled the sail. The wind caught it and yanked the ship forward. It crashed through a wave, sending a spray of cold water into the air, which splashed the three sailors. Reith shook his head to get the water out of his hair and off his face. The coolness of the water refreshed him and fully revived him from his sleep. It had a less sanctifying effect on Dema, who swore when the water hit her.

"Doesn't that just make you feel alive?" Morris yelled over the wind. Reith thought so, but he surmised that Dema felt differently.

To the east, a great forest dominated the land. In some

places, the trees seemed to even come to the water's edge. To the west, all was blue. The lake was an inland sea of sorts, with water stretching to the horizon. That morning, they saw no other vessel on the lake, but they did see a few deer drinking by the shore, and Dema swore she saw a bear retreating into the forest, but Reith and Morris didn't see anything.

The sun rose from their right, high into the sky and then began to sink to their left. Still the wind kept them moving forward at a swift pace. Reith and Dema delighted Morris with stories of their time among the elves and the dwarves.

"I'd love to see the Free Isles," Morris yearned. "I'm sure they're beautiful."

"They are," Dema agreed, "But we're not sure what all is left. The elves set fire to the isles."

"It's a shame, a damn shame," Morris said. "And for what? What good is a burned island?"

As Reith looked out over the water, he pondered that question. Solzar had set all this in motion. He destroyed a few towns, Coeden and Suthrond, and then whispered in the ear of Koinas, the king of the elves, and urged him to make war on the humans and the dwarves. The Free Isles were destroyed, as was the dwarven city of Balkh. Darren Shahr almost fell. And now that Solzar was no longer a Shadow, the Dark Powers had raised up other Shadows, one each it seemed, among the humans, elves, and dwarves. But with each of those three, they did not take power to destroy their cities. They took power to wage war on Galismoor and the last free kingdom of Terrasohnen. All three marched on the human capital city, and Reith could only assume they meant to destroy it.

The Dark Powers destroy all they cannot command.

It made sense to him. For so long, Reith saw the violence as senseless, but really it was calculated. The Dark Powers wanted power, but if they could not pull someone to their side and rule through them, they decided to simply destroy that place.

Are they raising up a Shadow in Galismoor?

The thought chilled him to the bone. For a second, he contemplated turning back to Galismoor to try and thwart the development of yet another Shadow. It would make sense that the Dark Powers tried to win the city through a Shadow on the inside. But if the other three Shadows were marching, perhaps that meant that no one had yet turned traitor.

Reith grasped the hilt of his sword and turned his attention northward. Ahead was a frozen river and some power that could restore Terrasohnen. His ring felt warm on his finger, reassuring him that he was going the right way.

North. No turning back.

———

Around midafternoon, they passed by a fishing village.

"With the wind strong, we can reach the next village before sundown," Morris said. "No use stopping now."

True to his word, it was about an hour to dusk when they pulled up to a dock at a small fishing village, that at first glance looked nearly identical to the one they had left that morning. After securing the ship to the dock, they entered the town, searching for the tavern.

It wasn't hard to find. Inside was a gigantic fireplace, which lit up the room and gave warmth. The tavern keepers, an elderly man and woman, were behind the counter, cleaning glasses. Beside them, there was a single patron, a man whose back was to them.

"Welcome!" the elderly man exclaimed. "Greetings, travelers. Come, relax. Can I get you something to eat and drink? We have cider, mead, and ale, all made here. There's a stew in the pot and fresh bread."

"That sounds wonderful," Morris replied. "Ale for me. And some of that stew and bread."

"Cider and the food," Dema said.

"I'll try the mead, and of course the stew and bread," Reith added.

Soon, steaming bowls of beef stew were laid in front of them, and their glasses of drink. The stew was delicious, the bread was soft and warm, and the mead filled Reith with warmth.

"Where are you from?" the elderly woman asked. "And where are you going?"

"We come from Galismoor," Morris declared. "But Galismoor is not where I am from. I am from a village a few days north of here. And we go north, even farther north than my village. These two have an errand near the frozen river."

"The frozen river? You don't say," the woman replied. "What sort of errand could two people as young as yourselves have up there."

Reith wasn't planning on speaking of their journey and what they hoped to accomplish. He assumed there would be no harm in telling, but he was caught off guard. He was saved from answering by the intrusion of the other patron of the tavern turning in his chair to speak.

"I expect that they are sightseers," he said, but his bright blue eyes pierced Reith. The man was perhaps forty years old. He had a full brown beard, and most of his hair on his head, though it had specks of gray. He wore a simple brown, hooded robe.

"I hear it's beautiful up there," the woman replied. "Plenty dangerous though. But pretty country." That seemed to turn aside her curiosity.

"Care to join us, brother?" Morris asked.

"I think I just might." The man stood, downed what remained of his glass, and gestured to the bar for another one, before sitting in the vacant chair between Morris and Dema and across from Reith.

"It's always welcomed to see a man of the robe," Morris said as the tavern keeper brought the man another drink. "What's your name, brother?"

"I am Brother Barnabas."

"Good to meet you, Barnabas," Morris replied, offering a hand to the man, which was accepted and shaken.

"I'm Dema." She offered her hand and then Reith introduced himself and his hand.

"Barnabas is a shepherd," Morris declared. "Except instead of sheep, he shepherds souls."

"A shepherd of souls?" Dema asked. "How does that work?"

"People are a lot like sheep," Barnabas replied. "Often times they don't care to look up and see where they are going. Sometimes they get themselves into trouble. That's where I come in."

"Barnabas, if I'm right in speculating," Morris continued, "runs chapel services here in town, and perhaps some other towns in the area."

"Right you are, Morris."

"Reith, here, worked for a lore master in an elven city," Morris explained. "In a temple."

"How interesting," Barnabas said, his eyes widening with interest. "I have always been fascinated by how our brothers and sisters among the elves and dwarves practiced their faith. Tell me, what was it like?"

Reith spent a few minutes telling Barnabas what he had told Morris earlier.

"Have you studied much of the religion, as the elves call it, of the God of Light?"

"I have studied some, but really, I have lived it."

"I have found living the faith is much more beneficial than

studying it," Barnabas replied. "Faith is meant to be lived, explored, tested, and practiced. You can't do that when your nose is in a book. But of course, the books have benefit too."

"I have seen things that I would never have believed even a short time ago," Reith replied.

"So do all who live their faith. Tell me, Reith, what have you seen?"

Reith paused for a minute. He did not really think Barnabas was asking for the whole story of his travels, though that would, of course, tell of all he had seen. So he pondered a simpler way of saying it.

"I have seen light beyond the brightness of the sun and darkness deeper than a moonless night. I have been chased by Shadows and I have seen a Shadow vanish as though the light came out from behind a cloud."

"How marvelous," Barnabas replied. "A Shadow who was and who is no more. None of the stories speak of such things."

"What stories of the Shadows do they tell in your chapels?" Reith asked.

"The being whom the elves call the God of Light, my people simply call Father, or Father of Light. And that's why we call others brother and sister, as we are all our Father's children. We tell of the Father creating the first two Guardians, shortly after the beginning of the world. Through these two Guardians, all the Guardians came into being, the first sons and daughters of the Father. Those first two Guardians, the first brothers, one was called Azaliah and the other Obeniah. Obeniah grew jealous of his brother, Azaliah. He thought Father loved Azaliah better, though that was not true. In rage, he rose and killed his brother, casting his body to the earth. Obeniah swayed half of the Guardians and became their chieftain. They grew in power and darkness until at last the Father cast them from the spirit realm. By his dark arts, Obeniah made the first Shadows. Of course, the power of creation belongs to the Father alone, and Obeniah cannot create anything from nothing. All he can do is twist and distort that which the Father has made. A Shadow is a distortion of a good thing made by the Father."

"I have never heard of Azaliah and Obeniah," Reith said, when Barnabas had finished speaking.

"It's not a tale in the elven lore," Barnabas replied. "Each of the races has bits and pieces of the narrative. It is only when they are placed together can the people of Terrasohnen know entirely the story of the Father."

"How did you know we are not mere sightseers?" Reith asked.

"The sword at your hip and the ring on your finger," Barnabas said simply. "They are ancient objects. No one takes ancient objects on a sightseeing vacation."

"Do you know where we are going?" Dema asked.

"I assume you are going to the Ice Temple," Barnabas replied. "That must mean the hour is dark, indeed."

"There are three armies, all led by Shadows, marching toward Galismoor," Dema stated. "They might have already begun the siege of the city."

"Three armies?" Barnabas asked, with confusion.

"The elves, the dwarves, and rebels in Kal-Epharion," Dema replied.

"That is ill news," Barnabas said, shaking his head. "And you are going north to seek what you can find in the Ice Temple?"

"I have been called to do so," Reith said. "Dema is my companion, Morris, our guide."

"Speaking of guide," Morris interjected. "What do you know of the lands north of the lake?"

"Well, a sailor like you knows the lake grows more treacherous the further north you go. There are many dangers, toils, and snares. Rocks lie unseen beneath the waves. Obey the beacons."

"What's a beacon?" Dema asked.

"You'll start to see them tomorrow," Morris said. "At treacherous points on the lake, towers have been erected along the shore. At the top, a fire is lit, and mirrors are placed behind the light to direct beams out onto the lake. They warn of danger and the light guides sailors to safety. And at the north end of the lake?"

"There are allegedly ice flows, so it remains to be seen how far north you can travel by water. The forest gradually fades into the mountains. There are dangerous beasts, icy rocks, steep cliffs. Few who travel that far ever come back south again. It's hard separating the fiction from the fact, as the area has an almost mythological reputation."

"Sounds like an easy, sightseeing trip," Reith said with sarcasm.

"Ordinarily, I would not recommend undergoing such a trip," Barnabas said seriously. "But as you say you are called, and your sword and ring attest to that calling, it seems the Father is in on this, calling you out of the books and stories and into a life of faith."

"Sometimes it feels like we're in a story," Dema said.

"Of course you're in a story," Barnabas said. "You're in your own story, but you're also in *the* story, the great story."

"How does it end?" Reith asked.

"Only the Father can say," Barnabas replied.

"Will it at least be a happy ending?" Dema asked.

"The great story will end in a happy ending, that is sure," Barnabas answered. "But is our part toward the end? Or is it simply a chapter?"

Reith pondered those words as he got ready for bed that night. He didn't like the idea that his story might simply be the end of chapter, where evil could get the upper hand for a time. The thought made him uneasy.

In the back of his mind, he had always had the idea that his errand would be successful. He had never really entertained the opposite. The road before him looked dark. He felt as if he were standing on the edge of a cliff, not knowing if there was a bridge in front of him or a steep fall into blackness.

His dreams that night followed a similar theme. He was running in the dark. He could not see even his feet. With each step, he wondered if the ground would simply not be there the next time his foot went forward.

SIXTEEN

Reith awoke to the soft tapping of rain on the roof and the window of the tavern. He lay there for several minutes with his eyes shut, wishing he could fall back to sleep. The bed was warm and comfortable, perhaps the best he had slept in since his own bed at Vereinen's house in Coeden.

Eventually, he forced himself to rise, dress, and head downstairs to the dining room of the tavern. Of course, Morris was there waiting for him.

"It's no good," Morris said, shaking his head. "The weather turned on us. We'll need to wait out this rain. Might not be able to leave until tomorrow."

Inside, Reith was glad for the respite. The days of travel were long, and the rain would make things unpleasantly cold aboard *Lake Ranger*.

"I'll let Dema sleep as long as she wants."

"I need to go check on the ship soon, make sure she's not taking on too much water. But you stay here, enjoy the fire, and your breakfast."

The elderly tavern keeper's wife brought Reith eggs,

bacon, and toast, as well as a steaming mug of tea. He thanked her and dug into the food. For a while, he was the only patron in the dining hall. He finished his meal and sat by the fire, where he was brought another mug of tea. It was so warm, and he was so comfortable, that he dozed off in his chair before the fire.

He awoke to a soft hand on his arm.

"Good morning."

The soft, gentle voice belonged to Dema, and she was smiling.

"Did you have a good nap?"

"It was great until you woke me up," Reith grunted in reply.

"It's time to go," Dema explained. "The rain stopped, and Morris said the wind is good again. I have lunch for us, and we'll eat on the ship."

Reith rose from his chair, taking it slowly as his muscles and joints protested. He and Dema thanked the tavern keepers and left to find Morris. He was onboard the *Lake Ranger*, reorganizing their hold and preparing the sails for the day. The sun was out now, and it was nearly directly overhead. Away to the east, Reith could see the remnants of the rain clouds.

"It's a good day for a sail!" Morris called to them as they approached the dock. "I'm glad that rain has moved on. It's a little chilly, but we should still make good progress today, even though it's half gone."

A quarter of an hour later, they were out on the open lake, running before a stiff wind from the south.

"These are the kinds of days sailors live for!" Morris shouted above the wind and the waves.

Reith and Dema sat in the front of the ship, enjoying the beautiful day. The coastline began to change. Where the forest used to reach the edge of the lake, now cliffs began to loom out of the water. They were small at first, five or ten feet, but as the day wore on, Reith noticed the cliffs were reaching twenty or more feet.

In the late afternoon, they entered a wide bay. At either end, the land jutted out into the lake. Reith saw a tall tower built at the edge of the first point as they passed and thought he could spy a similar one in the distance on the other point. The waves were smaller here. Inside the bay, they found a small town, like the ones they had stayed in before, and Morris declared this was as far as they were going today.

"We can make my town tomorrow evening, if the winds stay strong like this," he stated confidently.

As they pulled up to the docks, Reith noticed this town was larger than the other ones they had seen. There were perhaps a dozen fishing vessels at the docks, and a couple of other ships besides. There was a main street leading away from the docks, and this street had a couple of taverns, a chapel, a butcher shop, a tannery, a smithery, a cooperage, and an apothecary. Beyond the shops, Reith saw chimneys of houses. He guessed that two or three hundred people lived here.

"Welcome to the largest port town on the lake," Morris said.

They docked and entered the town. The sun was low in the west, and their bodies cast long shadows that stretched before them as they entered the town, an advanced guard of sorts.

"There are two taverns here," Morris explained. "Both are quite excellent. The Lion has the best drinks, but The Eagle has better food and softer beds."

"The Eagle it is," Dema replied.

Morris led them along the street until they reached a two-story building with a wooden sign out front. On it was painted an eagle, and Reith was impressed by the quality of the artwork. As they approached the door, Reith heard the merry sounds of voices and laughter. Someone was singing.

Morris pushed open the door, and they entered the crowded room. To their left was a roaring fireplace, and a man was rotating what appeared to be whole chickens on a spit. Across from them was the bar, and two women were behind it, pouring drinks for the customers. Beyond them, through a window, Reith saw into the kitchen and the smell of delicious baking things wafted toward them. All along the room were tables and chairs, most of them filled with merry townsfolk, some eating dinner and some simply having a drink after a long day. At the far end of the room stood a solitary figure on a raised platform. In his hand was a lute and he was singing. Reith could catch the occasional bit of the song as the sounds of the crowd ebbed and flowed. Near the stage sat a few interested persons, listening intently to the music.

Morris led them to the first empty table he could find. The room was so crowded that the table was near the singer. As they took their seats, the song ended, and several people broke out in applause. The singer smiled and gave a short bow. Now that they were closer, Reith noticed that the singer was not really a man at all, but a boy around his own age. He had long brown hair and a smooth, young face. He turned to Dema and saw her looking dreamily at the singer.

"Hey!" Reith exclaimed indignantly.

"What?" Dema asked mischievously.

"Keep your eyes to your own man," Reith said.

"Are you jealous, Reith?" Dema asked playfully.

He did not dignify that with a response.

"You know you're the only man for me," Dema said. "But if you could play the lute and sing, that would be wonderful."

Their conversation was interrupted by a serving girl who approached their table.

"Can I get you something to drink? Eat?" she asked. Reith couldn't help but notice that this girl, also about their age, was very pretty indeed. Her brown hair was pulled back in a ponytail, and her brown eyes were large and stunning. But it was her smile that drew him in.

"A round of cider," Morris said. "And I'll take half of one of those chickens over yonder. Got any bread?"

"Fresh baked," she replied.

"I'll have the same," Dema chimed in.

Reith missed this part of the conversation, as he was still enamored with the serving girl's smile.

After a long pause, the girl spoke up.

"And what will you have?"

Dema looked at him and elbowed him in the ribs.

"Oh, uh," Reith stammered. "I'll have what she's having."

The serving girl smiled and walked back to the kitchen.

"You filthy hypocrite," Dema scolded him.

"What?" he asked. "Are you jealous?" He gave her a wicked grin.

"Now, now, children," Morris said, with a smile dancing on his own face.

The serving girl came back with the ciders, which were delicious. A few minutes later, she returned with platters of chicken, roast potatoes, and fresh bread.

They dug in and ate silently, savoring the food, while also listening to the singer. From here, they could hear his song clearly. This one was a folk tune about an old rabbit who was very grumpy about his carrot garden. From time to time, the listeners would laugh at a particularly silly line in the song.

After a while, the serving girl returned to check on them, and Morris put in the request for three rooms, which the girl said she would arrange for them.

After about a half hour, the singer announced he would be taking a break, but that he would be back on later. As he descended from the stage, Morris shouted out, "Can we buy you a drink, lad?" The singer looked around, found them and sat at their table, directly across from Dema.

"Thank you, kindly," the boy said.

"What's your name?" Morris asked, as he raised his hand to attract the attention of the serving girl.

"Simon," he replied as the serving girl made her way over to the table.

"We'd like to buy this young man a drink," Morris stated. "Whatever he wants."

"Cider, please," Simon said to the girl.

Reith looked from Simon to the girl and then back to Simon.

"Are you two related?" he asked.

"Twins," Simon said, grinning. "That's Bella. Our parents own the place. We take turns serving and singing."

"It's a lovely establishment you have here," Morris said. "Can you join us for a drink too, Bella, or are you too busy?"

Bella looked around the crowded tavern.

"I'm due a break soon, let me go grab drinks and I can come sit for a bit. I'll let someone in the back know."

She left and soon returned with two ciders. She squeezed in next to her brother.

"Sorry, we didn't catch your name," Bella said.

"I'm Morris, this lovely lady is Dema, and this here is Reith."

"Pleased to meet you," Bella and Simon said together. "And thanks for the drinks," Simon added. He raised his cup to them and drank. Everyone at the table mimicked his gesture.

"What brings you here?" Simon asked. "You're not from around here." He said that last bit to Reith and Dema.

"We're traveling north, to the frozen river," Reith said vaguely. "Morris is our guide and captain."

"What on Terrasohnen would lead you to do something like that?" Bella asked.

"It's something I've been called to do," Reith said, and his hand instinctively went to his sword hilt.

"It's something you'll be cold to do, more like," Simon said with a grin. "It gets nasty up there, 'specially this time of year. Cold and windy. Plus, you get terrible beasts."

"What sort of beasts?" Dema asked.

"Snow wolves, ice bears, there's stories of giants," Bella said simply. "But they're just stories."

"What do the stories say about the giants?" Reith asked, genuinely curious.

"The stories say they are fifteen feet tall and can kill a man simply by squeezing him between their thumb and finger." He held up his hand and showed them the pinching motion. "There are only stories because folk who see them seldom live to tell the tale."

"Are the stories true?" Dema asked.

"There's truth in every story, lass," Simon explained. "Something someone saw once gets passed along, it encounters a bard like me, and we embellish the story a bit. That story gets passed on, details are changed, rearranged, and the story passes through more ears and more tongues. What's left? A story. A myth. But in that story, there's a kernel of truth."

"So giants might not be real at all."

"Who's to say, really?" Bella answered. "Maybe someone saw a rock that looked like a giant? Maybe there's a village made up of slightly above average people and the person who found it happened to be smaller than average? Or maybe there are actual giants out there."

"The point is, you'd have to be mad to try a journey like that." Simon looked from Reith to Dema and back again. "So who called you and why?"

Reith glanced at Dema, who gave him a slight nod.

"What do you know of Shadows?" Reith asked.

Both Simon and Bella looked startled at the change in subject.

"Shadows? Those evil things that creep along through the night looking to devour little children?" Bella asked. "Just stories, right?"

"These stories are real, or at least some of the details are," Reith explained. He briefly told them of Solzar's attack on his village of Coeden and Dema's village of Suthrond.

"There are more Shadows, and they're all attacking Galismoor as we speak," Reith finished.

"And you're running away?" Bella asked, with an accusatory look at the two of them.

"What? No, of course not," Dema replied indignantly.

"Since all this started," Reith began, choosing his words carefully. "I have gotten wrapped up in it somehow. There are prophecies and such, it's a long story. But it's got to be me. Someone is calling me north. There's something I need to find. Something that will help fight the Shadows."

"How exciting," Simon said, and Reith was confused for a moment before Simon continued. "It's a bard's dream to come across a story like this in person, while it's happening. If you make it back and win the war, you'll have to tell me the whole story and I will enshrine it in song forever and ever. The Tale of Reith and Dema. No, that's not it. I'll have to think of a better name."

"I promise," Reith replied with a grin.

"Oi! Bella! Simon!" a stern voice came from the back of the tavern. Bella swore under her breath.

"Gotta get back to work," she replied, standing up.

"And I need to sing," Simon said, following her.

"Thanks for the drinks!" Bella said. "They're on the house."

Simon ascended the stage, and there was a smattering of applause as he took his lute and tested its tuning. He tweaked the tuning pegs and then began a rowdy number that got the crowd clapping and stomping their feet to the rhythm.

"It seems you two have similar taste," Morris pointed out. "I saw the looks you two were giving Simon and Bella at first. Twins!" he let out a bellowing laugh. Reith and Dema grinned sheepishly at each other. Reith took Dema's hand and gave it a squeeze.

"You're the only one for me," he said.

———

The beds at The Eagle were as comfortable as Morris advertised, and Reith slept soundly. There was a hearty meal of shredded potatoes, eggs, sausage, and biscuits in the morning, but Simon and Bella were nowhere to be seen.

"They stay up late entertaining and serving the guests," their father explained. "We let them have a good lie in."

"It's a pity, I wished we were able to see them again before we left," Dema said.

"Well, Reith here promised to return one day," Morris pointed out.

"Only if he survives, we manage to find what we're looking for, and we destroy all the Shadows and the armies around Galismoor," Dema added.

"Well, if you put it that way," Reith said, "It sounds awfully simple."

Soon they were off again. The winds were strong and at their back as they left the bay and headed out to the open lake.

"I'd like to go back there," Dema said as they neared the northernmost point of the bay.

"We have some work to do first," Reith pointed out.

"I mean I want to go back there, forever," Dema said. "I want to live there. It seems like as good a place as any. What do you think?"

"I hadn't thought about it," Reith answered truthfully. He hadn't given much thought to what he wanted to do when this was all over. He was so focused on the path in front of him and what needed to be done next. For the first time in a long time, he let himself dream a bit.

He pictured himself in a small house on the lake. Dema was with him of course. Books lined the shelves of the home, and he was continuing the work he started with Vereinen. The thought filled him with pleasure.

"I think I would like that," Reith said. "What would you do?"

"I have no idea," Dema said. "But I like the idea of living here. It's peaceful. People seem so friendly. And it's beautiful on the lake. Maybe I'll open a tavern. Maybe a shop. Maybe we'll grow an orchard. What would you do?"

"I'd like to do what I originally set out to do," Reith said. "I'd like to be a chronicler."

"You'll have a lot to write about, just from personal experience," Dema said.

"I've seen and learned more in the past few months than I think Vereinen could have ever taught me," he said. "I'd like to honor his memory."

"Let's make our life here."

"I want nothing more in all the world."

Dema leaned in and the two of them shared a long, loving kiss.

"I love you," Dema whispered.

"I love you, too," Reith whispered back.

They sat silently, each lost in thought as they traversed the waves. Eventually, Morris called Reith to help him with something and the moment was broken.

As they traveled farther north, the air remained cool as it felt in the morning, even though the sun still rose in the sky.

"We'll probably need our coats tomorrow," Morris predicted.

Near evening, they saw a tower loom up out of the trees on top of a cliff. Reith saw it was a beacon, and beyond it the lake swelled out, so that the beacon was on a point, almost a peninsula.

"Here we are, my hometown!" Morris declared. There was a small village nestled into the crook of the peninsula, and Morris steered them toward it. Rather than take them to the main docks, Morris sailed a bit farther north, and Reith saw as they approached the shore that Morris had a private dock, and beyond that, he could just make out a house among the trees.

"Welcome to my humble abode," Morris said.

Seventeen

Morris' house was a three-bedroom cabin with a large living room and a kitchen. It was cozy and warm, and clearly well made by an excellent craftsman.

"Your home is lovely," Dema said.

"Oh, it's nothing," Morris replied, but his shining eyes told the story of how proud he was of this place. "Let me show you to your rooms."

He took Dema to the first room and Reith the second and pointed down the hall. "That one's my room. If there's anything you need while we're here, feel free to open every closet and cabinet. If you still can't find it, let me know. My house is your house. Make yourselves at home. I don't have many supplies here, so dinner will be at the tavern, and I'll need to run by the general store to pick up a few things. Let's leave in ten minutes, shall we?"

The plan was agreed to, and not having many possessions, Reith and Dema found seats in the common area of the house. Dema settled into a comfortable rocking chair and Reith sat at the dining table.

"I could get used to this," Dema said as she rocked back and forth.

"It's a wonderful home," Reith agreed. "Cozy and welcoming."

They sat in silence for a few minutes as they waited for Morris to return. At long last, he arrived.

"Ready to eat?" he asked them.

"Famished," Reith said.

Morris took them out the front door of the house. The door opened onto a well-trod path winding its way through the trees. In the few minutes they had been inside, it had grown significantly colder outside. Morris led them along the path, and soon their path met a wider road of packed earth. This road was generally straight, and Reith guessed that trees had been felled to make this path. After five minutes of walking, the road passed between two buildings before opening onto the town square. A few people walked to and fro, tending to their business. There was a tavern, a chapel, a general store that Reith could see, plus a few other buildings that may have been shops of some sort or another or they could have been homes.

Morris greeted everyone they saw by name, and several of them asked how he was and what he had been up to, and this led to lots of small talk where Reith and Dema stood sheepishly by waiting for it to be over. All the while the temperature dropped, and Reith and Dema stood there with teeth chattering. Morris did not seem to mind the cold, nor the interruptions to their errand. This happened so frequently that it was nearly an hour after they had left the house before they finally made it across the threshold of the tavern.

The tavern was brightly lit by candles and two large fireplaces, one on either end of the room. The warmth was welcomed by Reith and Dema, who each extended their hands toward the fire as they passed.

"Morris!" the barman called out in a loud voice. Everyone in the tavern turned toward the door and several of them raised a glass and echoed the barman's cry.

"Arty!" Morris called out heartily. "Good to see you!"

"What are you drinking, Morris?" Arty asked.

"A pint of your famous ale, of course," Morris replied.

"And who might these young people be?" Arty asked, noticing Reith and Dema for the first time.

"Friends I'm helping travel north," Morris explained.

"Any friend of Morris is a friend of mine," Arty said, holding out a hand to shake. "I'm Arty. And you are?"

"Reith."

"Dema."

They each shook Arty's hand.

"What can I get for you?" he asked. "I've got cider, mead, the aforementioned ale, whatever you like."

Reith and Dema ordered their drinks, and Morris ordered a round of Arty's famous perpetual stew for them, which he assured Reith and Dema was legendary in this part of the world.

Soon, they were sitting at a table near the fire enjoying their drinks, the stew, and some fresh warm bread and some delicious butter. As they ate, other patrons of the tavern would drop by their table from time to time to speak with Morris, same as had happened out in the square. During a brief lull in the visitors, Dema commented on it.

"You sure are popular around her," she remarked.

"Folk are just friendly around here," Morris answered as he slathered butter on his bread. "I guarantee, if you come back here, you'll get the same treatment."

"Folk might be friendly, but they are extra friendly to you," Reith replied.

"It's nothing," Morris said modestly.

"Nothing?" Arty had come near and had overheard the

last exchange. "Is it nothing that Morris, here, fought off a bear that was trying to attack a poor, old widow? Is it nothing that Morris sailed down the coast to the next town and back in a day with less than favorable winds, simply to get a lifesaving medicine for a child? Is it nothing that he charged into a burning house to save an entire family before running back and forth from the lake with buckets of water to extinguish the blaze?"

"It's what anyone would do," Morris grunted as he dipped his bread in his stew. "Nothing special about any of it."

"Morris is a hero around these parts," Arty explained. "Folks appreciate him and owe him a debt of gratitude."

"Y'all don't owe me nothing," Morris huffed. "It's called being neighborly."

"You keep telling yourself that, Mo," Arty replied with a chuckle. "You kids are awfully lucky to have Morris on your side."

Reith and Dema looked at Morris with newfound respect after that.

After they ate, Morris took them to the general store, where he picked up a few supplies for the house as well as the ship. It took an hour to get out of the shop as the shop keeper wanted to trade stories with Morris, but eventually they were on the road again to Morris's house.

They walked in silence for most of the way. It was cold and they walked quickly.

"You see why I decided to move to Galismoor for most of the year," Morris said softly. "I don't like being the center of attention like that, not often at any rate. They treat me like a god. But I'm just Morris."

"That's a heavy burden." Dema patted him on the shoulder. "I'm sorry you feel that way."

That night, Reith wondered about his future. The sword and the ring had come to him, the voice was calling to him. If he was successful, what would that be like? Could he show his face in Galismoor without being mobbed at every turn by well-wishers and admirers? Where could he go to have peace and be with Dema and his books?

Well, at least for now that's a big if. There's no guarantee I'll be successful.

The thought wasn't very comforting. But he made a resolution with himself.

I am Reith. Just Reith. That's all I'll ever be. They won't make a god out of me."

———

The morning was cold. Morris outfitted them with hats, coats, and gloves from the closet of his home, and soon they were off. It was a gray, overcast day, and the waves were a bit rougher than they had been. This jostled the boat quite a bit more, and Reith was glad to have developed good sea legs.

Morris expertly steered them through the waves, and they continued their way north. Talking was limited as each of the three tried their best to stay warm. Reith and Dema sat closely together, their backs to the wind. Perhaps because they couldn't see the sun, this day seemed longer than all the rest. The progress across the lake was agonizingly slow.

It was with great relief that they sailed into the harbor of another small lake town that evening. Morris took them to the tavern where they enjoyed warm drinks and food.

The tavern only had one room available for them, and Morris insisted that Reith and Dema took the bed while he made a bed on the floor with some extra pillows and blankets. Reith and Dema protested, but Morris wouldn't hear of it. Reith and Dema were glad to sleep beside each other, as the chill from the lake that day was still in their bones.

It was cold again the next morning.

"How much further do we have to go?" Dema asked.

"I hope to reach the northern lighthouse tonight," Morris replied. "And then we should be able to reach the frozen river the next day."

"And then the real fun begins," Reith said.

It was cold and gray again this day, and Reith realized with a start that afternoon that mountains were looming over the horizon to the north. He hadn't noticed as the snow and ice on the mountain tops fit in so perfectly with the colorless sky. They were getting close to the end of the lake.

Reith pointed out the mountains to Dema, and they marveled at how tall they were. These mountains were different than the mountains they had traveled through to the south. For one, there was more ice and snow on these. But these northern mountains looked more rugged, more unfriendly. Though the mountains to the south housed a great amount of danger, the mountains themselves were tall, straight, and stately. They almost looked carved. These northern mountains rose in jagged peaks and sharp points, not carved as though by a sculptor, but perhaps hewn from rock by a very large man with a club.

A frigid wind blew down from the mountains across the lake, chilling Reith to the bone. But he felt the ring on his finger gradually warm, and somehow it gave warmth to his whole body.

Find me.

The voice came again, and with it came a sense of peace. He couldn't explain it, but it felt as if his soul was calmed in an instant.

———

That evening, they pulled up to the northern lighthouse. It was on top of a cliff perhaps fifty feet above the surface of the lake and situated on a point jutting out into the lake. It was taller than any of the other lighthouses that they had yet seen along the lake. The tower was connected to a small house at its base, and Reith could see smoke rising from the chimney.

"Here we are," Morris said. "No other towns or settlements north of here. Really, only fishermen go further north than this. But it's treacherous waters around here. See those rocks?"

He pointed toward the base of the cliff, and Reith saw several jagged, black rocks sticking out of the water, and knew there must be more beneath the surface, based on how the waves tossed and swirled.

Along the side of the cliff, Reith saw a small dock, with a single small boat bobbing gently beside. There was space enough for their boat, and a staircase was hewn into the rock face. Morris expertly maneuvered the *Lake Ranger* to the dock, tied it, and they disembarked and climbed the stairs.

At the top, they found that the lighthouse was on a relatively flat plateau above the lake. Inland they saw trees and beyond that, the mountains. The house was sturdily built of logs, and firelight could be seen dancing in the windows. There was a small stable, which Reith guessed housed a horse or two. The lighthouse itself loomed over them.

The door to the house opened and a woman stepped out. She was matronly, with an apron, and gray hair tied up in a bun.

"Well, come on in," she called to them. "You'll catch a cold out here."

Morris led the way, with Reith and Dema in step behind him.

They entered the kitchen of the house, and there was a roaring fire and a pot simmering by it. A wooden table sat in the middle of the room with four sturdy chairs around it. At the table sat a man, balding, and what little hair was left was gray. He wore glasses and he was peering at a chart or a map spread out on the table. Upon their entry, he looked up, took off his glasses, and stood.

"Guests!" he said with a booming voice that did not seem to fit the man to whom it belonged.

"Yes, dear," his wife said.

"I'm Glen, and this is my wife, Diana," Glen said. "Welcome to our home, welcome to our table."

"I'll grab the spare chair," Diana said, bustling over to a door on the other side of the room and disappearing for a minute before returning with a chair.

All five were quickly seated at the table, and a pot of tea was set to brew.

"Tell us about yourselves," Glen said. "What brings you this far north? We don't get visitors very often."

"I'm Morris, and this is Reith, and Dema."

"Pleased to meet you," Diana said. "What brings young folk like you up here?"

"We're going to the frozen river," Reith replied. Glen and Diana exchanged meaningful glances.

"Do you seek the temple?" Glen asked seriously.

"What? How did you know?" Reith stammered.

There was a long pause as Glen and Diana looked at each other.

"In all my years, I never thought," Glen began, before trailing off.

"It's finally happened," Diana said, and tears welled in her eyes.

"I'm sorry," Reith apologized, though rather confused as to what he was apologizing for or why this bit of information had brought about such a reaction from the lighthouse keepers.

"No need to apologize, son," Glen replied, waving his hands in protest.

"It's just that, we've been waiting," Diana began, seemingly unsure of the words.

"For hundreds of years, my family has watched over this part of the lake," Glen explained. "Fathers passed it along to their sons, mothers to their daughters. Always, we'd pass down the knowledge of the lighthouse and the promise."

"What promise?" Dema asked.

"The promise that one day, someone would come north, seeking the temple of ice. And when they did, things would be put right in Terrasohnen."

"For generations, it's really been more of a legend," Diana added. "We didn't know if it were true, or if it would happen in our lifetimes. We were worried the promise would die with us."

"We're childless, you see," Glen said, and a look of pain crossed his face, and tears again came to Diana's eyes. "But now that you're here, all is well!" His face brightened, but the sorrow still lingered behind his eyes.

"Do you have any information or advice to guide us?" Reith asked tentatively.

"Even better," Glen said. "Hold on, let me get it."

Glen stood, left the room, and came back a few minutes later with a dusty wooden box, which he set gently on the table. He pushed it gently toward Reith.

"Go on, son," Glen urged. "Open it."

Reith pulled on the lid, but it wouldn't budge. He spun the box around to see if he was missing a clasp or a lock, but he didn't see anything.

"It's locked," he said, pointing out the obvious.

"Look!" Dema said, pointing to the lid. On the lid, Reith saw a small circle carved into the wood. He leaned in and blew away the dust. He ran his finger over the circle, and found it was deep.

"I wonder," he said thoughtfully, and he pulled the ring

from his finger. It suddenly flared incredibly warm, almost too hot to touch. He lined up the ring with the carved circle and placed it on the circle. Then he pressed it down. There was a satisfying click as the ring settled into the grooves. He tried the lid again, and this time found it lifted easily. Four other heads leaned in to get a look as the lid rose.

Inside, the box was lined with purple cloth and padded. In the very center was a small, round, golden object. Reith reached in and gently picked it up. It was warm to the touch, though it was metal.

"It's a compass!" he exclaimed, holding it up.

Everyone marveled at it, and Reith passed it around so that everyone could inspect it closely.

"Do you know anything of it?" Reith asked Glen as Glen peered at the compass.

"We didn't know what was in the box," Glen said. "It was locked, and you have the only key. We've wondered, we've guessed, but all we were told was to give the box to the one who came looking for the frozen river. I wonder ..." Glen trailed off and handed the compass to Diana. He rose and returned a moment later with his own compass.

"I wonder," he said again. He placed his compass down on the table, and the arrow pointed due north. He took the other compass from Diana and placed it beside his. It pointed slightly, ever so slightly west of due north.

"What does it mean?" Dema asked.

"It means," Morris explained, grasping the meaning. "That they are calibrated to different sources. Compasses work by homing in on the magnetic signal of metal in the earth, which we call due north. But this compass," he said, and pointed to the one that had been in the box. "This one is calibrated to something near the due north from where we are, but not exactly."

"It'll point the way a bit more accurately than my ring," Reith pointed out.

"It's marvelous," said Glen. "And all this time, it's been right here, waiting for the one for whom it was destined."

"That's enough excitement for now," Diana said. "Let's eat."

"I need to go light the beacon," Glen said.

"Can I come?" Morris asked.

"Of course!" Glen replied. "I'd be glad for the company."

Dema and Reith helped Diana set the table for dinner, which turned out to be a hearty chicken and bean soup, with fresh bread. It was delicious.

———

The next morning, the sun rose over the mountains to the east and bathed the whole lake in red, purple, and orange light. Reith rose, bundled up, and stood on the clifftop overlooking the lake. It was a cold morning, and his breath clouded the air in front of him. But it was so beautiful, he could not tear himself away. To his right, to the north, the mountains loomed over the northern part of the lake, and he thought he saw the north shore. Before him, the lake stretched endlessly. His shadow was long in front of him.

Presently Dema joined him.

"It's cold out here," Dema said. Her arms were folded in front of her, and she seemed to shrink into herself to block out the wind.

"But it's so beautiful," Reith protested.

"I'll give you that," she replied.

They stood and watched the waves crashing on rocks below for a while. Gulls swooped to and fro, alighting on the water.

"Thank you for coming with me," Reith said softly after a

while. "You didn't have to, and I don't think I could have done this alone."

"It's just been sailing so far," she replied. "You could do that alone."

"It's what's ahead that I don't think I could handle.

"You're wrong."

"What?"

"Not about not being able to handle it. You're wrong that I didn't have to come. Of course I had to come. After all we've been through? After separating to be ambassadors? Of course I had to stay with you. I hated being away from you when I was in Darren Shahr."

"Perhaps that had more to do with your being a prisoner," Reith replied with a half grin.

"Well, yeah, that was awful. But before then, when I was free, I really missed you."

"I missed you in Sardis, too."

"Ready for the final leg of the journey?"

"No."

"Good, me neither. Now come inside before we both die of hypothermia."

Glen and Diana had prepared them a wonderful breakfast of biscuits, eggs, and bacon. After breakfast, they presented Reith, Dema, and Morris each with their own pack. Reith opened his to find a warm blanket, a coat, a woolen hat, and a pair of thick, leather gloves.

"Thank you so much. Your hospitality has been wonderful."

"Don't mention it," Glen replied. "Just remember to give those things back once you come back this way."

Before they knew it, they were back on the *Lake Ranger*, and waving goodbye to Glen and Diana as they sailed out to the open lake.

"Goodbye! Thanks again for everything!" Reith yelled.

"It's not goodbye," Diana called back. "It's see you later."

As they sailed north, they saw two figures standing on top of the cliff, waving.

"Glen and Diana are good people," Morris said. "Good people. Well Reith, what does your compass tell us?"

"Oh!" Reith had almost forgotten about his compass. He scrambled to retrieve it from his bag. He stood at the front of the ship and pointed his arm slightly left of where they were headed. "It says go that way."

"Aye, aye, mister navigator," Morris said, adjusting the tiller slightly, and they surged forward out into the waves.

"You know," Morris began a few minutes later. "I think I'll take Glen up on his offer."

"What offer?" Dema asked.

"They're getting older, and they need someone to look after the place, someone to tend to the lighthouse and keep her going. Glen asked if I'd consider it. And I have."

"You'd be great at it," Dema beamed.

By mid-afternoon, the wind picked up and the first flurries began to fall. Reith was glad of his extra gear loaned to him by the lighthouse keepers, and he and Dema stayed bundled together on deck. Morris had his blanket wrapped around him as he kept the ship on a steady course. Every quarter hour or so, Reith checked his compass to make sure they were going the right way. Morris was excellent at his job and Reith didn't have to correct him.

The mountains still loomed large in the distance, but Reith didn't feel like they were making any progress. They didn't seem to be growing any closer.

"I think we'll need to spend a night on board," Morris called out as the afternoon wore on. "I can't imagine we'll be anywhere near where we need to be when night falls. I'm going to steer us northeast and we'll find a quiet spot to stop and drop anchor."

The plan seemed good to Reith and Dema, and soon they were in a small bay, protected by points on either side. The waves were gentle. Morris dropped anchor and they broke into their supplies for a meager dinner. Compared to the food they had eaten at taverns and at the lighthouse, this meal was poor.

"Better than nothing, I suppose," Morris offered.

As the sun set, they went below to sleep on the hammocks. Reith kept his coat and hat on and pulled the blanket on top of himself. The ship gently rocked them to sleep, the only sounds being the waves gently lapping against the hull and the creak of the hammock ropes straining.

The next morning, they discovered with shock that the lake had frozen around their boat in the night. There was a thin layer of ice holding them in place.

"We can use the oars to break free," Morris said, and he and Reith spent a few minutes slapping at the ice until they were free again.

"That could have gotten nasty," Morris said once they were safely back on the lake and sailing north again. "I don't fancy becoming an icicle."

———

They reached the mouth of the frozen river at noon. Like their bay, there was a thin layer of ice on the lake at its northernmost reaches. The mountains loomed over them. The river was a solid white mass of ice, curving away around the nearest mountain. Reith and Dema broke the ice as Morris eased them forward toward the shore. He managed to find a flat, sandy area to land.

"Quickly now," he said. "I don't want to freeze here. I'll head back out, and I'll stay nearby. I imagine I'll have my hands full keeping this ship from freezing into the ice, but it'll give me something to do. When you need me, light a big fire here on the beach, and I'll be by to get you as soon as I can."

"Thanks Morris," Reith said. "We owe you."

"You don't owe me nothing," Morris replied, shaking his hands at them. "It has been my pleasure. Best of luck, you two. I'll see you again real soon."

Reith and Morris shook hands and Dema gave him a big hug. Morris clambered back into the ship and Reith gave him a push back out into the lake.

"Good luck!" Morris called to them and he gave them a wave before he turned to his work and rowed back out.

Reith turned around and surveyed the frozen river.

"Ready?"

"It's now or never."

And with that, the two of them left the lake behind and began their hike along the frozen river.

EIGHTEEN

The ring was more help than the compass now that they were back on land. The constant warmth of the ring on his finger was a comfort to Reith and was very useful at keeping the cold at bay.

Reith and Dema traveled along the eastern bank of the frozen river. It was rocky, and occasionally they had to scale large boulders as the river climbed into the mountains. It was icy in places and very slow going. About an hour before sundown, they started looking in earnest for a place to camp. They found a relatively flat area near the river that was protected on three sides by boulders and a cliff wall of a mountain. They decided to risk a fire and Reith offered to take the first watch of the night so Dema could sleep. She pitched the tent and was soon fast asleep.

Night fell on them, and Reith sat with his back to the fire so that his eyes could see in the darkness in front of him. He heard a moaning howl sound and didn't know if it was the wind whistling through the mountains or something more sinister. Every sound, every shadow put him on edge.

The stars overhead were dazzling bright. He found as

many constellations as he could remember and spent the hours daydreaming of warm places.

When he judged the moon to have traveled far enough for the night to be held gone, he gently woke Dema and settled down to sleep.

He dreamed he was soaring on the back of a great winged creature, gliding in and out of valleys, around mountains, and over a river. They rounded a bend and before him stood a large cathedral carved from ice. *Find me,* rang a voice in his head.

———

"Good morning, sleepyhead," Dema said as she gently rubbed his shoulder. "Rise and shine!"

He rolled over, stretched, and came to a sitting position.

"How was your watch?" he asked.

"Uneventful, though I may have heard wolves. It could have been the wind though. If they were wolves, they seated a long way from me."

"I thought I heard them, too, but I wasn't sure."

They ate a quick breakfast from the provisions they carried with them, then packed the camp, made sure the fire was out, and began again.

Around midday, they came upon a fork in the river. One part of the frozen river turned north and west; the other fork turned east. From where they stood, each way led higher up into the mountains. Reith pulled out the compass, which pointed to the left most part of the fork, the one going northwest.

"This way," he said, and led the way past the fork. The ring on his finger began to pulse, growing warmer and then cooler and back again. Somehow, he knew that the ring was approving his direction. A few minutes later, they came to a large, flat rock that overlooked the fork they were on, as well as the fork they had skipped. They took a break, and Reith took the opportunity to look back to the east.

"Look!" he whispered as forcefully as he could to Dema, who rose to her feet to see what he was pointing at.

To the east, up the fork of the river, they saw movement. Large, white creatures moved slowly along the bank of the river. Reith could just make out two or three of them, it was hard to tell as the creatures blended in with the snow and ice.

"What are they?" Dema asked.

"They look sort of like bears," Reith said, squinting to get a better view.

"But one of them is walking around on two feet, instead of four."

It was true. One of the creatures was walking like a man, while the others went about on all fours.

"Giants?" Reith asked.

"Could be," Dema agreed. "Not very human like giants, but maybe some sort of man and bear hybrid."

"I'm glad we're over here," Reith said. "If we had to go that way, we would have walked right into them before we knew what had happened.

"We need to be careful. Who knows what lurks around every bend?"

They continued on, but with caution. Reith practiced drawing his sword, as he felt that he would be unable to use his bow and arrows with gloves on.

They traveled uneventfully that day, though the going was much slower than Reith or Dema would have preferred. Reith did not have the slightest idea how much further they had to travel.

Dema took first watch that night, and Reith went to the tent to sleep.

He had another dream. He was walking purposefully, his sword at his side. It took him a minute to realize he was in the streets of Galismoor. Evidently his dreaming self knew exactly where he was and where he wanted to go. He strode forward to the palace, to the throne room. Nobles and courtiers lined the walls as he marched up to the empty throne. Humans, dwarves, and elves stood side by side in harmony. He ascended, received a crown from someone, and sat down. Thunderous applause broke out, and the crowd chanted, "Long live King Reith!"

And then a voice spoke to him in his head.

"All this can be yours," it whispered. He couldn't tell if it was a man or a woman, or even if it were a person at all. Come to think of it, he couldn't tell if it was a single voice or a multitude. But it was seductive. "All this will be yours, if you would turn back to Galismoor."

The dream shifted.

He was aboard a ship. In the distance, the Free Isles loomed over the horizon. The dream skipped forward, and he was walking into the library, which looked damaged by fire, but still stood. Inside, workers restored the library and worked with the books, taking them down for restoration and re-shelving books that had been restored already.

"You can save the library," the voice whispered again. "If you abandon your quest and return now."

The dream changed again.

This time he had no idea where he was. He was somewhere he had never set foot before. He was in a dark room that held many secrets. He knew it deep in his bones.

"Reith," a familiar voice called out to him. He whirled and saw Vereinen step forward into the torch light.

"Vereinen!"

Reith rushed to his old master, and they embraced.

"How are you here?" he asked Vereinen.

"You called me here," Vereinen replied. "Don't you know even the dead listen to your command?"

"You can bring him back," the voice whispered in his ear again. "You can bring Kydar back. You can bring back anyone you wish. We have power to give you, if you would just follow us."

The dream faded and he dreamed no more.

———

Dema was shaking him awake. He sat up with a start, not knowing where he was. Then it all came crashing back down. The frozen river, the quest, his sword, ring, and compass.

"It's okay!" Dema said soothingly. "It's just me. It's your turn for watch. You were sound asleep. I hated to disturb you. Were you having a dream?"

The question caught Reith off guard. His mind remembered the three dreams in a flash.

"I ... no," he said after a stammering pause. He didn't know why he lied, but he did not feel like disclosing what his dreams had been about.

They switched places, and Reith took his spot under the stars with the fire behind him.

His shadow stretched forward, and he replayed the dreams slowly in his mind.

Were they just dreams? Or something more?

He decided that there was something more to the dreams than what his unconscious mind could create for him. He was dedicated to his task, why would his mind concoct dreams about abandoning the quest?

Someone wanted him to turn around and go back to Galismoor. Someone didn't want him to go forward and reach the temple.

Two questions pressed against his mind, each demanding an answer, both competing to be answered first. Who sent the dreams and were the offers real?

The offers tempted him. He was offered a crown. He was offered the ability to restore the library in the Free Isles. He was offered the chance to bring back people from the dead. *I could bring back Vereinen. I could bring back Kydar. I could bring back everyone who's been killed in this war.*

That, more than anything, was tempting to him. He had never gotten to say goodbye to so many people. He could restore so many families.

Could he though? Who had the power to raise the dead? And could they really grant that power to him?

A kingdom and a restored library were easy compared to the third thing. He allowed himself to daydream about what his kingdom would be like. It would be a unified kingdom of humans, dwarves, and elves. He would enact justice across Terrasohnen. His kingdom would be good. There would be no war. He would rule well. And when the time came, he would pass along his kingdom to his children. He would make a fine king, of that he was sure.

But are these real offers?

He let the visions of grandeur gradually fade, and he turned to the other question. The more he thought, the more he knew that the Dark Powers had sent the dreams.

He watched his shadow dance in front of him as the fire danced and crackled behind him.

Shadows just stand in the light.

He didn't know where the thought came from, but it came to his mind all the same. And it caused him to wonder. *Has everything I've heard about Shadows been a lie?*

It wouldn't be the first time in history that people lied to protect their power. The Guardians and their followers of course would want to put their side on the good side. Every side tries to paint their deeds in gold.

Could he have been wrong this whole time? What if

Shadows, instead of blocking the light, were simply basking in it?

The question gave him a sinking feeling in his stomach. He had traveled so long, seen so many things. If he were wrong about this, what did that mean? He knew the Guardians and the Dark Powers were the same sorts of beings, but he had always assumed, or been told, the Guardians were good, and the Dark Powers were bad. What if they were simply two sides of the same coin?

If that were the case, he could be confident that whoever it was that sent him the dreams was able to fulfill their promise. He could truly become the king of Terrasohnen.

Images and visions of all the good he could do came rushing back to him. He'd be a good king, a king for the people. He'd stop war, make things fair, keep taxes low. How he longed for it!

King Reith.

He liked the sound of it. He liked the idea of the crowds all chanting for him. He liked the idea of a unified Terrasohnen. He could put backwards people like Pryderus in their place forever. That thought raised his spirits, and he spent several exciting minutes devising punishments of Pryderus that matched his moral ineptitude.

Soon, the weight of the choice came back to him. He could go forward; continue the journey he had started. Or he could turn around and become king. He wondered how Dema would feel about that.

It was the thought of Dema that turned the tide in his heart. His love burned for her. He loved her deeply. He wanted to make her happy.

A Shadow killed Kydar.

Dema's love for him was matched only by her grief over her brother, her brother who had been killed while Solzar had chased them while a Shadow. If it wasn't for the Shadow, if it wasn't for the Dark Powers, Kydar would be alive.

At that moment, he noticed that the darkness began to lift. The sun was rising.

It doesn't matter if the Dark Powers can raise the dead if they were the ones to do the killing in the first place. The offer of resurrection lost its luster when it was offered by the murderers themselves. What if they turned around and killed again? Or what if they lied about the resurrection power?

Vereinen had given his life for the sake of a Shadow. Not to join it, but to transform it.

Tears began to flow down Reith's cheeks, and they froze on his face. He turned back toward the fire and was struck by the warmth and the light. A Shadow can only be seen when blocking the light, but nothing can match the warmth and brightness of the light itself.

He let Dema sleep until the sun was fully up and then woke her. When she emerged from the tent, she looked at his face and saw he had been crying.

"What's wrong?" she asked, worry covering her face. "What happened?"

"I almost made a horrible mistake."

For the next hour, he recounted for her his dreams and his thought process the night before. She listened patiently, seldom interrupting.

"And I almost did it," he said. "I almost believed them and turned back."

"But you didn't," she said softly. "You didn't. And that makes all the difference."

"I hate that I was so tempted."

"It's not a bad thing to be tempted," she replied. "Temptation is just another word for a choice. We face choices all the time. A temptation is a choice between a good thing and a bad thing. It's not wrong to be faced with choices. It's what makes us who we are. Choices give us a chance to grow."

"Thanks for understanding, Dema," he said, and wiped away fresh tears.

"You know what this means, though, right?"

"What?" he asked.

"It means that the Dark Powers are going to try even harder to stop us."

"What can they do?"

"I don't know, but we'd better be ready."

———

True to Dema's word, trouble arrived that very day. They ascended a steep rocky face along what used to be a waterfall before the water froze, and when they reached the top, they came face to face with a nightmare.

The carcass of some animal lay in the snow, thirty feet away, staining the ground crimson. The animal was so mangled and savaged that Reith could not tell what it was.

Crouching over the carcass was a giant creature with white fur all over. Its mouth and paws were stained red, but something was odd about the paws. Reith looked closer and noticed they looked more like a man's hands than an animal's paw. The creature was snarling and growling as it devoured the meat from the remains. It had four sharp fangs at the corners of its mouth, two on top and two on the bottom.

All this Reith and Dema took in quickly. Then the creature lifted its nose, which was flat against its face, and sniffed the air. It stood to its hind legs and towered above them, perhaps seven feet tall. Then it turned toward them, and Reith saw red eyes. The eyes widened when the beast spotted them, and the creature opened its mouth and let out a bellowing roar. The fangs gleamed in the sunlight and dripped blood.

Reith unsheathed his sword as the beast dropped to all fours and sprang at them with surprising agility. In one bound, it covered half the space that had separated them. Reith did not have time to swing his sword. He sprang sideways, diving out of the way, tucking and rolling to the ground. He shrugged off his pack and regained his feet. Dema had jumped the opposite way and now the beast was roughly in between the two of them.

The creature roared in frustration, looking this way and that, trying to decide which of its prey to attack first. Reith gripped his sword with both hands.

"Hey! Over here!" he bellowed at the monster.

The great white beast turned toward him and sprang forward, arms outstretched, ready to grab him. Reith stepped to the side and jumped forward, past the outstretched hand. As the beast flew by him, he swung his blade across the creature's back, and saw a line of red break through the white fur.

The beast stopped, stood on its hind legs and bellowed a cry of pain to the mountains, which reverberated around and around, nearly deafening Reith.

The monster turned, snarling at Reith. Reith retreated to where Dema stood ready with her long dagger in hand. This time, the creature went slowly, instead of springing forward. It had learned a sharp lesson in steel. Blood dripped from it as it stepped toward them, leaving dots of red in the snow behind it.

"Stay close," Reith whispered to Dema.

Slowly the thing came onward. When it was just out of reach from their blades, it started pacing back and forth, testing their defenses. If the wound on its back was bothering it, Reith could not tell.

"What now?" Dema asked as the creature paced.

"Try to gain the upper hand," Reith said softly. "I'm going to attack, make it mad. I wonder if we can trick it into running off a cliff?"

"It's worth a shot," Dema said. "What do you need me to do?"

Reith briefly outlined what he was thinking and then counted to three. On three, he leapt forward and jabbed at the forearm of the beast. He surprised it and managed to land a blow. The creature swatted his sword away with its other arm, but then screamed in pain as Dema's dagger found a home in its side. It lunged back, and Dema had no choice but to let go. The monster retreated as far away as it could, and used its surprisingly human hand to pull the dagger free and dropped it to the ground. Blood poured from its wounds and the beast hunched over, panting.

"Do you trust me?" Reith asked.

"Of course," Dema replied calmly.

"I need you to take my sword," he said, handing it to her.

"Why? What will you fight with?"

"Your dagger."

"You mean my dagger that's over there at the feet of the thing we're trying to kill?"

"That's the one."

"How are you going to get it?"

"You're going to get it for me."

Again he explained the plan. She agreed to it, and he went over to his bag. He dropped his gloves and took a single arrow and notched it to his bow. He retreated as far back as he could, separating from Dema.

The beast was licking its wounds while keeping a vigilant eye on the two humans.

He drew the bow back and sent an arrow flying through the air. It was true, and struck the monster in the side, the side opposite the one Dema had stabbed. The beast roared and turned toward him. He reached for a second arrow and sent that one after the first, and it hit the beast in the chest. Dema hurried along around toward the place where the monster had been as the beast approached Reith. He sent one more arrow and this one found the stomach. He dropped his bow and sprinted in the direction Dema had gone. The monster started to turn back toward them.

There was a rock that stood three or four feet tall that Reith sprinted toward. He leapt toward it and pushed himself off of it, launching himself into the air. As he did that, two things happened at once. Dema screamed and drew the beast's attention back upon herself. At the same time, she tossed the body dagger in the air, point down and hilt up. At the full height of his jump, Reith grabbed the dagger with both hands. The monster's indecision landed it right where Reith was about to land, and Reith fell upon its neck, driving the point of the dagger deep into the neck of the animal. It tried to scream but gurgled on blood and staggered. Reith pushed himself away, leaving the dagger in the back of the animal's neck. He hit the ground hard and rolled away as fast as he could. He rose in time to see the creature stumble and fall to the ground, a pool of blood spreading for its various injuries. It gave a strangled cry and then breathed no more.

"How did you know that would work?" Dema asked as she handed him back his sword and went to retrieve her dagger.

"I didn't," he said with a manic grin.

Nineteen

That afternoon, the going got a lot easier. They were still going steadily uphill along the bank of the river, but the terrain was smoother. They put many miles between them and the monster they had killed. They couldn't decide on a proper name for it, as it was different from any type of animal they had ever encountered. They were agreed that it was cross between a bear and human-like creature.

They found a small cave to camp in that night. It was more of a hollowed-out space in the wall of the mountain, and only went back a half dozen feet or so, but it had a roof over their head and was relatively protected from the wind. As a bonus, it was easily defensible in the event of an attack.

They lit a fire and decided the cave gave them enough protection from the elements to not have to pitch the tent. Reith took first watch.

There were more sounds this night. In the distance, he heard wolves howling and hunting. He heard the cry of creatures like the one they had fought that day. Every few minutes, another sound would join the chorus. In this part of the mountains, the animals were active.

An hour after he started his watch, he could have sworn he heard distant voices. The voices were deep and unintelligible from where he sat. Every so often, the wind would carry the odd word down to him, but the words he heard were no language he had ever heard before.

They did not seem to be nearby, but it was hard to tell because of the way sound bounced off the walls of the mountains. The voices could be miles away, or just around the corner a hundred yards away.

To pass the time, he fidgeted with his ring, spinning it on the flat ground. All around, the world was quiet now. The sound of voices and animals had died away.

He reached for the ring again and recoiled in pain. It was scorching hot. He put his gloves back on and took it again, and alarm bells went off in his head. Somehow, the ring was telling him to move. He sprang over to Dema and quickly shook her awake.

"We've got to go," he hissed. "Quickly! And quietly!"

Surprisingly, she woke quickly and sprang into action. Their belongings were in their bags and because they hadn't pitched the tent, they were ready to move a minute after Reith had woken her. They kicked some snow on the fire, which hissed and went out. It took a minute for their eyes to adjust to the darkness.

Reith led them along the river. Luckily, the moon was nearly full, and the stars were out in full force. As their eyes grew used to the light from the heavens, more and more of the world came into focus. The light bounced and danced on the snow, illuminating the whole world.

After about ten minutes, Dema spoke up.

"Why did we need to leave?" she whispered to him.

"My ring," he said. The ring was back on his finger now, having cooled off. It was its normal warm temperature now, the temperature that told him he was going the right way. He told her about the ring growing hot and about the animals and the voices he had heard.

"People?" she asked.

"Maybe, but their voices were low and deep."

"Giants?"

"I hope we don't find out."

They continued in silence for a few more minutes, before the ring suddenly cooled on Reith's finger.

"Hold on," he said. They stopped and he retrieved his compass from his pack. Looking at it, he saw the arrow was pointing directly to their right. He turned and only saw the black mountain wall.

"What?" he said aloud, perplexed. He turned and walked over to the cliff, keeping one eye on the compass and one eye on where he was going. The ring grew warm again.

Sure enough, the compass pointed directly to the wall.

"Are we supposed to climb it?" Dema asked, her tone betraying her disbelief in their climbing abilities. Reith had to admit that the cliff was beyond their skill. He walked left along the cliff face with his hand on the wall. The ring grew colder again. He turned back to the right and the ring immediately warmed. Just a few feet on, he gasped.

There, entirely hidden from view unless you stood right in front of it, was a narrow fissure in the cliff. It opened to a path wide enough for two to walk abreast.

"Dema!" he whispered excitedly.

"What?" she asked, and he knew she still couldn't see it.

"Look!"

"At what?"

She came forward and then also gasped.

"A secret path!"

"The ring and the compass agree," Reith said. "This is the way."

They slipped between the rocks and entered the new path.

The cliff walls were narrowest at their feet and widened as they ascended. Even though it was narrow, and the mountains loomed large above them, it was not stifling.

The path wound its way through the mountains, steadily heading uphill. For about an hour they climbed before the two cliffs seemed to fall away and they reached an open area. They were on top of one of the smaller mountains now and had a view of the river valley below them.

Down below, perhaps three hundred feet below them, Reith saw the light of dozens of torches. Each torch was held by a large person, much larger than the average human. Little black things flitted about in between the large creatures. They looked like dark shadows.

"So there are giants," Dema said in awe.

"What are those things running around between them?" Reith asked.

Just then they heard a howl from far below them and they knew.

"Wolves," the said in unison.

"How are the giants friendly with wolves?" Reith asked.

"The real question," Dema said, "Is what they're doing out and about with torches in the middle of the night?"

"Hunting?"

"For what?"

Neither of them supplied the answer to that question, and Reith shuddered.

"The ring saved us, then," he said.

"It seems so."

Reith checked his compass once more and it pointed them away from the giants and wolves below, and Reith was grateful for that.

"I wonder if the giants can even access the path we took," he mused as they continued their way. "They might track us to the opening and then have to give up."

"Or they can send the wolves."

They quickened their pace. The compass and the ring led them downward now, and Reith guessed that they were descending to another part of the mountains, perhaps a part that was only accessible through the narrow path they had followed.

Twice, Reith slipped and fell onto his backside and slid forward a few feet before he was able to stop his descent. Both times, Dema laughed at him as he flailed about helplessly. When it was finally Dema's turn to slip and fall, Reith returned the laughter right back.

They continued at a brisk pace, wanting to put as much time between them and the giants and wolves as they could. Reith checked his compass at regular intervals to make sure they were going the right way. The ring was a steady warm temperature which let him know he was on the right path.

Judging by the moon and stars, it was perhaps an hour before the first traces of dawn.

"I need a rest," Reith said, and they found a spot nearby with rocks to sit on. They had been there for nearly five minutes when their blood ran cold. A howl split the cold night air, a howl that was a lot closer than either Reith or Dema cared for.

Immediately, they were on their feet again, racing down the path as fast as they could go. It was treacherous running through the dark. After Reith collided with a rock he didn't see until it was too late, they had to slow their pace, but they kept going as fast as was safe.

Reith's knee and elbow ached where he had run into the rock and went sprawling, but he didn't let those injuries slow him down. They needed to put as much space between them and the wolves as they could. Dawn could not come soon enough.

They did not hear the wolves howl again, but it was small comfort. A wolf pack is silent as they hunt.

They came to a rise in the path. By the time they reached the top, their lungs were screaming, and their hearts were pounding even faster than before.

"Give me a minute," Dema gasped as she bent nearly double with her hands on her knees.

"We might not have a minute," Reith said, turning to look back down the slope.

"I can't keep going," Dema panted. "We must make a stand here. We wait for dawn, or we wait for the wolves."

Reith threw down his pack and surveyed the top of the hill. If the wolves were coming after them the way they came, they would have to come to them nearly single file, which would work to their advantage as defenders. But behind them was more open. *I wonder if they can get around to the other side? If they can, we're in trouble.*

He stilled his heart to listen for the sound of approaching paws, growls, howls, and labored breathing from running. Suddenly, something hit him, and he fell to the ground, dazed.

Images flashed through his head, and he couldn't open his eyes or raise any part of his body off the ground. It was like he was held there by some invisible force. The images were of wolves running, snarling, biting. He saw red, so much red, and realized it was blood. His blood. Dema's blood.

You don't have to die, a voice whispered in his ear. *The wolves are tracking the scent of the sword, ring, and compass. Drop them all, and leave, and you will be safe.*

The force continued to hold him down, and he was helpless before it.

You can live, the voice hissed. *You can be free. You can have power.*

The images in his mind shifted. Now he was standing tall, surrounded by wolves. The wolves were not attacking him, they were revering him. They awaited his command. They were his to control. He was powerful.

No one will ever remember you, Reith, son of none. You are nothing. If you die here, your corpse will be covered in snow and ice, and no one would ever know. But give up your quest and take the power we offer, and you will be immortal. They will sing songs of Reith the Conqueror. They will write stories and poems about your legendary deeds. You will become a legend.

Now the images changed again. He saw a statue of himself in the city square of Galismoor. He was in the library and saw the spines of books that read things like, *Tales of Reith the Great, The Chronicles of Reith the Mighty,* and *Reith: Hero of Legend.* He was in a tavern and a bard sang a ballad about Reith the Valiant, and his mighty deeds. The melody still floated in his head as the images slipped away.

All this can be yours. You know what to do.

The voice left him, and the images stayed away. But he was still pinned to the ground by something which awaited his answer. The ballad about himself was catchy, and he hummed the melody to himself as he lay there. He replayed for himself all the images he had seen.

And in that moment, he was honest with himself. He wanted those things. He wanted to be remembered. He wanted to be in songs and books. He wanted artists to carve his image in stone. He wanted to be a legend. It felt good to admit what he wanted.

Darkness began to sweep over him as a wave. He embraced it, felt it, cherished it. He felt the change begin to overtake him.

And he found that he was able to open his eyes.

The stars were bright overhead. Out of the corner of his eye, he could see the sliver of the moon. His eyes were drawn to the spaces in the sky between the stars. He craved the dark, craved the blackness, craved the shadow where no light shone.

He was hungry, so hungry. He would devour kings and kingdom, lands and realms. He would cross the sea and consume the lands beyond the horizon. And then he would eat the stars themselves. The thought gave him a grim satisfaction.

He found he could move his hands now and brought them together. He pulled his ring off and held it between his thumb and index finger. All he had to do was let go.

And then, from a thousand miles away, came another voice.

"Reith!"

The call was urgent. *Dema.*

And then she came into view. She was radiant, a beacon of hope in the darkness. He tried to reach for her, but he couldn't. Unconsciously, he slipped the ring back on his finger and tried to rise.

"Reith! The wolves! Get up!"

She was shaking him, trying to wake him up, even though he was already awake.

"Help me!"

And the illusion of all the empty promises was broken. He had been so close to giving in, so close to letting go of everything. But Dema had brought him back from the brink. But he still couldn't move.

He heard the howl of hunting wolves. He was going to die here, unable to protect himself or Dema. He would have to watch her fight off wolves by herself until she inevitably fell before their ferocious attack.

He let out a visceral scream of anger, frustration, and hurt. Dema was started by this and jumped to her feet, leaping away from him.

"I can't get up!" he screamed, as panic set in. He felt trapped, and he felt the world itself was closing in on him. He was being smothered by the sky.

Dema's eyes shifted off him and toward something he couldn't see behind him.

"They're here," she said softly. She gave him one last look. "I love you."

She took a sword in hand and walked out of his line of sight. He struggled against his invisible bonds, still unable to move. Even his hands had gone still again.

He was drowning. He felt as though his head were underwater and he could not breathe. The pressure squeezed his lungs, and he couldn't even take a breath. Iron bars crushed his chest and he felt himself grow smaller and smaller.

"God of Light, help us!" he screamed at the heavens.

There was a blinding flash of light and Reith knew no more.

———

The first thing he was aware of was the hard ground beneath him. His back was sore, and his shoulders ached. The second thing he knew was the cold. The ground was cold, the air was cold, he was coldness personified. He shivered and found that there was a blanket over him, but it wasn't doing much good at the moment. He felt firelight dancing on his eyelids and knew a fire was nearby, but he was too far away to feel the warming effects.

He opened his eyes and tried to sit up. He was able to move, but his body was stiff and sore, so he groaned as he rose.

"What happened?" he asked groggily. He shook his head to clear the fog that had settled between his ears and then looked around.

The fire crackled merrily nearby, next to a shelf of rock that jutted out from a cliff. He realized that he was not on the hilltop anymore. He spun around on the spot, trying to see where he was, but also to catch a glimpse of Dema, who was nowhere to be seen.

He mentally debated the intelligence of calling out for her. She had to be nearby, but he had no idea what else might be nearby. He tried to piece together what had happened the night before to get clarity, but he would reach the flash of light and from that point on, he knew nothing.

He decided to sit and wait for fifteen minutes by the fire to let his body warm up and to hopefully un-stiffen his aching muscles. If she wasn't back by then, he vowed to go looking for her.

Reith pulled himself slowly to his feet, and every muscle in his body protested, even some he hadn't previously known to exist. He walked over to the cliff beside the fire, hobbling like an arthritic old man. He lowered himself down with his back to the cliff and again his body nearly rebelled against the command. He fell down the last foot or so, banging his tailbone on the hard ground. He winced in pain and collapsed against the rock. If anything tried to attack him now, he would be utterly useless in a fight.

Reith closed his eyes and rested his head back. He was exhausted, even though he had been passed out for a considerable amount of time. He did not know how many hours or even days had passed since he had last been conscious.

Warmth began to fill his arms and legs. He massaged his sore muscles and stretched a bit. Presently, it was thirst that was the most intense feeling within him. He opened his eyes and looked around. He saw his pack leaned against a rock on the other side of the fire. He struggled to his feet again and hobbled over as he rubbed his bruised tailbone. Retrieving the pack, he brought the whole thing back to where he had been sitting.

He rummaged through the pack until he found what he was looking for: the water bottle. It was half full, and he made the mental note to melt down some ice and snow. He took a few sips and sighed contentedly. In his brief moment of peace, he wondered anew where Dema was.

He gave her the full fifteen minutes, and then fifteen more for good measure. But now, he was worried. So reluctantly, he rose to his feet. He wondered for a moment whether he should break camp and take everything with him or if he should leave the fire going and anything not absolutely necessary.

He walked out in a spiral working outward from the fire, hoping to see some sign of where she had gone. He easily found the direction from which they arrived at this new camp. There were long lines roughly parallel in the dirt and snow that he knew had to have been made by his feet as Dema dragged him. The foot dragging tracks led back up a hill and out of sight.

She must have only dragged me downhill.

He kept looking, and only saw muddled footprints, his own and hers when she set up camp. There were a couple of sets leading away from the camp and another set coming back in. He deduced she had left briefly, perhaps to get firewood, or maybe ice and snow for water. But she had gone again, on some unknown errand.

He began to assemble all their possessions. It was then he noticed something missing from his pack. The compass was gone.

Terror and dismay gripped his heart. He dumped out his pack and frantically searched through the contents, trying desperately to find it. It wasn't there among his things. He looked through the few things Dema had left behind and couldn't find it there either. He rushed up the hill where his feet had left ruts trying to see if it had fallen out as he was dragged along. He didn't see it along the hill, but soon reached the top. What he saw astounded him.

In the center of the hill was a gigantic black scorch mark,

as though fire had fallen from heaven and smote the earth. Around the scorch mark were the corpses of a dozen or so wolves. There was not a mark on them, but they were dead all the same. Reith knelt to examine the nearest one, and for a split second, had the idea to make a coat from the fur. But it would be too time consuming, and plus, there was no running water to wash the blood off him or the fur. And he had no way to dry the pelt and treat it.

It was astounding to him what had happened. The flash of light, the wolves dying, he didn't know what to make of it all. Perhaps Dema could give him more answers.

Amid the carnage, he did not find his compass.

Reluctantly, he trudged back down the hill.

He scattered the fire and kicked some dirt and ice on the embers. He shouldered his pack with all his possessions and the few things Dema had left behind and went to inspect the tracks leading away from the camp. One set led off toward the left and one toward the right. Looking left, he saw a grove of pine trees not far away and assumed that was the way Dema had gone to get firewood before returning. To the right, the footprints led around a corner into some valley or canyon in the mountains.

He went right and followed the tracks. He kept one eye on the tracks to make sure he was going in the right direction and looked around to see if there were any other tracks, perhaps made by giants, wolves, or something worse. But here, the snow was undisturbed except for the tracks Dema had made. The ring clung warmly to his finger, and he felt reassured that he was going the right way.

Reith continued for about a half hour. The path led him into a canyon, and the walls of it towered above him, perhaps a hundred feet or so above the canyon floor. Dema's tracks continued beside a narrow, frozen river.

The hair on the back of Reith's neck stood on end, and he

felt goosebumps rising on his arms and neck. He turned slowly, feeling that there were eyes on him. But behind him, he saw nothing except the river and the canyon. The feeling did not dissipate, and he warily looked every which way, including up to see if something or someone was on the top of the canyon. But still, he saw nothing. There was nothing to do except press on.

He quickened his pace while trying to keep his footsteps silent so that he could listen for noises. It turned out to not be very easy to be quiet and rush, so he slowed his pace down again. He rested his hand on the hilt of his sword, ready to draw it and throw his pack down in an instant if action were required of him.

The screech of some bird of prey high above him almost gave him a heart attack. The sound echoed around and around the canyon, up and down the crevice in the earth, sounding to Reith as if a whole flock of murderous falcons were descending on him. But high above, he saw just the one bird, perhaps an eagle.

His heart was pounding, and adrenaline coursed through his veins, and he couldn't listen intently anymore, so he tripled his pace and was practically jogging down the canyon. Still, Dema's tracks led on.

And then Reith had a truly awful idea. What if the tracks he was following did not belong to Dema? What if Dema had left the camp to get firewood, but had never returned? What if she was attacked, and her assailant came back to the camp, took the compass, and was leading Reith deeper and deeper into this canyon?

The thought caused Reith to stop in his tracks. Icy terror flooded his heart and he stood there petrified. He hadn't thought to check the other set of prints. *What if she's injured in that grove of evergreens? Or worse?*

He didn't want to think about what his carelessness and inattention to detail may have cost them.

But he still didn't know if these thoughts were true. Perhaps he was indeed following Dema, and she had some purpose or reason for traveling as far down the canyon as she did.

And then he felt the eyes again. He whirled around, but again he couldn't see anything or anyone.

"Who's there?" he called down the canyon, and his voice reverberated back to him. Panic began to rise in him and he felt like screaming at the sky and collapsing in a puddle of sobs all at once. He choked down the feeling and kept spinning on the spot to see if he could spot anything unusual.

Reith drew his sword, and the steel caught the light, which reflected around and around on the snow and ice, turning Reith into some sort of human beacon.

He turned back the way he had been traveling and saw a dark shape running toward him. He sprang forward with a war cry and was ready to land the killing blow when he realized who it was.

"Dema!" he said, and he let the sword fall to his side.

"Watch what you're doing!" she said, angry at almost being skewered.

"Where have you been?" he asked accusingly. "You left me!"

"Reith," she said breathlessly, with excitement in her voice. "I found it. I found the Temple of Ice."

TWENTY

"What?" Reith asked, not comprehending what was going on.

"I found the Temple of Ice," Dema repeated more insistently. "It's about ten minutes further down the canyon."

"Hold on, back up," Reith replied, shaking his head in confusion. "Why did you go looking by yourself? Why did you leave me unconscious? And while I'm on the subject, what happened to make me unconscious?"

"I'll tell you on the way," Dema said, and they began walking up the canyon again. "First of all, I have no idea what was going on with you last night. You were frozen to the ground."

"I think the Dark Powers were holding me down. They wanted me to stop my journey, to put down the ring, sword, and compass. I could only move when I tried to take my ring off."

"But then you stopped," Dema said, her face changing to a frown. "Why? What happened?"

"You called to me," he said simply. "And you needed help."

"Is that when you called out to the God of Light?"

"I guess so. The last thing I remember was a flash of light and then everything went dark."

"There was a lightning bolt that came down and struck the ground right beside us," Dema explained. "When it hit the ground, individual bolts shot out at each of the wolves, but none touched you or me. Let me tell you, we were ten seconds from death. The wolves were almost on us. And with just me fighting, it would have been over quickly."

"I think that's what the Dark Powers wanted. They wanted me to give up or they wanted us to die."

"Thank the God of Light," Dema replied in a hushed, awed voice.

"Then what happened?" Reith asked.

"Well, I had no desire to remain on that hill with the dead wolves. I left you for a minute to scout out a camp and found a good spot nearby. I dragged you down, set up camp, and tried to sleep for a bit, but it was dawn by the time I got the fire lit and everything situated. You were unconscious, but breathing, so I wasn't too worried about you."

"I can't believe you left me up there alone with the dead wolves," Reith said incredulously.

"I can't believe you laid on your back while I was about to fight off a dozen bloodthirsty wolves by myself," Dema shot back. "I think that makes us even."

"So, why did you leave the camp?" Reith asked, chaining the subject.

"Well, first, I got bored waiting for you to wake up. So I looked through your pack and inspected your compass for a bit. While I was doing that, I heard a voice, as plain as day, like we're talking now. It said, 'You're almost there.' And then I felt this uncontrollable urge to look for the temple. The compass led me straight there."

"And did you once stop to think about the wisdom of

leaving your unconscious boyfriend alone in treacherous mountains?"

"Only once or twice, but I got over it," Dema replied slyly. "I think the Guardians want us to find the Temple today. If I hadn't come when I did, who knows when we would have set out for it. It's almost night already, and you wouldn't be this close if you hadn't come looking for me."

"What's the temple like?" Reith asked.

"Well, I didn't go in," Dema explained. "As soon as I saw where it was, I knew in my heart that I had to go looking for you and bring you quickly. But from the outside, it was glorious. You'll see in a minute, it's around this bend."

They pressed on, quickening their pace as they rounded the last bend. Slowly, the temple came into view.

It was a massive structure, carved of ice and the mountain itself. Gigantic pillars of ice lined the front of the building, and behind those, Reith saw a black, obsidian door.

His ring pulsed warmly on his finger, and it spread through his body from head to toe.

"This is as far as I got," Dema said. They stood on the edge of her tracks.

"Let's go," Reith said, and he took her hand in his and led the way toward the gigantic black door.

They slowly approached the temple, not wanting to disturb the solemnity of the place. Reith realized as he approached that the canyon ended just past the temple. He vaguely wondered how long it had been since someone had stood where they currently stood.

At the giant pillars, he stopped to place his hands on them. The ice was intricately carved with patterns and shapes etched into them. They were so translucent; he could see all the way through them. Finally, he turned his attention to the door.

The obsidian door was twice the height of a man and about the width of three men standing side by side. There was no handle to be seen, just smooth, black stone, perfectly chiseled. He placed his hand on it, and to his surprise, found it was warm. He pressed against it, hoping it would open, but the stone stood firm.

He stepped back and looked for any hint of a seam or a mechanism to open the door, but he didn't find anything. Dema stepped forward and placed her hands on the door too. She ran them along the surface of the stone.

"Here," she said, stepping back, but leaving one finger pressed against the door. "There's a narrow crack."

Reith stepped forward again and placed his hand on the spot Dema indicated. He felt the barest trace of a crack in the door. It was perfectly straight and perpendicular with the ground, so he knew it was not there by accident. He pulled his sword out and placed his cheek against the rock beside the crack and raised the sword level with it. He poked the tip of the sword in and then stepped back to thrust the sword in slowly with both hands. It slid in easily and soon was all the way to the hilt. Even then, nothing happened.

"Maybe it's like a real key and needs a turn," Dema suggested.

He grasped the hilt and twisted the sword ninety degrees to the right. There was a loud click as the bolt of the lock slid back from the door. Reith pushed against the door with his shoulder and found it swung quite easily inward. Beyond the door was the inky blackness of the temple.

Reith felt excitement rise within him, as well as a fair amount for fear and trepidation. He knew that whatever happened, once he crossed the threshold, there was no going back. He turned to Dema.

"It's beautiful, but I'm not a big fan of the location."

Dema looked at him like he was an idiot but then burst out laughing.

"You're making a joke at a time like this?"

Reith shrugged in reply. Then he took a deep breath and turned serious again. "Let's go."

He pushed the door as wide as he could, and the light from the outside flooded the temple. There was a blue glow inside as sunlight came in through the ice at the front. It sparkled and twinkled, and made the temple look even colder than it felt, which was surprisingly warm considering the location and the plethora of ice in the structure.

The floor was ice, but it was not slippery. It was the texture and transparency of expensive glass. The room they entered was perfectly square, perhaps fifty feet by fifty feet. Looking up, Reith guessed the ceiling was probably close to fifty feet high as well. Against the two side walls stood carved tables made from ice. These were the only things in the room beside the door they entered and a similar door directly across from the entry way. Reith stepped over to inspect the tables. They were waist high, and perhaps four feet long and two feet wide. Nothing adorned the tables, but they sparkled like diamonds.

"I think we need to go in the next room," Reith said softly. His voice echoed around the room, making it sound much louder than he had initially spoken.

Reith and Dema turned to the second door and grasped hands. They walked slowly across the antechamber. At the door, Reith dropped Dema's hand and reached out and placed his plan flat against the door. He did not see a handle and assumed it would be like the first room. He was not wrong.

In the center of the door, there was a small circular engraving. He knew what to do.

He pulled the ring off his finger and fitted it gently in the hole that was made for it. He pressed it in and heard a click. He gently pushed and the door swung inward, revealing firelight flickering beyond. With a deep breath, Reith grabbed Dema's hand again and led her through the door.

The firelight came from two twin fireplaces, one to the left and the other to the right. This room was identical in size to the first, but all the walls here were black rock. The floor was a bright, white marble.

Reith's breath was taken away. At the other side of the room lay something huge. It stretched nearly from one wall to the other, and even laying down, it was ten feet of the ground. Its scales were a golden orange, and they gleamed in the firelight, giving the impression the thing was moving. Reith saw legs as thick as tree trunks, and a curvy body that was lithe and muscular.

And then the thing moved.

Like a snake uncoiling, it straightened out and rose from the floor, its head rising impossibly higher and higher in the air, until the thing was looking down at him from thirty feet up.

Reith had never seen a dragon before, but all the descriptions he had read could not have done the creature before him justice. It was more majestic and more terrible than he could have imagined.

He didn't realize his knees were shaking until they gave out and he sank to the floor on his knees. Beside him, Dema lowered herself to the ground as well, though her motion was smooth and entirely voluntary.

"You found me."

The voice rumbled deep within the dragon and reverberated around the room. The flickering of the firelight stuttered and changed for a moment as the sound crested in a wave. It was the exact same voice Reith had been hearing in his head for months, now in physical form.

"I am Reith," he stammered up at the dragon, not knowing what else to say in the presence of a dragon. Manners around dragons were never part of his education with Vereinen.

"Welcome, Reith," the dragon replied in greeting. "And welcome, Dema. Long have I waited for our meeting."

Then, all the stories Reith had ever heard of dragons came flooding into his head, all at once, like a mob pushing and shoving to the front. His mind's eye pictured dragons soaring over villages and towns and setting fire to the buildings. He saw dragons hoarding gold, silver, and gems in caves, and robbing people. He saw dragons swooping over Erador and burning the city to a crisp. The stories were clear: the dragons could not be trusted.

"Who are you?" was all he could manage. Of all the things he had expected, a dragon was not one of them.

There was a rhythmic rumble from the dragon, and it took Reith a few seconds to realize he was hearing the dragon chuckle. The sound terrified him even more.

"The better question, young Reith, is *what* am I? And that, is a long story."

The dragon settled down a bit, bringing its head closer to eye level for the humans, though it was still ten feet up. It was almost as if it were sitting.

"Why are we here?" Dema asked, finding her voice.

"Another good question," the dragon replied. "I suppose you two are full of them. So before you go on asking more, let me tell you a story. It should answer all your questions. Please don't interrupt."

"Once upon a time," the dragon began, "There was the Light. And the Light made the world, and the Light filled the world with wonderful creatures, and plants, and mountains, and valleys, and oceans, and rivers, and everything else, including three types of being that reflected the glory of the Light. They of course, were the humans, elves, and dwarves. To look after the world the Light had made, the Light made another set of beings, supernatural, immortal beings, gifted with powers, and commissioned to guard over the world. After a time, some of these Guardians decided that they did not like ruling under the Light, they wanted to rule over the world themselves. So they rebelled against the Light, and Darkness and Shadow spread through the world, marring the reflected glory of the Light. These Dark Powers worked against the Light wherever they could, and recruited some of the humans, dwarves, and elves to aid them in their plan. They built a huge, magnificent city on the shore of the sea, and there they aimed to set up a Kingdom of Darkness. The Light sent the Guardians to thwart the plans, and the Guardians succeeded. But the Darkness was not destroyed. It continued on. And one day, the Light knew the Darkness would return in full force with a vengeance and steps were needed to protect the future of the world. So the Light and the Guardians devised a plan. A boy of the future was chosen, and a path laid before him on which to trod. He would be called to this place, to awaken one whom had volunteered to remain captive by the Darkness, for that was the brilliance of the plan. The Dark Powers were led to believe they had honestly captured the most powerful of the Guardians. But it was a trap, and a plan long thought of, and a long time in the making."

The dragon stopped his story there, and Reith couldn't get his head around it.

"But the dragons are the bad guys!" he said with frustration in his voice. "All the stories say so! You can't be a Guardian!"

The dragon peered at him, pondering its next move.

"Where do you think all those stories came from, Reith?"

He thought back to all the fairytales he had heard as a child in the tavern. He thought of the later reading heeded with Vereinen. All the stories had a ring of truth to them, perhaps a shadow of the truth. And then it hit him.

"For a thousand years, the Dark Powers have poisoned the

minds of the peoples of Terrasohnen against the Guardians," the dragon explained.

"How can I be sure?" Reith asked. "I need to know."

"What happened after you retrieved the key sword from Erador?" the dragon asked.

"I went to Suthrond," Reith said.

"Yes, but what happened everywhere you went for a time?"

Reith thought back to his travels with Aspen. He thought of riding through the woods, and of fruit he fed to the horse, and the fruit trees that had sprouted up around them from the seeds of the fruit.

"The miracle trees," he answered finally.

"I like that name for them," the dragon replied. "The miracle trees. That wasn't the Dark Powers doing. They couldn't possibly bring about anything of the sort. The trees and the stream responded to the one the prophecies told about coming and claiming the key sword for his own. There was hope that filled the air when you were fulfilling your calling. And hope is contagious. All across Terrasohnen, right now, there is new growth. The Guardians destroyed Dragonscar as a warning, but now everything is being put right again. New creation is spreading to the corners of the world, a sign that wrongs are being righted, that the time of the Light's favor is drawing near."

"What good are a bunch of fruit trees?" Reith asked.

The dragon eyed him, as if trying to decide if it was a legitimate question or if Reith was just being insolent.

"Beauty is the weapon the enemy most fears."

"Beauty is a weapon?" Reith asked, perplexed.

"Beauty is intrinsically tied up with goodness, joy, and life. By planting trees along your way, you were fighting against the spread of darkness throughout Terrasohnen. If you could but soar over the lands of Terrasohnen, you would see the green path that you walked. Where your foot trod, the world, in a small, seemingly insignificant way, became new again. That is the good that you did. That is the weapon that fights back against the tide of darkness."

"You keep talking about this path that I am on," Reith changed the subject. He didn't mean to be so antagonistic, but he needed answers, and the questions burned inside him so fierce and hot that he had to get them out quickly or risk the heat. "So I've just been a pawn this whole time? I had a calling, I was chosen, and I had to walk that path, no matter what?"

"It was foreknown that you would walk this path," the dragon said simply. "And you have freely chosen it for yourself."

"But you called to me," Reith protested. "Who knows what would have happened if you hadn't done that?"

"No one is ever told what may have come to pass. You were called, yes, and you freely chose the path, as the Light knew you would."

"Then I didn't really freely choose, did I?"

The dragon sighed, and if you have ever heard a dragon sigh, you know it's quite the ordeal. The air was hot as it filled the room, and Reith felt the temperature rise by a few degrees.

"Did you ever feel as if you were being controlled or manipulated in all your journeys? Did you ever feel as if your feet moved forward due to a will other than your own? You are a special, not because you were chosen, but because your heart led you on the paths you chose to trod, a path that was in step with the Light."

Reith thought on this for a minute, and didn't have anything to add, so he changed course again.

"What is your name?"

The dragon chuckled again.

"I have had many names, and most have been forgotten by

time. Some are names for only myself to know, granted but the Light. In time, you will also discover the name the Light has given to you. I have been called Brightscale, the Bane of Shadows, the Terror of Darkness, the Herald. You, however, may call me Anxo."

"How do you discover the name the Light gave you?" Dema asked.

"The Light tells you," Anxo said simply. "Walk in the Light long enough, and you will hear the voice."

"What is the name of the Light?" Reith asked, suddenly curious.

"You have asked a question where Guardians fear to tread. We do not know. It may yet be granted to the races of Terrasohnen to embrace the deep mysteries of the Light. Now, onto business. We have much to do and little time to do it. Have you satisfied your curiosity? Have you satisfied yourself to my identity?"

Reith and Dema nodded. *This is beyond my wildest dreams*, Reith thought.

"What are we going to do?" Dema asked. "There are three Shadows leading three armies at the gates of Galismoor as we speak. The battle may soon be over."

"All is not yet lost," Anxo replied. "Greater is the one for whom the Guardians fight than the many they fight."

"Are you going to swoop in and breathe fire on them?" Reith asked.

"Don't be so crude," Anxo said, affronted. "Have I not said that beauty is our weapon of choice?"

"So, what, you'll throw flowers at them?" Dema asked.

"In time, Dema, you may come to know the ways of the Light better than that. No, there will not be flowers. Just the simple beauty of a soul given over to the light."

Reith and Dema looked at each other in utter confusion.

"In time, you'll understand," Anxo added, seeing their

look of confusion. "Now, I must break out of my prison. Have you the compass?"

Reith pulled it out of his pocket and held it up. It gleamed in the firelight.

"Good!" Anxo said, rising higher. "It, too, is a key, like the sword and the ring. There is a keyhole for it in the center of the floor." Anxo pointed a claw at the ground near where Reith and Dema stood. "Place it there and press it in."

Reith bent to a knee and found the spot. He placed it gently, and it fit like fingers in a perfectly crafted glove. He pressed it in, and there was a loud click, followed by a horrible scrapping sound of stone against stone. Reith sprang to his feet, worried the temple was falling upon itself.

Light flooded the room, and Reith looked up to see the roof of the temple splitting in two. The sound was so deafening that he had to cover his ears.

At last the grinding stopped, and he stood blinking in the sudden sunlight. Anxo reared up on his handlers and stretched to the blue sky.

"Cover your ears," he warned. Without waiting for a reply, he roared a terrible roar and breathed fire into the sky.

"Come, get on my back."

"What?" Reith stammered.

"You think we'll walk to Galismoor? Or sail? No, we can be there tonight if we fly. You will be perfectly safe."

Anxo crouched and stretched out a leg for them to climb up on. Reith went first, and settled on the dragon's back, just below the neck. He found that he was quite secure. The scales were quite warm to the touch. Dema clambered up and sat behind him with her arms around his waist.

"Hold on, children!"

With a tremendous jump, Anxo propelled himself to the sky. Before Reith even knew what was happening, they were above the temple. Anxo's great wings stretched out and flapped in the wind, propelling them higher and higher. And then Anxo dove.

He barreled down, catching speed. Reith thought for a moment that they would crash into the canyon floor, but Anxo straightened out and flew low to the ground through the canyon, effortlessly making each twist and turn. At the end of the canyon, he pulled up and went twisting through mountains and valleys. Terrain that had taken them days to cross flew under them dizzyingly quickly. They flew through a low valley and heard the shouts of giants and the howl of wolves. Anxo didn't go out of his way to antagonize them but blew a warning blast of fire that warmed Reith and Dema. This infuriated the giants and the wolves even more, and Reith and Dema laughed as they soared past their enemies below.

They found themselves flying low over the frozen river, and Anxo blew fire as they went, melting the river. And so there was a wall of water below them, crashing down toward the lake as they flew, a trumpet sounding their arrival.

Within minutes, they exited the mountains and soared out over the lake. Anxo flew low, dragging his claws in the waves as they went, sending up a spray of water behind them. He did not fly in a straight line, but relished in the flight, swerving this way and that, climbing and diving. Out on the lake, they saw a small ship.

"Fly near the ship!" Reith yelled over the roar of the wind in his ears.

Anxo glided out toward the ship, slowing down so that the wind wasn't as loud in their ears. On the ship, they saw a figure rise.

"Morris!" Reith and Dema called out in unison.

Anxo glided around the small boat, and Reith saw Morris' face light up in recognition.

"You did it!" Morris shouted at them. "Yah-hoo! I knew you would! My eyes, a dragon!"

"Thanks for all your help!" Dema shouted down to him.

"Make sure you visit Glen and Diana before you go back south!" Morris yelled up at them. "But don't give them too much of a fright!"

"Farewell, Morris!" Reith yelled, as Anxo turned away from the boat.

"Farewell!"

Scarcely a minute later, they were at the cliffs where Glen and Diana's lighthouse stood. Anxo landed gently on the edge of the cliff, and the two humans slid off. They saw Glen and Diana approaching warily.

Reith and Dema rushed over to them and embraced the two older people.

"Well, I'll be," Glen said, peering over Reith's head. "Is that a dragon?"

"A dragon and a Guardian," Reith replied.

"Is it safe?" Diana asked quietly.

"Depends on who you are," Dema said. "For you, I think it will be safe. Come on, we'll introduce you."

But there was no introduction needed.

"Glen, Diana," Anxo said in his low, deep rumble of a voice. "Long have you served. Well done, good and faithful servants of the Light."

"We don't know what to say," Glen said, and tears began to leak down his face.

"Your task is ended," Anxo said. "Short is the time you have left. Soon you will enter the courts of Light, hand in hand, with trumpets to herald your arrival."

"Thank you, sir," Diana replied, bowing her head in reverence. "It is more than you deserve."

"It is more," Anxo agreed, "but it is also less."

The words made little sense to Reith, but they seemed to

make all the sense in the world to Glen and Diana, who each nodded. Reith filed them away in his head to ponder later.

"Until we meet again, may the Light go with you," Anxo said solemnly.

"May the wind be at your back," Glen replied.

Reith and Dema gave back the things that had been loaned to them and embraced the older couple one last time.

"Thank you," Glen said to them.

"No, thank you," Reith and Dema insisted.

"Come, young ones," Anxo beckoned, and they soon were in place upon his back.

"Galismoor calls for aid."

With that, Anxo left off the cliff and they hurtled down toward the waves. He caught them with the air and flew south, even faster than they had yet traveled.

And Reith realized he had no sword anymore. His was in the keyhole of the temple.

PART FOUR
ELLAMORA

Twenty-One

Pinpricks of light dotted the landscape around Galismoor. Thousands of campfires and torches stretched away as far as the eye could see, showing the magnitude of the problem facing King Calmon and the defenders of the city.

From high atop the walls, Ellamora gazed down at their foes. The fighting hadn't started yet, but the tension was in the air. The armies had each arrived earlier that day. The humans of Kal-Epharion arrived first, in the late morning. The elves arrived by mid-afternoon. The dwarves arrived last of all near twilight.

Galismoor was shut tight against the invaders. Men lined the walls, and a brutal schedule had already been assigned to them, as King Calmon expected the siege to last some weeks. The men had been divided into three groups. Two groups would be on duty at all times while the other group slept. Sixteen-hour days were about to become the norm for the men.

Ellamora had her bow slung on her back. The invading forces were too far away for an arrow attack, but she was ready if the need to shoot would arise. As one of the only elves in the city, she was not assigned to the rotation of the troops. In fact, she wasn't really expected to fight against her countrymen at all, but that's not the sort of warrior Ellamora was. She had defied her stepfather, Pryderus, when justice called for it.

Beside her stood Laneras. She had burst into loud, hysterical sobs when a small door by the gate had been opened to allow Laneras, Pallin, and a few elves from Crain to enter. They had born a white flag and had pelted toward the city a few hours ahead of the elven horde. They had swept wide to the west to avoid the human camp of Kal-Epharion, and upon their approach, Calmon had sought her out to see if she knew them and whether they were trustworthy. Her answers had led to the door being opened, before being shut and blockaded again.

Upon their arrival in the city, they were questioned by Calmon as to the size of the elven army and their weaponry. After the questioning, they were released into the custody of Ellamora, and they were allowed to retain their weapons, despite some of the Galismoorians being none too thrilled at this development.

Laneras and Pallin and their men insisted on fighting, and they patrolled the walls facing the armies.

"Did you ever think you'd end up here?" Laneras asked her.

"In Galismoor, or facing an army of our people?" Ellamora replied.

"Both, I suppose."

"No, never."

"Neither did I. How did we get to this point?"

"Darkness, Shadows, evil. Take your pick," Ellamora replied. "And for me, doing the next right thing placed in front of me."

"I'm afraid this is where it will end for us," Laneras said

quietly. "If we win, who knows what King Calmon will do with us. If we lose, well, we'll be executed as traitors to our people."

"I do not think we need to fear King Calmon," Ellamora said. "He is a good man."

"A good man who will have to decide what to do with a few dozen elves who betrayed their kind to fight for him. We can't really go back to our own lands, not after that. That means we'll be here."

"Why did you come?" Ellamora asked.

"Because it was the right thing to do," Laneras said. "We heard rumors that the elves were marching north yet again. Pallin gave a rousing speech, implored our soldiers to not fight against Galismoor if the army form Sardis came recruiting. And then he said that he was going to help the defenders, and asked if anyone would go with him."

"Of course that's what you would do," Ellamora said tenderly. She took his hand in hers.

"What are our chances?" Laneras asked as he surveyed the assembled enemy armies.

"Slim. We are in the hands of the God of Light."

"Those are pretty good hands to be in."

"And Reith's hands."

"Of those hands, I am less sure."

Ellamora snorted out a laugh that was much louder than she had intended and caused humans and elves alike to glare at her.

"Oh, Laneras, I missed you."

———

At dawn, a trumpet sounded from the camps outside the city. The siege of Galismoor had begun.

All three armies began to march methodically forward.

Elves carried a battering ram for the city gate. Various ladders could be seen in the hands of the attackers. In the distance, some of the soldiers could be seen constructing siege towers to roll up against the walls.

When the advancing armies were in range, the archer master ordered all to shoot high arching shots over the hordes.

"On my command! One, two, three, shoot!"

The first volley rose nearly silently, with the only sound being the twang of bowstrings. Before the first round struck home, the order had already been given to reload, and the second volley was in the air right before the first struck.

Out of the corner of her eye, she saw a few attackers stumble and fall as arrows pierced them, but the number was a woefully small percentage of the overall force. Six volleys had been shot before the commander authorized them to fire at will, as the armies were now at the base of the wall.

Ellamora chose her targets carefully. When she had shot in the volley with the crowd, she had no idea if her arrows found the mark or not. But this time, she did not miss.

She shot a human through the neck. She shot a dwarf in the stomach. She shot an elf in the chest. With precision and speed, she mowed down attackers, but still more and more came. She focused her attention on those who were climbing the ladders, hoping that their falling bodies would crush or hurt those below. She hated the work.

Beside her, Laneras was similarly efficient. Below them, the ranks of the attackers thinned, both by the losses they sustained by the bows of Ellamora and Laneras, but also because the attackers recognized that this section of the wall meant death for them.

There was a loud thud that shook the wall beneath them. The battering ram had struck its first blow against the city gate. The gate was sturdy and would stand for a long time, but not forever. Ellamora turned her attention toward the gate and began to shoot the elves who carried the ram. She and Laneras began to pick off the bearers one by one, and twice the ram fell to the ground. As the elves scrambled to pick it up again, they managed to take down several more as they bent in a vulnerable position.

The battle raged on all morning. The attackers made very little progress but hadn't suffered tremendous losses. Around noon, the attackers pulled away, giving all parties a brief respite.

"They've been toying with us," Laneras said, breathing heavily from the exertion. "They wanted to test our defenses."

As they pulled away, Ellamora saw the dead and injured on the ground below, but that number was perhaps only one in one hundred of the retreating armies.

"They took some losses, but now they know more about us," Ellamora said. "And they'll be back."

"It's just a matter of when," Laneras agreed.

They left the wall and went to the living quarters. Ellamora showed Laneras into Reith's room, and she went to hers, and they got a few hours of sleep in the break in the fighting. She knew she would need as much sleep as she could get in the coming weeks.

They awoke refreshed late in the afternoon. All was quiet. The fighting had not yet begun again.

"Are they waiting for dark?" Ellamora asked Laneras as they watched the workers below continue to construct their towers.

"That's what I would do," Laneras replied grimly. "The city will be illuminated by torches and firelight, giving enough light for the attackers, while they move silently and invisibly in the darkness. Makes it hard for people like us to shoot them."

"That's a good strategy," Ellamora admitted, not liking it in the slightest.

"We'll have to resort to arrow volleys and dropping things off the walls on their heads," Laneras said. "And if they get those siege towers up and running, we'll have to fight them off by hand."

"Good thing I had a good teacher on the sword," Ellamora replied with a grin.

"Should we grab a bite to eat before the fighting begins again?" Laneras suggested.

"Might as well," Ellamora answered. She felt useless at the moment. There were enemies all around the city and she was stuck inside, waiting for them to attack. She wished she had been able to go with Reith and Dema.

They're doing something that might make the difference in this war.

She felt resentful of them, getting permission to travel off to the north to seek help, with her left behind. She had gotten so used to their company over the previous months, traveling to Sardis, Amisos, the Free Isles, Balkh, Darren Shahr, and Palander. All their adventures, which started when these humans interrupted life in Crain, had brought her close together with Reith and Dema. They had laughed together. They had fought together. They had lost close ones together. And now, she felt abandoned.

In the mess hall, they each got a plate and then they found Ellyn sitting by herself, a plate of food in front of her ignored as she read a book. At their approach, Ellyn noticed them, closed the book, and seemed surprised that her uneaten food was still in front of her and took a bite.

"Good afternoon, Ellyn," Laneras greeted.

"Come, join me!" Ellyn said, placing her book in the center of the table and gesturing to the empty seats nearby.

Ellamora sat beside her while Laneras sat across from Ellyn. "How are you liking Galismoor?" she asked Laneras.

"I'd like it a lot better if three armies weren't camped outside the walls," he replied darkly.

"Well, yes, there is that," Ellyn agreed. "But other than that, how do you like it?"

"Fine, I guess. Haven't had much time for sight-seeing."

"You should really try to," Ellyn said seriously. "You need to understand what you're fighting to save."

"It's not just this city," Laneras replied. "I know what I'm trying to save. I'm trying to save Terrasohnen. Elves, humans, and dwarves. I'm trying to save the goodness of the world."

"If only there were more like you," Ellyn said, shaking her head.

"Why are these armies following these Shadows?" Ellamora asked. "That part hasn't made sense to me."

"For the most part, why would any soldier fight in any army?" Laneras asked. "Because they are told to. Think of what it would mean for these soldiers to refuse. They would lose their livelihood. They would be forced to flee their homes or else face imprisonment or death. There's great shame in refusing an order from a superior officer."

"And you have to think that the Shadows are using persuasive language," Ellyn added. "We've seen some of that at work, villainizing outsiders, puffing up their listeners, that sort of thing."

"It's pretty easy to guess what each of the three Shadows is telling their armies," Laneras continued. "The Kal-Epharion Shadow is probably spinning a tale of oppression from Galismoor and revenge. The dwarf Shadow is probably talking poorly of Reith and Dema, blaming Dema in particular for an assassination of their queen, and that revenge is needed. Koinas is probably blaming the humans for interfering in elven matters, and it's time to fight back."

"Those things would be plenty persuasive to the common soldier," Ellamora agreed. "But they're not true."

"When have tyrants ever cared about the truth?" Ellyn asked. "The truth is inconvenient for those who want to demonize other people. No, all they care about is power, and they'll tell any tale to get it and keep it."

"It's not just a physical war then," Ellamora replied.

"It's physical, ideological, and spiritual," Ellyn said.

"May the truth win out," Laneras said, holding aloft his cup.

"To the truth," Ellyn and Ellamora responded. And they all drank.

———

The attack did not begin at dusk. It came a few hours later when the sun had completely set, and all was dark. The only warning the defenders had was changes in the torches and firelight as soldiers passed in front of them on their way to the walls. But the defenders were ready. Flaming arrows were sent this time, with the hopes that small fires would start and illuminate the attackers, as well as cause temporary night blindness as the fire flashed before the attackers' eyes.

Ellamora stood on top of the wall and the wind gently tousled her hair. She stood beside a pile of arrows whose tips were wrapped in cloth. To one side was a small bowl of oil and to the other side was a torch. For each arrow, she placed it on the string, dipped it in oil, lit it aflame, and then quickly drew back and shot it into the night. With the torch so close, her night vision was terrible, but she knew the general distance she was required to shoot and felt reasonably sure her efforts were accomplishing something.

Laneras stood beside her. They shared a torch between them, but his bowl of oil was on the other side. There wasn't much need to speak, and they silently went about their work. There was the occasional gasp as someone let the flaming arrow linger too close for too long to fingers, but other than that, there wasn't much talking on the wall other than the occasional shout about the movements of the enemy.

Soon, the thud of the battering ram could be heard and felt, and a commander on the wall instructed archers to send flaming arrows at it in hopes of burning it. Even though the ram was soon peppered with arrows, none of them caught fire.

Maybe they doused it with water, Ellamora thought grimly.

Instead of the ram, she focused her attention on those carrying it again, and was pleased to push a few men off the ram as they howled with pain as a flaming arrow stuck out of them.

It was grim work, and it soon began to take its toll on Ellamora. She felt her head spin, and she shook it to try and clear it, but it didn't work. The world was spinning. She felt her throat tighten and air became difficult to come by. Her heart pounded in her chest and her eyes gave her tunnel vision.

"I need to take a break," she announced to Laneras in the middle of the night. "I need to sleep."

She went back to her sleeping quarters and tossed and turned for several hours. Each time she shut her eyes, all she saw were the people she had shot bursting into flame. Their screams echoed in her ears.

Right around dawn, she managed to finally drift off to sleep and she slept most of the morning, though her dreams were haunted by screams of the dead and dying.

When she awoke, she laid in bed for quite a long time.

You're weak, she chided herself. *It's just war. You've done this before.*

And it was true, she had done this before. She had been in battles. She had been on its walls during a siege. She had killed people before. But something about it was catching up to her now.

She couldn't face Laneras now. He was a soldier, he was trained for this, this was his job. No, she needed someone else.

She opened her door and peeked out. She saw a maidservant walking away down the hall.

"Excuse me," Ellamora called down the hall. The woman gave a start and turned to look at her.

"Yes, miss?" she asked.

"Could you fetch someone for me and bring them here?" She gave the name, description, and where might this person be, and the servant rushed off. A few minutes later, there was a knock at the door. Ellamora rose, opened it, and let Ellyn into the room.

"Thank you for coming, Ellyn," Ellamora said, as she gestured to a chair for Ellyn to sit in. She herself sat down on the edge of the bed.

"Of course," Ellyn replied. "To what do I owe the pleasure?"

Ellamora fumbled with her words for a few moments, not exactly sure how to say what she wanted to say.

"It's okay, Ellamora," Ellyn said softly. "I'm here to listen. Imagine we're at the temple in Crain if that puts your mind at ease."

Ellamora's mind went to the quiet solitude of the temple, with the flickering candle lights and burning incense and her heart began to find peace.

"I'm afraid I'm losing it," Ellamora said finally. "I had to leave the wall last night in the middle of the fighting."

"Why did you leave?" Ellyn asked. From anyone else, the question might have sounded judgmental, but from Ellyn, it was simply what it was, a question.

"I couldn't take it anymore," Ellamora replied. "I couldn't take the screams. I couldn't kill anyone else."

"And that makes you think you're losing it?" Ellyn asked. "By 'it' do you mean your mind? Your heart? Your touch?"

"Something like that," Ellamora replied. "It's weakness. I used to be able to do this. I've fought in battles, I've protected cities, I've killed soldiers before. I don't know what's happening to me."

"Why do you think it is weakness?" Ellyn asked, and again, there was not an ounce of judgement in her question, just the desire to know more.

"Because I know I can be strong. I know I can fight. I know I can kill. I am a warrior."

"Is that all you are?"

The question hung over the room like a fog.

"Well, no," Ellamora said finally.

"Let me tell you a story," Ellyn said. "Once, there were two men. The first man was a warrior. He was strong of blade and strong of bow. He never met an adversary he could not beat. Whatever obstacle that was placed before him, he dispatched of it with an arrow or a sword. In the course of time, this man married, and for a while, he was happy. But after a time, he and his bride began to fight and bicker. The warrior viewed each fight as a battle to the death, like his wars he fought. And he won all of them with the same determination and drive he used in his physical battles. One day, his wife left him, and in despair, the man took his own life. He had finally lost a fight, a battle that he had won."

"The second man was a farmer. He did not pick up the sword or the bow, but the plow and the sickle. Like all men, from time to time, he procured an enemy for himself, but when a fight would break out, he sat by his enemy and reasoned with him. And he won over more than he lost. There was one stubborn enemy that refused to be won over. So the man made it his mission to love his enemy. He entered his enemy's employ as a servant. Day after day, he waited on his enemy, devoting himself to the work. He took care of all his enemy's needs. One day, he knelt to wash his enemy's feet. When he had finished, his enemy pulled him to his feet and embraced him as a brother."

"Tell me, which of the two men was stronger: the warrior or the poet?"

"The farmer," Ellamora answered.

"Maybe you're not so weak as you thought," Ellyn said, and she rose and left the room, leaving Ellamora to ponder the story.

Twenty-Two

Over the next few days, Ellamora kept Laneras company on the walls, but she did not fire an arrow. She didn't even bring her sword or her bow.

"Will you help me?" Laneras asked that first evening in between arrow shots.

"I will aid you however I can, but I will not take up arms," Ellamora said calmly.

"I don't understand," Laneras replied.

"Neither do I," Ellamora said with a shrug.

And she really didn't know why. But the thought of taking up arms was suddenly appalling to her. So she made herself useful in other ways. She ran for supplies or more arrows. She brought news of the enemy's movements to the command center in the city square, supplying Calmon and his generals with important strategic information. Her heart was fully invested in the outcome of this battle, as her life might hang in the balance.

She found herself spending more and more time with Ellyn. Ellyn had not devoted herself to fighting in the war and made herself useful in similar ways to Ellamora.

The most pressing concern for the defenders of Galismoor was the integrity of the gate. Throughout each night, the attackers slammed their battering ram against the gate. Huge piles of rubble, debris, and trash were heaped up against the gate, hoping to slow down the attack if the enemy gained entry through the gate.

On the fifth night, the siege towers came rolling through the night toward the city. They were upon them almost before the defenders realized it. Of course, they had seen the progress made on them during the days, and the generals had prepared for such an attack. But the siege towers rolled silently. A great shout went up where the first one appeared. As many men as could be spared were sent to fight off the attackers, and for the first time, enemies gained a place within the city itself. But they could only come across a few at a time, and the defenders managed to drive them back. Oil was dumped on the siege tower and a torch was tossed onto it and the whole thing quickly went up in flame, a blazing beacon in the night. While all eyes were on it, disaster struck.

Laneras had not gone to defend against the first tower, and instead stood by his usual post and kept firing arrows as he had the whole battle. Ellamora sat behind him, watching the bonfire of the siege tower.

Out of the darkness, a second siege tower emerged, this one laden with many troops. Laneras called out a warning but then found himself fighting for his life. Other defenders came to his aid, but they were outnumbered. Too many had gone to fight the other siege tower. Enemy soldiers poured onto the wall, humans, elves, and dwarves; they had sent a full assortment. Bells were ringing, and captains urged their forces to fight. Eventually, the attackers were beaten back, and the last ones on the wall were either killed, taken captive, or jumped back to the siege tower. It went up in flame too.

Ellamora rushed to the aid of the injured. She kept a

medical kit nearby and she was glad of it. She surveyed the scene to determine who had the most severe wounds. She saw one soldier lying face down with blood pouring from several cuts. She saw his chest moving with breathing and she rushed over.

She turned the man over onto his back, and she gasped. Laneras was almost unrecognizable. She quickly inspected him and was relieved to find that most of the blood appeared to not be his own. His sword was still clutched in his hand, and it was stained red. But he had several nasty wounds of his own. He had several slashes along his arms, not very deep, but they needed to be stitched up. The one that worried her the most was a stab wound he had in his abdomen. It wasn't very deep either, but she knew any sort of stab wound to the belly area was a recipe for disaster. She called for a stretcher, and Laneras was taken to the hospital ward where injured soldiers were sent.

Everything in her wanted to rush off after the stretcher, but duty kept her on the wall. She stitched up some wounds, bandaged others, and helped as best she could. When the last of her charges was taken care of, she ran off to the hospital. She gave a nurse quite the fright, as she was covered in blood.

"I'm looking for an elf," she said earnestly. "He was brought here a short while ago."

"Over here, dear," a matronly woman said briskly.

Ellamora rushed over and found two nurses tending to Laneras' wounds. He was unconscious, and that was probably for the best. He was white as a sheet from blood loss.

"Is he going to make it?" Ellamora asked quietly. She felt so small.

"Remains to be seen," one of the nurses replied. "He's in a bad way now. If he makes it through the next twenty-four hours, I like his chances. Unless infection sets in."

The other nurse shot a nasty look at the one who had spoken.

"What?" she said defensively. "I'm telling it like it is. I don't want to give false hope."

"No, thank you," Ellamora replied. "I'd rather know the truth. Can I stay with him?"

The two nurses looked at each other and engaged in a wordless conversation.

"There's not really a place for you to stay, miss," said the one who had yet to speak. "It's crowded and busy."

"I'll stay out of the way," Ellamora said quickly. "I'll sit here on the floor against the wall."

The nurses looked at each other again.

"It's not really our call to make," the first nurse said. "If you stay, you promise us to say it was all your idea and you just decided for yourself to stay, alright?"

"I promise," Ellamora said. She stood by watching them finishing their work on Laneras, and when they moved on to other patients, she sat against the wall near the head of his bed. From this place, no one could see her unless they happened to be standing directly in line with the gap between Laneras' bed and the one next to him. Ellamora's head was below the top of the bed and was well hidden unless someone was trying to look for her.

Thus began some of the longest hours of Ellamora's life. She had experienced plenty of long hours in recent months, waiting in the dungeons of Sardis for her fate to be decided, waiting all night for Romulus and Remus to take control of the elven force at Darren Shahr. And her mind went back to other long nights, like when her father died, and she stayed awake for days, alternately crying and staring at the wall, refusing to be comforted. Or when her mother married Pryderus, and she refused to attend the wedding. She had punched a hole in her wall on that occasion.

But this was different. In those other occasions, she had been passive. Others had made or were making decisions and all she could do was wait to see how the cards fell. Now, she felt in on it. Laneras' life hung in the balance, and she felt if she could stand guard over him, he would make it. It gave her a sense of calm and purpose.

All her attention was focused on the still body of Laneras, her friend.

But that's not right.

Laneras was more than a friend. A brother.

That's not it either.

She hadn't ever really considered how she felt about Laneras. He was a few years older than her and had really been a mentor of sorts, but the feelings she had right now were more than that.

She gazed into the future and tried to see where Laneras fit in that picture. Of course, he was there. In her ideal future, he didn't die in Galismoor. But then what?

Slowly it dawned on her.

I love him.

And that made the horribleness of the situation even worse.

"Don't die," she whispered. "I'll never forgive you."

———

For hours, Ellamora stood vigil over Laneras. After about six hours, his breathing grew more labored, and she flagged down one of the nurses who had been tending to him when she arrived.

"Good thing you're here," she said as she checked his bandages. "We need to rewrap some of these."

A short time later, the bandages had been removed and

new bandages were added. Ellamora was shocked by how much blood covered the old bandages.

"These wounds are starting to clot," the nurse said. "That's a good sign. He's a fighter."

The next day, Ellyn came to see her and Laneras. Laneras was still unconscious, but his coloring was better, and his breathing was more even. Ellyn came bearing food and drink for Ellamora.

"How is he?" Ellyn asked, concern radiating off her face. She sat down beside Ellamora.

"He's better than he was a few hours ago." She recounted the scary moment they had had.

"How are you?" Ellyn asked.

"I really don't know," Ellamora replied. "I'll be a whole lot better if he recovers."

"Why don't you go get some sleep? I'll wait here beside him until you return."

"No," Ellamora replied, a bit more forcefully than she had intended. "I mean, thank you for the offer, but I'm fine. I want to be here when he wakes. Or if he ..." she trailed off. "I would never forgive myself if something happened while I wasn't here."

"I'll come back to check on you both from time to time," Ellyn said, getting up to leave. "And really, I don't mind staying by his side if you need that at some point."

"It's really fine," Ellamora replied.

"I hope so," Ellyn said, and she gave Ellamora a knowing look.

Ellamora resumed her vigil, waiting for any sign that Laneras would awake.

A few hours later, after another visit from Ellyn, her patience was rewarded.

She heard a low groan from the bed above her and sprang to her feet. She took Laneras' hand gently in her own, and watched as he winced, groaned, and finally opened his eyes.

"Ellamora!" he said, with a hoarse, croaky voice.

"Shhhh, don't talk now," she said softly. "You're in the hospital. You got hurt during the fight. You're awake now, so I hope that means you're recovering."

He tried to sit up, but he gave up and clutched at his stomach and moaned loudly.

"I feel like I got run over by a horse," he groaned as he sank back down to his pillows.

"Close," Ellamora replied. "Just tried to fight off a few too many soldiers."

"Did we get them?" Laneras asked. "Did we hold the wall?"

"We beat them back," Ellamora said. "It was a near thing, but we managed."

"I need to get back out there to fight," Laneras said, again trying to it up.

"Not likely to happen," Ellamora answered. "The only way you're fighting in this war again is if the battle itself comes to the hospital ward. Either way, the battle will be over by the time you're able to lift a sword again, let alone swing it."

"Ellamora," Laneras said weakly. "Do you think we'll win?"

"I hope so."

———

Now that Laneras was awake and talking, Ellamora allowed herself time away from the hospital wing. She spent the majority of each day there but would leave for meals and to sleep. Ellyn stayed with Laneras during the few waking hours Ellamora was gone.

Laneras progressed steadily over the next few days, but

Ellamora wished she could say the same for the war effort. Whenever she went out of the hospital, she saw exhausted men everywhere. The constant effort and little sleep was wearing on everyone, and she didn't know how much longer they could keep it up. The attacking armies continued their nighttime barrage against the walls and the gate. From each report she heard, the attacks were getting more numerous and more successful, with one managing to keep attackers on the walls for fifteen minutes before they were beaten back. The gate wasn't faring much better, and in overhearing muttered conversations at mealtimes, Ellamora surmised they would only stand for another day, two at the most.

She let her mind wander to Reith and Dema and prayed to the God of Light that they would be back soon with help. The prospect of their return was really the only thing keeping her going now. She tried to avoid the walls at night, partly because it was getting too dangerous up there for anyone without a weapon, and partly because the scope of the enemy's camps was too much. It overwhelmed her, and she despaired.

If they come soon, we might have a chance.

She didn't know what help they would bring, but she knew her spirits would lift if she could just see her friends again.

One night, eight nights after Reith and Dema had departed, she took Laneras on a walk.

"Don't be gone long," one of the nurses scolded severely. "He needs rest, but a quick walk will do him some good."

After Ellamora and Laneras promised profusely to be back soon, they were allowed to depart. Laneras requested to be taken up to the city wall.

"That is not going to be a quick trip," Ellamora said, uncertainly.

"What are they going to do?" Laneras replied. "Come on, I want to see."

They walked slowly through the city. Laneras needed no assistance on flat ground, but Ellamora remained close and kept a hand on his arm.

"I really do like this city," Laneras said, his eyes sweeping the surroundings, taking everything in. "And this sure beats being stuck in a bed with nothing to look at but Nurse Glares-at-me."

"She only glares because she cares," Ellamora replied, and burst out laughing at the rhyme she had made. Laneras started to laugh, and it almost did him in. He clutched at his stomach and bent over, making noises that sounded like a drowning rat.

"Don't do that!" he said when he finally got his pain under control.

"What? Be my normal, hilarious self?"

"Yes, that. Don't do it."

"I'll try to keep my razor-sharp wit put away where it can't hurt you."

They continued on again, slightly slower this time. As they walked, Ellamora stole regular glances at her companion.

Despite being injured, his eyes were bright with wonder. It wasn't lost on Laneras that he was in a foreign city full of strange people and strange sights. The architecture was different than the elven cities. And the feeling in the air was different. Of course, the people were different, but not so different as she would have thought. But the wide-eyed wonder of Laneras was contagious, and it caused her to open her eyes anew to the wonders of Galismoor.

"This is the sort of place worth fighting for," Laneras said at last as they neared the stairs that would take them to the northern wall of the city overlooking the lake. "It's the sort of good place that is worth sacrificing for."

"You think places are worth dying for?" Ellamora asked.

"Places, and people, together. A package deal," Laneras explained. "You should understand. You've been everywhere."

She had been everywhere. The elven kingdom, the dwarven kingdom, and now the human kingdom. Even the Free Isles. And in each place, she had struggled and fought. For the people, for the place. For the goodness of Terrasohnen, the goodness that the God of Light had filled the world with at creation.

"There are good people and good places all over Terrasohnen," she agreed. "And they are worth protecting."

"Are you still against taking up arms?" Laneras asked. The way he said it made Ellamora think it had been on his mind a long time, since before he had been injured.

"Killing repulsed me," Ellamora replied honestly. "I had spilled so much blood. Something hit me the other night, and I couldn't do it anymore."

"Will you ever fight again?" Laneras asked.

"Maybe, maybe not," Ellamora answered. "I can't really say. I feel at peace without a weapon in my hand for the moment. The situation may change though. Galismoor does not need my bow or my sword at the moment."

"The time may come when it is required of you again," Laneras said solemnly. "I hope that you are ready if that time comes."

"I'll be ready." She said it mostly to ease Laneras' mind. She didn't say the rest of what was on her mind.

I'll be ready to die.

She didn't want to die of course, but she felt it would be better to be killed weaponless than to fight and kill again.

Maybe I feel this way now, when danger is not quite so near. Maybe I'll feel differently when someone is trying to kill me.

Ellamora decided in that moment that above all, she wanted to be strong. Not warrior strong, like in Ellyn's story, but strong in the sense of peace.

They slowly ascended the stairs and looked out over the lake. The moon was full and reflected on the still surface of the water. Somewhere out there, Reith and Dema were looking for help. Now was the moment they were needed. Now was the darkest hour.

———

The next night, Ellamora vowed to stand on the wall and offer medical aid to any who needed it. It was something she had not done since Laneras had been hurt, but she felt that she must do something for the war effort, even if she wasn't going to pick up a weapon.

Be strong. Bring peace. Heal, not harm.

It was a mantra that she took up and repeated to herself throughout the night. She bandaged several wounds and escorted a couple of soldiers to the hospital to receive extra care that she could not provide for them. All in all, it was a quiet night, but she wondered when the gate would finally give, and the enemy would swarm the city.

The gate finally gave way the tenth night after Reith and Dema had departed. Fighting on the ramparts was brutal and fierce, as the enemy seemed to devote even more effort to the attack this night. Ellamora was within feet of attacking soldiers and hoped her medical purpose would spare her from random violence. She trusted the men beside her to keep her safe, even as she tried, in her own way, to keep them safe.

When the gate was finally battered down, the fighting was too fierce on the walls to send reinforcements. All was chaos. All was confusion. Everywhere she looked, she saw humans, elves, and dwarves swarming into Galismoor, while the valiant defenders tried to stem the tide. Down below, she saw fierce fighting at the city gate. The enemy surged forward, trying to gain entry into the city, and with each surge, Calmon urged his men to meet it.

And still, Ellamora kept to her work. There were so many wounded, and many dead littering the wall. She tried to help those who she could save, but there were too many. She should have been terrified, but she had a strange sense of calm in her soul.

Be strong. Bring peace. Heal, not harm.

Suddenly, the chaos and confusion multiplied a hundredfold. There was screaming from soldiers on both sides, and a great jet of flame split the sky above Galismoor. In the darkness, Ellamora saw something huge blocking out the stars behind it.

More flames shot through the air, lower this time. Every eye was on this strange sight, and no one knew quite what to make of it.

"Dragon!"

A solitary shout rang out over the fighting, and soon the word was on ten thousand lips.

We're doomed.

Ellamora knew the stories of course. She knew of Erador and the dragons' fury which laid it to waste.

The dragon landed inside the city, a score of yards from the gates. All soldiers trained weapons on it, not knowing which side the beast was on.

But then Ellamora saw two figures slide off the dragon's back.

We're saved!

It was Reith and Dema on the back of the giant dragon. The dragon roared and spit fire again, and the defenders realized their salvation was at hand. They turned and fought hard, driving back the attackers, clearing the gate area. The defenders on the walls returned to their fighting with renewed vigor. Ellamora laughed at the absurdity of it all. They were saved! Reith and Dema were back, and on the back of a dragon.

The light of her laugh never left her face. Icy steel split her back, and before she knew what had happened to her, she was on the ground. The sounds of battle faded away, and she saw a light. The light grew bigger and brighter and overwhelmed her whole being. Peace and calm washed over her, and the pain subsided. And the last thought Ellamora had on this side of death was this: *I was strong.*

PART FIVE
REITH

TWENTY-THREE

Upon landing on the ground, Reith was shooting arrows as quickly as he could get another on the string. With Dema beside him and Anxo roaring and breathing fire, they quickly pushed back the attacking forces. The gate was useless, but when the enemy was gone, fleeing back to their camp, new fortifications were piled up in front of the gate. Anxo was helpful in this, as he was able to sweep debris against the hole where the gate had stood with his tail.

"Reith!" King Calmon said happily. "I am so glad you are here! But, what a shock!"

Calmon looked toward the dragon, and he bowed in a courtly, majestic way to Anxo.

"Welcome, dragon!" he called up to Anxo. "Any friend of Reith's is a friend of mine."

"Greetings, King Calmon," Anxo spoke in his loud, low, rumble of a voice.

"I'm afraid that we do not have accommodations in Galismoor for, uh, one such as yourself," Calmon said diplomatically.

"I require nothing of mortals," Anxo replied. "I will tend to myself."

"Reith, you must tell me everything," the king said, obviously still overwhelmed by the presence of a dragon who knew his name. "A dragon! A dragon in Galismoor! And on our side! Extraordinary. Come to my study. Dema, you are welcome to come with us. Dragon?" he called up to Anxo.

"Ask what you will, O man," Anxo replied.

"Tell me your name."

"I am Anxo, greatest of the Guardians. Go with the human youth, we will speak soon."

At the mention of the Guardians, a shiver ran through the assembled crowd.

Anxo spread his wings and took to the sky, circling the city once, twice, three times, and then alighting on the walls overlooking the camps.

King Calmon practically bounced all the way to his study.

"I can't believe it," he said. "I really can't believe it. If I hadn't seen it with my own two eyes ..."

They reached his study and Calmon ushered Reith and Dema in.

"Tell me, quickly, of all your adventures these past days since you left."

Reith recounted their voyage with Morris, skipping over most of the journey until they were at the northern lighthouse. The compass intrigued Calmon, but Reith informed him that all three items were left at the Temple of Ice.

"That's a pity, it was a marvelous sword."

Reith spent more time on their journey up the frozen river and the strange creatures and foes they met along the way, with Dema stepping in to supply some much needed detail if Reith left it out.

"And then we entered the Temple, met Anxo, and flew back to Galismoor."

"Did you know you were on a quest to find a dragon?" Calmon asked.

"We had no idea what was in there," Reith said. "A dragon wasn't even on our minds."

"And now we have one, a Guardian. That does throw a wrinkle into the all the old stories of Erador."

"It makes sense though," Reith replied. "Erador is in full bloom now. There's a connection."

"Did Anxo say anything about what he plans on doing for us?" Calmon asked. "Frankly, I don't know how best to deploy a dragon in battle."

"We haven't talked about that," Reith said. "I assume he'll swoop down and smite our foes before us."

"Well, when it comes to dragons, it's best to assume nothing," Calmon replied wryly. "I don't know much about dragons, but that much I do know. Now, is there anything else you need to tell me before I go and speak with him?"

Reith and Dema looked at each other and then shrugged in unison.

"I think we told you everything, or at least everything important."

"Well then, I am off to speak with the dragon himself," Calmon declared, and showed them out of his study.

As Calmon trotted off to meet Anxo, Reith and Dema were surprised to find Ellyn was waiting for them, and there were tears streaking her face.

"What happened?" Dema asked.

"It's Ellamora," Ellyn replied with a sob. "She didn't make it."

Ellyn hurried them along to the city square where bodies were lined up waiting for removal. At the far end was a familiar one, covered in blood, with the echo of a laugh on her face.

Dema dropped to her knees and wept bitterly. Reith stood behind her as tears flowed freely down his own face. Ellyn knelt beside Dema and embraced her, and the two women wept together.

Ellamora's face was radiant in death. But as he gazed at it, Reith felt anger rising within him. This was another death in the long line of deaths the Dark Powers and the Shadows had caused. The evidence was right before them. How many lay beside Ellamora? And how many others had died?

His heart and mind took him back to Vereinen, and he felt the wound that Vereinen's death had caused open up again. How many more would have to die?

He found his gaze drawn upward, where he saw the huge shape of the dragon outlined against the dark sky. He could not see Calmon from where he was standing, but he knew the king was up there.

Hopefully they're figuring out a way to end the war.

As he watched them, it struck Reith that he felt like he was an outsider to the story now. He had played his part, united the sword, ring, and compass, found the temple, done his duty, and brought the Guardian back to Galismoor. What part was he to play now that he no longer had a mysterious sword at his hip?

He felt naked without a sword and thought about getting a replacement form the armory. But he knew that no blade would match the sword he had carried for months.

Maybe I'll just stick with my bow for now.

His gaze dropped back down from the lofty heights and fell again on Ellamora, and he mentally beat himself up over thinking about swords and his part to play in the war while his friend lay freshly dead before him, and his girlfriend mourned nearby.

"Come on," Ellyn said. "We need to leave the body for the men who will take care of her. Let's get a bite to eat and a warm drink.

Ellyn led Reith and Dema through the city, and Reith walked as if in a dream. He let her steer, while he let his mind wander. Part of him wanted to turn back and race out of the city and storm the enemy camps. Part of him wanted to crawl under the covers of a soft bed and let grownups deal with all the problems in the world, as if he were a child. Part of him wanted to break down and weep. Part of him wanted to remember the good times with Ellamora and laugh. All these thoughts and feelings were completely him, all of it, all together, wrapped up in one confused person.

He found that a plate was laid before him, and his hands were holding a warm cup of some sweet-smelling liquid.

"To Ellamora," Ellyn said, raising her own glass. Reith automatically raised his in reply, but Dema's mind was a thousand miles away. The drink was hot mead and it burned his throat as it went down, stirring up some life in him, even as they remembered the dead.

They sat in silence, sipping their drinks and picking at their food, of which Reith remembered very little. When his drink was gone, Reith announced he was going to go to bed, and took Dema by the hand and escorted her to her room. Ellyn bade them goodnight.

Dema said nothing as Reith tucked her into bed. He kissed her on the forehead, and then left her to her own grief, while he went to attend to his own. His room was as he had left it, and it felt homey and comforting. He hadn't realized how exhausted he was, and almost as soon as his head hit the pillow, he was asleep.

———

The sun was up by the time Reith awoke. He stretched in the soft, warm bed, feeling content and happy after a good night of dreamless sleep. And then reality crashed down on him. He had to spend a few minutes sorting through all the thoughts, feelings, and memories to remember what was true.

He and Dema had found the Temple of Ice. *True.*

A Guardian, who was a dragon was there, named Anxo. *True.*

Ellamora was dead. *True.*

It was a lot for him to process. On this side of a night's sleep, he felt his emotions were less raw, as if a scab had formed over them. If he picked at it, it would bleed again, and time was the only thing that would heal it, though a scar would remain.

He bathed, and it was a glorious bath he desperately needed. The road weariness washed away with the dirt and grime, and he felt refreshed, like he was a new man.

He dressed and left his room. He was surprised to see Solzar walking down the hallway toward him. Beside Solzar was an armed guard. As they approached, Reith noticed the guard was eyeing him with more suspicion than Solzar.

The guard is here to protect Solzar. I bet a lot of people here want him dead.

"Reith!" Solzar called to him as they approached. "Just the man I wanted to see!"

It was still a disorienting thing for Reith to see Solzar after everything that had happened. Gone was the Gray Man, but the features were the same. Weirder still was the genuine smile gracing the face of the man who had been a Shadow. Reith didn't know if he would ever get used to the man's presence.

"King Calmon let you out?" Reith asked, looking from Solzar to the guard and back again.

"The dragon wanted me free," Solzar replied with a shrug.

"What a Guardian wants with a former Shadow such as myself, I do not know."

"Have you spoken to him?" Reith asked.

"No, I have not. Calmon implied that I would be summoned sometime soon to stand before Anxo, but I do not know when or for what purpose such a meeting will be held. Frankly, I am quite nervous."

"Anxo is good," Reith replied.

"What hope can one such as I have to stand before such goodness?"

"About as much hope as the rest of us."

"In your time with Anxo, he didn't say anything about his strategy for fighting the Shadows?" Solzar asked anxiously.

"No, he didn't. How would you fight a Shadow? Or three?"

"The king has asked me the very same question. Having a Guardian in the flesh is helpful for our cause. I don't know what Anxo will do or how the Shadows will respond. And Reith," he added, abruptly changing the subject. "I am so sorry about your friend, Ellamora."

Emotion welled up in Reith, though tears didn't come to his eyes. He was choked up enough to prevent a verbal response, so he simply nodded.

"And for what it's worth, I am so sorry for the part I played in this whole mess," Solzar said softly.

———

Nothing much happened that day. The hole where the gate had been was filled with rock and rubble, and hot tar was poured over it to seal it up. Preparations were made for another night assault on the city.

Reith found Dema, Ellyn, and Yaz sitting in a quiet corner of a courtyard around noon, and the four of them sat together, not talking much, but taking comfort in the presence of the others. As the shadows grew longer, Reith left to prepare for the night's battle. He planned on being on the wall with his bow.

At dusk, he ascended the wall and took his place. He was surrounded by unfamiliar soldiers, which left him alone with his thoughts.

As night fell, the torches and fires of the enemy camps gleamed brighter in the distance. They stretched on endlessly, and Reith began to despair. They were outnumbered, and the gate had already been broken down. Another night or two of all-out assault and the battle would be over.

He heard gasps all around him and turned to see men running out of the way as a massive dragon glided overhead and landed beside Reith. Anxo folded up his gigantic wings and settled down on top of the wall.

"Good evening, Reith."

"Hello," Reith replied, still not entirely sure of himself around this ancient Guardian.

"What's on your mind tonight?" Anxo asked.

"It all just seems so hopeless," Reith said. "Look at all of them out there. There are so many of them, and we are so few. What are we going to do?"

"It's not as hopeless as you might think," Anxo replied softly. "Do you want to see what I see?"

"I don't know what that means," Reith said hesitantly.

"Let me give you dragon sight."

For a split second, the world went black, but when he blinked, his vision was restored. He noticed that his point of view had shifted upward. He looked around and saw himself standing there on the wall.

You are seeing with my eyes now, Anxo whispered softly into his heart. *What do you see?*

Reith looked around. He saw the men on the wall, most

keeping their distance from the dragon. He looked out over the camp and saw the thousands of torches and fires that marked the enemy's camp. With the dragon's eyes, he could actually see the Shadows. All three were together, perhaps planning their attack. They appeared almost black, the absence of light.

And then Reith looked up.

High in the air, flying back and forth, surrounding the city and surrounding the camp of the enemy were hundreds of dragons, perhaps thousands of dragons. His vision went dark and when he blinked again, he saw with his own eyes. All was the same, but the dragons were gone.

"Are the Guardians here?" Reith asked.

"Of course," Anxo said. "The Guardians are always nearby."

"Then why aren't they doing anything?"

"Who said they are not doing anything?"

"They're just flying around!" Reith protested. "Why don't they attack?"

"Oh, we could," Anxo replied. "But the battle for the soul of Terrasohnen does not occur when we fight. No, the battle is fought in the hearts and minds of the peoples of Terrasohnen."

"So you're not going to do anything?" Reith asked, feeling anger rising within him. "You're going to let the Shadows keep attacking us, keep killing us, and eventually win?"

"We have no such intention," Anxo replied. "But the battle must be fought and won by humans, dwarves, and elves."

"What are you going to do?"

"You have seen with the eyes of a Guardian. You have seen that our army vastly outnumbers theirs. Trust in the Light, Reith. Even though your eyes do not now see, trust in the light. Now, I would like you to go and fetch King Calmon and

Solzar and bring them back to me. There are matters we all need to discuss."

Reith left the wall very perplexed. Seeing the Guardians through Anxo's eyes was quite the experience, and he wrestled with the belief in their existence in his heart, fixing it there, keeping it there, though his normal eyes could not see.

He quickly found Calmon, and a messenger was dispatched to retrieve Solzar, and soon the three of them ascended the stairs to where Anxo sat on the wall.

"Greetings, Anxo," Calmon called to the dragon as they approached.

"Thank you for attending to Reith's summons," Anxo replied.

"What did you wish to talk to us about?" Calmon asked. "Strategy for the war?"

"Of a sort," Anxo replied. "As you know, there are three Shadows out there, plotting our downfall. It is the Light's desire that the battle be fought not among the Guardians and the Dark Powers, but by the peoples of Terrasohnen. I will not fight for you."

"What?" Calmon protested, dismayed.

"Tell me," Anxo went on, as though Calmon had not spoken. "What is the opposite of a Shadow?"

"Light?" Calmon answered with little certainty.

"Close," Anxo replied. "A Shadow simply blocks the light. The opposite of a Shadow would not block the Light, but magnify it, focus it, direct it."

"A lighthouse!" Reith answered. "A beacon!"

"Quite right," Anxo answered.

"There are three Shadows, so we need three Beacons," Reith continued, beginning to connect the dots in Anxo's plan. There were three of them here after all. He began to wonder what it would be like to be a Beacon.

"Again, Reith is close to the mark, but not entirely

correct," Anxo replied. "There are three Shadows, but only one Beacon is required."

"Who will be our Beacon?" Calmon asked.

"A Shadow is one who has given him or herself over to the Dark Powers completely," Anxo continued, ignoring Calmon's question for the moment. "The Shadow becomes their tool, their puppet. It's but a cruel imitation of what the Guardians do with a Beacon. A Beacon is someone who wholly gives themselves over to the Light, but they maintain their freedom of will. A Shadow consumes the individual, but a Beacon becomes more their true self."

"So Beacons are greater than Shadows," Reith pointed out.

"In more ways than one," Anxo agreed. "We need Solzar to become our Beacon. The power of the Light will flow through him."

"Me?" Solzar protested. "I am such a weak vessel, my lord. Choose someone else instead."

"You are indeed a weak vessel, Solzar. And that makes you worthy."

"I have done horrible things!" Solzar protested.

"And the Light will get so much more glory when you right your wrongs and do great things."

"Then, I am yours to command," Solzar replied softly after several long seconds of interior deliberation.

At once, the sound like a rushing wind came upon them and Reith felt goosebumps rise on his skin. Solzar stood up straight and threw his hands to the sky. Suddenly, a light, brighter than the sun, flashed all around them. Reith fell to the ground, closing his eyes and throwing his arms around his head to block out the light, for it overwhelmed him. For several long seconds, the light drove everything else from his senses. And then it gradually dimmed, and he was able to open his eyes. He saw that Solzar was glowing like a star, a beacon in the night. His light swept over the enemy camp and over the whole city. And then the light dimmed, and all that was left was the radiance of Solzar's face.

Solzar laughed with such joy. "I can see!"

Reith and Calmon stared in wonder at the radiant face of Solzar, the former Shadow.

"I do not think there will be an attack on the city tonight," Anxo said with satisfaction. "We have given the Shadows much to think about. Calmon, order as many men as can be spared to sleep. Tomorrow, you will ride out of the city and bring the fight to them. We are done with allowing the Shadows to dictate the fighting. We will take it to them in the light of day. Reith, try and get some sleep as well. You will be needed in the battle as well. Solzar, come and speak with me."

TWENTY-FOUR

At dawn, the cavalry was assembled in the city square. As Anxo had predicted, there was no attack that night. The city had one night of peace.

Reith was astride Aspen, and the horse and boy were quite happy to be reunited. A replacement sword was belted to Reith's hip. It was a fine weapon, but not nearly the equal of the great key sword. It felt off balance in his hand, and he vowed to himself to stick with the bow on this charge as much as he could.

The plan was to surprise the enemy with a morning charge right to their camp. Of course, the enemy had horses, but with a surprise charge, they could hardly be able to get their defenses ready and a solid formation with spears, so Calmon was confident they could sweep through. As to Solzar and Anxo's part in the battle, Reith and Calmon had no idea.

Anxo landed in the square beside Calmon and Reith.

"Remember, the Light is with you. Attack with strength and speed. We will take care of the Shadows."

Anxo took off and went back to the wall, where Solzar was

standing waiting for him. Even from here, Reith could see the glow on Solzar's face.

Dema arrived with Ellyn and Yaz to see him off to the battle. Dema really hadn't wanted Reith to risk himself, but when she was told that Anxo had requested his presence in the battle, she acquiesced. For Reith's part, he was glad that Dema was staying behind in the city.

"May the God of Light protect you," Ellyn said, patting his arm.

He dismounted to give Dema a hug and a kiss.

"I'll be back soon," he promised.

"Be safe," she said. "If you die, I'll never forgive you."

"I don't plan on getting anywhere near the fighting," Reith said. "I've got my bow, and I'll cause a great amount of mischief from a distance."

Soon, it was time for the all-important battle to begin. Calmon signaled up to Anxo, who flew down and readied himself to clear the gateway. The dragon pushed the debris through the gate and out to the field, and then the charge was on. Calmon led the way with several of his closest generals and advisors. Reith came near the rear, so that he could break off to the side and shoot at the enemy from a distance. All told, Calmon mustered about a thousand men on horseback for the charge. Even with their advantage on horseback, they were still horribly outnumbered.

The ground flew past them as they charged toward the enemy camp. A great shout came up from their enemies and Reith could see there was a flurry of activity as they rode. The enemy soldiers were in disarray. A few had spears, but there was no cohesion in their movements, no coordination in their defense. The camp had not been set up with the possibility that Galismoor might ride out to attack.

The first wave of cavalry swept through, breaking in deep to the camp. Countless soldiers fell before them. Reith urged

Aspen off to the right, where he loosed arrow after arrow on the enemy from a full gallop.

The momentum of the first charge was wavering, and the enemy was becoming better organized by the minute. Reith heard a trumpet blast and the cavalry swept away from the camp out to the plain to gather for another charge. This time, the spearmen of the Shadows were ready. They formed a tight formation, and from the side, Reith tried to take out as many as they could as the charge came from Calmon's men. This second charge surged through the ranks, cutting down men, elves, and dwarves left and right, but it was not nearly as successful as the first charge. The fighting was fierce, and Calmon's men began to take losses.

But then, a shadow like a great cloud rushed over the camp, and Reith turned to see Anxo flying out over the camp. He did not blow fire, but Solzar was on his back. From what he could see, Solzar was unarmed. Anxo landed on the far side of the camp, and Solzar dismounted. Three dark figures approached the Guardian and the Beacon. Of all the cavalry, only Reith was disengaged from the fighting to see what was going on.

Solzar walked forward, toward the three Shadows. His arms were outstretched, and his face was glowing. Anxo stayed back. Reith saw King Koinas, a woman who must be Malowe, and the other Shadow, the one from Kal-Epharion. In unison, the Shadows raised their swords and struck.

A blast of light emanated from Solzar, blinding everyone within a ten-mile radius of the Beacon. Reith turned in the saddle and shielded his eyes. Aspen brayed with shock and fear, and Reith heard men and horse making noises of distress in the distance.

Reith's vision began to slowly come back, but there were still black spots on his eyes, and he could not see clearly. He tried to see where Solzar and Anxo were, but his eyes couldn't focus. Then, a familiar voice entered his head.

It is done.

It was Anxo's voice of course, and Reith's vision unexpectedly cleared. On the battlefield, men and horses were blinking in the light, trying to get their vision to refocus. Some blindly swung their sword this way and that, but for the most part, the fighting had ceased.

Reith looked to the far side of the camp, but there was no one there. No Anxo, no Solzar, no Shadows.

"The Shadows are vanquished!" Reith shouted and urged Aspen forward in a gallop toward the king's forces. "The Shadows are vanquished!"

As the eyes of the men cleared, they saw it to be true, and Reith's cry began to be echoed throughout the cavalry. From behind them, a shout came up from the walls of the city.

"The Shadows are vanquished!"

The shout crested into a roar as every man, woman, and child from Galismoor shouted their deliverance. Renewed by what had happened, Calmon's men began to fight again.

The battle was over in five minutes. When the attacking armies realized their Shadows were gone, some threw down their weapons and surrendered. Some fled. Some continued to fight, but these were quickly subdued.

When the fighting was over, Reith took Aspen around the camp to the place where the Shadows, the Beacon, and the Guardian had disappeared. There was no trace of them, except the three Shadows' sword lay in the grass. Each blade was shattered into a thousand little pieces that gleamed in the sunlight. And Reith marveled at what had happened.

———

Upon entering the city, Reith saw Dema, and he leaped down from Aspen as she was still trotting. He embraced Dema and kissed her as he had never kissed her before.

"We did it!" she said when they finally broke apart.

"No more Shadows," Reith said, with a huge grin on his face.

"And no more quests," she said. "I'd like to find a place and stay there."

"Me too," Reith agreed.

There was great rejoicing in the city that night. The enemy camp was raided of any weapons, and the captured soldiers were allowed to remain camping there until it was decided what to do with them. A guard rotation was set to watch over them, but the fight was gone from them, and they were a docile group.

With the siege lifted, rations were eliminated, and a feast was called for. The feasting and drinking and dancing and celebrating lasted long into the night. For Reith, it was a blur.

The next day, Calmon bestowed upon Reith and Dema the honor of knighthood. They would remain in the king's pay, but due to their services already, would be free to pursue what they wished.

Calmon had much to figure out about sending the captured soldiers back to their homelands, and who should rule the two kingdoms. It was discovered that Romulus and Remus had both been killed in their father's coup, and with Koinas gone, there was no one left in that line to ascend the throne. Queen Kalis' children were still alive in Darren Shahr, but they were not old enough to rule either. And of course, Kal-Epharion was still in rebellion against the crown.

But Reith concerned himself with none of these things. He enjoyed trips to the lake with Dema, Ellyn, and Yaz, and eventually Laneras when he was fully healed.

After a few weeks, Calmon decided it was time to send the

captured peoples back to their lands, except for the men from Kal-Epharion. Pallin was appointed temporary leader over the elves and took the captured elven soldiers back. Laneras accompanied him, as well as Ellyn. It was a sorrowful goodbye when the three elves departed, but Reith and Dema promised to visit eventually.

Yaz was sent back with the dwarves, and Calmon appointed her as the regent of the dwarves with instructions to raise Rendar and Kalis' children to rule over the dwarven kingdom. It was yet another tearful goodbye when Yaz departed a couple days after the elves.

Reith and Dema found themselves alone in Galismoor. They were assured by Calmon that they could stay as long as they liked, but neither of them felt settled.

"We can go back to Suthrond for a bit," Dema said.

"Yes, it would be good to see Heth and the others," Reith replied.

"But more than that, we need to find a home," Dema said. "An honest to goodness home, a place where we can stay and plant roots and grow old together."

"You want to grow old with me?" Reith asked.

"There's no one else I'd rather grow old with."

———

Reith and Dema ended up spending a year in Suthrond. A month after their arrival, they married, and it was a joyous celebration among the weary people of Suthrond. They helped around the new town, planting and harvesting, but also taking time to leave and visit their friends. Crain was not far away, and they spent some weeks there with Ellyn and Laneras. Pallin was in Sardis dealing with the fallout of the end of the royal family.

But when the year was up, they still felt restless.

"This isn't our forever home," Dema said softly to Reith one night as they lay in bed. "I still want to live on the lake."

"Me too," Reith said.

Preparations were made, and a week later, Reith and Dema were on the road again. There were many tearful goodbyes in Suthrond but promises of visiting were made.

With Suthrond behind them, Reith turned to Dema. "Shall we go home, my dear?"

"I'm always home when I'm with you."

EPILOGUE

2 years later...

1   "Are you coming out?" Dema asked Reith. It was a sunny day in the middle of the summer. The breeze off the lake was cool and refreshing. The smell of the lake mingled with the smell of the apple and peach trees surrounding their home. The children were already outside, and Reith could hear them laughing and yelling as they played in the waves.

"I'll be out in a bit," he said. "I'm almost done."

Dema came and stood behind him, her hands resting on his shoulders as she looked down at his work.

"After all this time," she said. "I'm so proud of you for almost being done. We must celebrate tonight."

"Give me a few minutes," Reith said. "I promise, I'll be right there."

Dema stooped down and gave him a kiss on the cheek before gracefully leaving the room and going outside with the children.

Reith looked down at his life's work. It was a large, leather-bound book, and he had been working on it for twelve years.

He dipped his pen carefully and then neatly wrote out the last four words. "He was finally home."

Reith gently blew on these last words to dry the ink. He didn't want any smudges, not now, not at the end.

He set down his pen and leaned back in his chair and let out a breath he didn't know he had been holding. The wind from his lungs rustled the pages. He reached forward and shut the book. The words, "The Chronicles of Terrasohnen" looked up at him from the cover. Beneath them was written, "Reith Vereinenson."

As hard as the project had been for him, he had one last part to write. This part was the hardest yet, and he still didn't know exactly what he wanted to say. He opened the book to the second page, a blank page. The inscription page, the dedication page. It needed to be just right.

He closed his eyes and leaned back again. He thought about all that he had been through, all that it had taken to write this book. He knew who he wanted to dedicate it to, but he just didn't have the words.

For a long minute, he thought. Words came to mind, and he edited them in his head, mentally scratching some out, adding others, and rearranging until it was just right. Then he leaned forward again, took up his pen, and wrote.

For Vereinen,

Your memory will live on forever and ever, and the love you showed to a boy is a testimony to your life. I will be always your son. History will remember you; I have made sure of it. We will meet again someday.

It wasn't perfect, but it was true and good. Reith set his pen down for the last time. As the ink dried, tears fell down his face. They were a mixture of sorrow and love flowing down, mingled together.

At last, the ink was dry and the tears stopped flowing. Reith closed the book and placed it gently, reverently, on the shelf. Then he left his study to spend some well-earned time with his wife and children, Kydar and Ellamora. They would splash in the waves and enjoy the summer day. Reith was content and happy with his life. He was finally home.

THE END

Author's Note

Thank you for joining me on Reith's adventures in Terrasohnen. For me, this journey began in 2017, seven years before the publication of this book you hold in your hands. You may be wondering: will there be more stories in Terrasohnen? As I write this, I have no plans to return to Terrasohnen. I have said all that I need to say in Reith's story. What remains unsaid, I leave to you to fill in the gaps. Open your imagination and wonder! But have no fear, I will return with more stories of one sort or another someday. During this journey, I have discovered that I am a storyteller, and that's a vocation that cannot be set aside.

I have many thanks to give. First, to my wife Haley, and our boys, for lending me to Terrasohnen and Reith's story. To Brian for his help and encouragement on early drafts of these stories. For Jean and the CJM team for believing in this story and taking a chance on me. And lastly, to you, dear reader, for doing what readers do: picking up a book and reading it. The response from the readers has been incredible. Thank you.

Until we meet again. May the Light be with you.

NKC

2024

About the Author

N. K. Carlson is a storyteller and pastor living in Texas with his wife and sons.